NAOMI'S CHRISTMAS

Center Point
Large Print

Also by Marta Perry and available from
Center Point Large Print:

Amish Suspense Series:
  Murder in Plain Sight
  Vanish in Plain Sight

Pleasant Valley Series:
  Katie's Way
  Hannah's Joy
  Sarah's Gift

**This Large Print Book carries the
Seal of Approval of N.A.V.H.**

NAOMI'S CHRISTMAS

A Pleasant Valley Novel
Book Seven

MARTA PERRY

CENTER POINT LARGE PRINT
THORNDIKE, MAINE

This Center Point Large Print edition is published in the year 2012 by arrangement with The Berkley Publishing Group, a member of Penguin Group (USA)

The recipes contained in this book are to be followed exactly as written. The publisher is not responsible for your specific health or allergy needs that may require medical supervision. The publisher is not responsible for any adverse reactions to the recipes contained in this book.

The text of this Large Print edition is unabridged. In other aspects, this book may vary from the original edition. Printed in the United States of America on permanent paper. Set in 16-point Times New Roman type.

ISBN: 978-1-61173-574-1

Library of Congress Cataloging-in-Publication Data

Perry, Marta.
Naomi's Christmas / Marta Perry.
pages ; cm.
ISBN 978-1-61173-574-1 (library binding : alk. paper)
1. Amish—Fiction. 2. Lancaster County (Pa.)—Fiction.
3. Christmas stories. 4. Large type books. I. Title.
PS3616.E7933N36 2012b
813′.6—dc23
2012022199

This story is dedicated
to my children and grandchildren,
with much love.
And, as always, to Brian.

List of Characters

Naomi Esch, a beekeeper, eldest child of Sam Esch

Nathan King, widower, a dairy farmer; Ada, his late wife; his children: Joshua, six, and Sadie, almost five

Ezra King, Nathan's father

Sarah Schultz, Nathan's sister

Emma Miller, mother of Nathan's late wife, mother of Elizabeth, Jessie, and Seth

Elizabeth Miller, middle sister of Nathan's late wife

Jessie Miller, youngest sister of Nathan's late wife

Seth Miller, brother of Nathan's late wife, Englisch

Elijah Esch, Naomi's oldest brother; Lovina, his wife

Isaiah Esch, Naomi's youngest brother; Libby, his wife

Sam Esch, Naomi's father

Betty Shutz, Sam Esch's new wife

Anna and Sara, Naomi's sisters

Paula Schatz, Mennonite, runs Pleasant Valley's bakery

Hannah Brand, protagonist of *Hannah's Joy,*

Paula's niece, partner in the bakery; William Brand, her husband

Leah Glick, protagonist of *Leah's Choice*; Daniel Glick, her husband; their children: Matthew, Elizabeth, Jonah, and Rachel Anna

Katie Miller Brand, protagonist of *Katie's Way*, quilt shop owner; Caleb Brand, her husband, furniture shop owner

Rhoda Miller, Katie's sixteen-year-old sister

Rachel Zook, protagonist of *Rachel's Garden*; Gideon Zook, her husband; their children: Becky, Joseph, Mary, and Josiah

Joseph and Myra Beiler, Leah's brother and sister-in-law

Anna Beiler Fisher, protagonist of *Anna's Return*; Samuel Fisher, her husband; their children: adopted daughter Grace and baby David

Barbara Beiler, Leah's sister-in-law

Bishop Mose, spiritual leader of the Pleasant Valley Amish

Glossary of Pennsylvania Dutch Words and Phrases

ach. oh; used as an exclamation

agasinish. stubborn; self-willed

ain't so. A phrase commonly used at the end of a sentence to invite agreement.

alter. old man

anymore. Used as a substitute for "nowadays."

Ausbund. Amish hymnal. Used in the worship services, it contains traditional hymns, words only, to be sung without accompaniment. Many of the hymns date from the sixteenth century.

befuddled. mixed up

blabbermaul. talkative one

blaid. bashful

boppli. baby

bruder. brother

bu. boy

buwe. boys

daadi. daddy

Da Herr sei mit du. The Lord be with you.

denke. thanks (or *danki*)

Englischer. one who is not Plain

ferhoodled. upset; distracted

ferleicht. perhaps

frau. wife

fress. eat

gross. big

grossdaadi. grandfather

grossdaadi haus. An addition to the farmhouse, built for the grandparents to live in once they've "retired" from actively running the farm.

grossmutter. grandmother

gut. good

hatt. hard; difficult

haus. house

hinnersich. backward

ich. I

ja. yes

kapp. Prayer covering, worn in obedience to the Biblical injunction that women should pray with their heads covered. Kapps are made of Swiss organdy and are white. (In some Amish communities, unmarried girls thirteen and older wear black kapps during worship service.)

kinder. kids (or *kinner*)

komm. come

komm schnell. come quick

Leit. the people; the Amish

lippy. sassy

maidal. old maid; spinster

mamm. mother

middaagesse. lunch

mind. remember

onkel. uncle

Ordnung. The agreed-upon rules by which the

Amish community lives. When new practices become an issue, they are discussed at length among the leadership. The decision for or against innovation is generally made on the basis of maintaining the home and family as separate from the world. For instance, a telephone might be necessary in a shop in order to conduct business but would be banned from the home because it would intrude on family time.

Pennsylvania Dutch. The language is actually German in origin and is primarily a spoken language. Most Amish write in English, which results in many variations in spelling when the dialect is put into writing! The language probably originated in the south of Germany but is common also among the Swiss Mennonite and French Huguenot immigrants to Pennsylvania. The language was brought to America prior to the Revolution and is still in use today. High German is used for Scripture and church documents, while English is the language of commerce.

rumspringa. Running-around time. The late teen years when Amish youth taste some aspects of the outside world before deciding to be baptized into the church.

schnickelfritz. mischievous child

ser gut. very good

tastes like more. delicious

Was ist letz? What's the matter?
Wie bist du heit. how are you; said in greeting
wilkom. welcome
Wo bist du? Where are you?

Chapter One

Naomi Esch froze in her seat at the family table, unable to stop staring at her father. Daadi had just tossed what felt like a lightning bolt into the middle of her thirtieth birthday celebration. Around her, she could feel her siblings and their spouses stuck in equally unbelieving attitudes.

"Ach, what is wrong with all of you?" Daadi's eyes narrowed, his beard seeming to bristle as he glared at his offspring. "This is a reason to celebrate, ain't so?"

Lovina, her brother Elijah's wife, was the first to recover, her calm face showing little of what she felt. "We wish you and Betty much happiness." She bounced Amos, her two-year-old, on her lap, hushing him. "Wilkom, Betty."

Betty Shutz, a round dumpling of a woman with a pair of shrewd brown eyes, nodded and smiled, but the glance she sent toward Naomi was cautious.

Isaiah, the youngest and most impetuous, said what everyone was thinking. "But what about Naomi? If you and Betty are marrying, what is Naomi to do?"

The question roused Naomi from her frozen state. What *was* she supposed to do, after fifteen years spent raising her siblings, tending the house and garden and her beehives, and taking care of Daadi?

Daadi's gaze shifted, maybe a bit uneasily. "Naomi is a gut daughter, none better. No one would deny that. But newlyweds want to have time alone together, ja? So we . . . I was thinking Naomi would move in with Elijah and Lovina. They are both busy with the dry-goods store and two young kinder besides. It would be a big help to you, ja?"

Elijah and Lovina exchanged glances, and then Lovina smiled at Naomi. "Nothing would please us more than to have Naomi with us, but that is for her to say, ain't so?"

"Denke, Lovina." Naomi found that her stiff lips could move, after all. "But what about my beehives?"

Odd, that her thoughts had flown so quickly to her bees in the face of this shock. Or maybe not so odd. The beehives were the only thing she could call truly hers.

"I've already talked to Dick Holder about the hives, and he'll be happy to give Naomi a gut price for them." Daad spoke as if it were all settled, her life completely changed in a few short minutes.

"I will not sell the hives." Naomi could hardly believe that strong tone was coming out of her mouth. Everyone else looked equally surprised.

Maybe they'd never heard such firmness from her.

Daad's eyebrows drew down as he stared at her. "Komm, Naomi, don't be stubborn. It is the sensible thing to do. Betty is allergic to bee stings, so the hives cannot stay here. And Elijah's home in town isn't suitable. The money will give you a nice little nest egg for the future."

A babble of talk erupted around her as everyone seemed to have an opinion, but Naomi's thoughts were stuck on the words Daad had used. *Her future.* He clearly thought he knew what that future was to be. She should move from one sibling to another, helping to raise their children, never having a home or a life of her own.

She was engaging in selfish thinking, maybe, and it was unfitting for a humble Amish person. But . . .

She looked around the table. Elijah, two years younger than she, whom she'd comforted when bad dreams woke him in the night. Anna and Sara, the next two in the family, who had traveled by bus with their husbands from the next county for her birthday today. She'd taught the girls everything they needed to know to be Amish women, overseen their rumspringas, seen them married to gut men they loved. And Isaiah, the baby, the one whose first stumbling steps she'd guided. Were they to be her future, as they had her past?

Much as she loved them, her heart yearned for

15

more. Marriage might have passed her by during those years when she was busy raising her siblings, but she'd looked forward to a satisfying future, taking care of Daad, tending her hives, enjoying her part-time work at the bakery.

Amos slid down from his mother's lap and toddled around the table to tug on Naomi's skirt. A glance at his face told her he'd detected the strain in the air. She lifted him to her lap, running her hand down his back, murmuring soothing words. He leaned against her, relaxing, sucking on two fingers as he always did before going to sleep.

Lovina met her gaze from across the table and smiled. "Naomi is wonderful gut with children."

"For sure," Betty said, her first contribution to the conversation. "A widower with kinder would do well to have a wife like Naomi."

Somehow, that comment, coming from Betty, was the last straw. Naomi had to speak now, and quickly, before the rest of her life was set in stone by the family.

"You are all ser kind to give so much thought to my life. But as dearly as I love my nieces and nephews, I have no wish to raise them. And I will not give up my beehives. So I think I must find this answer for myself."

She took advantage of the ensuing silence to move the drowsy child to his father's arms. Grabbing a heavy wool shawl from the peg by the back door, she walked out, closing the door gently behind her.

Mid-November, and it was ser chilly already, a hint of the winter to come. Even the hardy mums on the sheltered side of the house had succumbed to frost. Clutching the shawl more tightly, she walked across brittle grass to the gnarled old apple tree that had once held a tree house when the boys were young. It was a relief to get out of the kitchen, too warm from all the cooking that had been done today for her birthday. This day had certainly turned out far different from the celebration her sisters had so lovingly planned.

She stopped under the tree, resting her hand against the rough bark. No point in going farther —she couldn't escape her family, and she wouldn't want to. Soon someone would come out to talk to her, and she would have to explain and justify and try to make them understand. But for this moment she was alone with her thoughts.

The family had one thing right. She did have a gift with children, and she couldn't deny that gift. But to raise someone else's children again, to grow to love them so dearly, but to know that she always took second place in their hearts . . . no, she couldn't. But when she tried to think how to carry out that brave declaration she'd made, she found she was lacking in ideas.

It was Isaiah who came out to her. Maybe they thought the youngest would be most likely to soften her heart. But Isaiah was a man grown now, married for just a year, and so much in love with his Libby. Not a baby any longer, but he still seemed so young to her with his round blue eyes and his corn-silk hair. The beard he was growing as a married man was as fine and silky as his hair.

He leaned against the tree next to her, his eyes serious as he studied her face. "Are you all right?"

Naomi managed a smile, though it probably wasn't very convincing. "Ja. I will be, anyway. I guess Daad's news was a shock."

"For sure." Isaiah shook his head. "It wonders me that none of us saw this marriage coming, but we didn't. I guess we all figured that if Daad had been going to wed again, he'd have done it years ago."

"Then Betty would have had the raising of you." Her smile was more natural this time.

Isaiah seemed to shudder. "Ach, I'm sure she's a gut woman. But I'm glad it was you who brought me up, Naomi."

For an instant she was surprised almost to tears. "Denke," she whispered, her throat tight. She'd never say she loved one more than another, but Isaiah was especially dear, both because he was the baby and because of his sweet nature.

She tilted her head, watching him, wondering how he would react to the question she was about to put to him. "What about you, Isaiah? Do you think I'm being selfish not to do what Daadi wants?"

He blinked, eyes wide and innocent. "Ach, Naomi, everyone knows there's not a selfish bone in your body, no matter—" He stopped, looking as if he'd bitten his tongue.

So that was what someone had been saying, once she'd left the kitchen. Well, she wouldn't put Isaiah in the middle by noticing.

"I guess the first thing is to find a place for my beehives," she said, deliberately turning the subject. "It's not going to be an easy job, moving them all."

"I'll help," he said instantly. "And I was thinking that I should ask Nathan King if you could have them on his farm. With Libby and me living right on the property, I could keep an eye on things for you."

Naomi hesitated. Isaiah enjoyed working for Nathan King on his dairy farm, and she didn't want to cause any difficulties between them by asking for something Nathan might not be so eager to grant. Nathan could have plenty of reasons not to want her beehives on his property.

"I wonder if that's wise," she said, careful to keep her voice neutral. "Ada and I were such close friends, and Nathan still mourns her so deeply even after two years. He might not want to have me around, reminding him of her."

Vertical lines formed between Isaiah's brows.

"It's true he's still grieving for Ada. But as for reminding him . . . well, he seems to be thinking about her all the time anyway."

"Poor Nathan," she murmured. And poor Ada, gone far too early, it seemed, in such a freak accident, leaving Nathan and two young kinder behind. Naomi accepted it as God's will, but she couldn't help wishing it had been otherwise. As for Nathan—well, she doubted he would ever be able to accept his loss.

Isaiah straightened, pushing away from the tree. "Let me talk to Nathan about it, anyway. I won't push. I'll make it easy for him to say no, if that's what he's of a mind to do. But he might well say yes."

She was still doubtful, but she nodded. "I guess it can't hurt to ask."

"That's right. And if he says no, we'll find someone else." Isaiah put his arm around her shoulders. "You're cold. Let's go inside."

She hung back. "That's not a gut idea. Daadi will just start trying to persuade me again, and I don't want to provoke a family quarrel on my birthday." Although maybe she'd already done that very thing.

"He won't say a word." Isaiah sounded confident. "Betty told him it was best to let you think about their marriage and get used to the idea of moving out without him pushing you."

"And he agreed to that?" It didn't sound like

Daadi at all. Once he'd made up his mind, he was like a rock.

"He did." Isaiah grinned, blue eyes twinkling. "Seems like Betty can manage him better than the rest of us put together. So don't lose heart. This is all going to turn out for the best, you'll see."

Naomi nodded as they started toward the house, not wanting to lay her burdens any more heavily on Isaiah. But she doubted this situation could possibly turn out for the best . . . for her, anyway.

Nathan King slid the harness over the back of Coal, the sturdy pony standing patiently between the shafts of the pony cart. He'd promised Joshua and Sadie a ride in the cart this afternoon, and he'd best get at it. Days grew short in November here in Pleasant Valley.

His father moved out of the shadow of the barn door, glancing up at the weak sunlight. "Giving the kinder a ride, ja? Are you sure you don't want me to stay around to help you with the milking?"

Nathan shook his head, feeling an inward pang at the stiffness with which Daad moved. It was impossible to keep him from helping on the dairy farm, but Nathan tried to spare his father as best he could.

"You go on home before Sarah is scolding me for keeping you late." Since Daad was living with Nathan's sister, she could be tart with Nathan about Daad doing too much, but he'd noticed she didn't have any better luck getting Daad to slow down. "Isaiah said he'd be back in time for evening milking."

"They were having a birthday party for Naomi, ain't so? I must remember to wish her happiness." Daad shook his head, the wind ruffling his beard, more gray now than brown. "I can't see her without thinking of your Ada, that's certain-sure. They were gut friends, ain't so?"

Nathan nodded, feeling his face stiffen. He didn't like talking about Ada, not that he ever stopped thinking about her.

He glimpsed movement from the corner of his eye, and his heart jolted.

"Joshua!" He snatched his small son from under the pony, where Joshua was reaching for the harness strap. "What are you doing?" He held the boy close for a moment and then set him on his feet. "You know better than to mess around the horses."

"But I can help, Daadi. I watch you and Grossdaadi all the time. I know how to harness Coal. She likes me."

"Whether she likes you or not isn't the point. You are too young to be harnessing her."

Nathan could sense his father's gaze on him, no doubt disapproving. Joshua stared at him with changeable hazel eyes so like Ada's that it cut to the heart to see disappointment in them. But keeping Joshua safe was more important than anyone's approval.

"But, Daadi . . ."

"Go back to Grossmammi. I will bring the cart up to the house in a moment."

Joshua pressed his lips together. Then he turned and walked back toward the farmhouse, his small shoulders drooping.

"The boy is six already," Daad commented. "When you were his age you were doing more than harnessing a pony."

Nathan's jaw set. "He's too young. When he's older I'll show him how." He turned to the patiently waiting pony and fastened the straps.

Daad put a hand on his shoulder. "Just because you lost Ada to an accident . . ."

"Don't." He was instantly sorry for the harshness of his tone, but he couldn't help it. He couldn't listen again to someone telling him that it wasn't his fault Ada died trying to get the horses out of the blazing barn. Or telling him, as people seemed to want to do, that after two years it was time he started living again.

He couldn't get over Ada. He couldn't undo the past. All he could do now was protect the children she had given him with all his strength.

"I'm sorry, Daad." His voice was tight.

"It's all right. You must deal with grief as best you can." Daad cleared his throat. "Have you settled on who is to take care of the kinder when Ada's mother is away?"

Worry settled on Nathan like a wet, heavy

blanket. "Sarah will komm a couple of days a week. She offered to have Joshua and Sadie stay with her every day, but I don't want them away from home so much. I'm still trying to find someone to watch them here for the rest of the time."

He could hardly fault Ada's mother for going to help Ada's middle sister with her new baby, but how was he to get along without her? She'd cared for the kinder every day of the past two years.

Realizing that his father was looking at him with concern, he shrugged. "I will find someone. You best get on home. Isaiah will be here soon."

"Isaiah is here now," a voice announced, and Isaiah Esch walked toward them with his long, loping stride. With his lanky body and wide grin, Isaiah still looked like the boy he'd been when he first came to work for Nathan instead of the married man he was now.

Daad nodded to him. "You had a gut birthday party for your sister, ja? Give her my best wishes when you see her again."

"Ja, denke, I will." Isaiah still smiled, but Nathan thought he detected something at odds with the smile in Isaiah's normally open face.

"I will be off now," Daad said. "No need to make Sarah fuss more than she already does."

He walked toward his buggy horse. Nathan knew better than to offer to help him. Daad resented any implication that he couldn't do what he'd always done.

Nathan turned toward Isaiah. "Was ist letz?" *What's wrong?* He knew Isaiah well enough to realize when something wasn't right.

"Ach, you're not going to believe it." Isaiah patted the pony absently. "It's my daad. He's going to marry Betty Shutz. Can you imagine? Announced it right in the middle of Naomi's birthday party."

Somehow the timing of the announcement didn't surprise Nathan as much as it seemed to have Isaiah. Sam Esch had always struck him as someone who put his own wants ahead of everyone else's.

"So Betty said yes to him. Well, if anyone can handle him, she can."

Isaiah blinked at this way of looking at his news. "Ja, you might be right about that. But it doesn't help Naomi much."

"No, I suppose not." It hadn't occurred to him how this change would affect Naomi, and it should have. "Maybe it will be all right. With Betty taking over the house and your daad, Naomi will have more time for her job and her beehives."

"If only," Isaiah said, the Englisch phrase a hangover from his rumspringa years. "Daad expects Naomi to move out. He acted like it was all set without even asking her. He said she should move in with Elijah and Lovina to help with the kinder. And he'd even set up for someone to buy the beehives."

A vague idea drifted through Nathan's thoughts. "And will she?"

Isaiah shook his head, his expression one of surprise. "She says not. Says she'll decide for herself what she's going to do. Mind, it's how I'd have felt if Daad did this to me, but I didn't expect it from Naomi. Nobody did." He grinned. "Least of all Daad."

"I can imagine." Sam wasn't used to his children refusing his ideas. "So what is Naomi going to do, then?"

"She says the first thing is to find a place for her beehives. Then she'll worry about herself." Isaiah's forehead wrinkled.

"She can't keep them at your daad's place?" Surely not even Sam would be that unkind just because Naomi didn't like his plans for her life.

"Apparently Betty's allergic to bee stings. Not that she'd be likely to get stung, not with honey bees, unless she poked a stick in the hives. But there it is. Naomi has to move the hives." Isaiah came to a stop and looked at Nathan. Expectantly.

So that was where this conversation had been headed. Isaiah hoped he would offer to have Naomi's beehives here.

Well, why not? He had plenty of available land, and the beehives wouldn't have to be close to the house. The only deterrent was that he would be brought into closer contact with

26

Naomi, with her inevitable reminders of Ada.

Still, as he'd thought when Daad had mentioned something about their friendship, he didn't stop thinking about his Ada anyway. And Naomi . . . the whole valley knew how gut Naomi was with children. He made a quick decision.

"Have Naomi stop by to talk to me about it. Maybe we can find a solution to that part of her problem, at least."

In fact, maybe he'd found a way to solve both of their problems.

Naomi discovered that her stomach was tied up in knots when she drove her buggy up the lane to Nathan's place the next day. The lane was both wide and well-kept, since the milk truck came in to pick up milk from the dairy operation. Nathan had made a thriving business from his dairy farm, but Ada wasn't here to share it with him.

Thoughts of Ada and Nathan plummeted her right back to an incident she tried to hide, blocking even her own memory of it.

She'd been sixteen, of an age to start her rumspringa years, but shy and uncertain, unlike Ada, who hadn't been able to stop talking about it.

Ada had been everything Naomi wasn't . . . pretty, lively, full of laughter and eager about life. But it was Naomi whom Nathan had approached that Sunday after worship; Naomi who'd heard Nathan asking if he could take her home from the singing that night. She had looked into his golden brown eyes and felt herself sinking into their depths. She would have done anything to be able to say yes.

But she couldn't. She wouldn't be going to the singing. She'd be staying at home to take care of the young ones, and so she'd had to say no.

Nathan had taken Ada home from the singing that night, and they'd tumbled into love with a suddenness that made it seem inevitable. Certainly Ada had never had any doubts.

She had confided in Naomi, of course. They were best friends. And Naomi had suppressed whatever envy she'd felt and encouraged her friend. When the time came, she'd been the one to help Ada's mother with the wedding, she'd been one of Ada's side-sitters, what the world would call a bridesmaid, and she'd rejoiced when Ada started her new life with Nathan.

It was as it should be, Naomi reminded herself now, stopping the buggy horse at the hitching rail by the back porch of the farmhouse. Nathan loved Ada with single-minded devotion and still did, even two years after her death.

Other people thought Nathan should move on, that he should marry again and give his kinder a mammi, but he wouldn't. Naomi understood that. Nathan would never betray his first love.

Naomi slid down from the buggy seat, shaking her skirt to straighten it, and turned toward the porch to discover Nathan and Ada's two children standing there, watching her.

"Joshua. Sadie. I am ser happy to see you." She bent to give each of them a hug, her heart touched as always by their resemblance to Ada. Joshua had hazel eyes just like his mother's, while Sadie, almost five now, had her pert, lively expression, with a smile always tugging at her lips.

"How are the bees?" Sadie held on to her for an extra second. "Did you bring us some honey?"

"You shouldn't ask," Joshua chided. Then he darted a glance at Naomi, eyeing the basket she carried.

She laughed, and he grinned back, knowing she'd caught him. "For sure I brought you some honey. I would not forget you." She handed the basket to Joshua. "Do you think that's enough?"

He peered at the three jars of amber honey. "For a while," he said, making her laugh again. "Daadi says he will be out in a minute, and we should keep you company."

"I can't think of any better company," she said. She sat on the top step, and the children sat on either side of her, Joshua holding the precious basket of honey jars on his lap.

"So what have you been doing? Do you have your sled ready for the first snow?"

Joshua nodded, studying the sky earnestly. "I wish it would snow. Do you think it will soon?"

"Well, November is a little early to get much snow," she said, careful not to promise what she couldn't deliver. "But it is gut to be ready for when it comes."

Sadie leaned against her. "Grossmammi says I am ready for a saucer all my own this year."

"If Grossmammi says it, it must be so," Naomi said. She put her arm around the little girl, irresistibly reminded of sitting on the back step, heads together with Ada, exchanging secrets.

"Grossmammi is going on a trip," Joshua informed her. "She is going to stay with Aunt Elizabeth for a while, and she says we must be very gut while she is away." He sat a little straighter, as if accepting that responsibility, making her think how like Nathan he was in temperament.

"I don't know why she has to go away." Sadie sounded a bit fretful. "I want her to stay here."

Naomi knew why Ada's mother was headed for Ohio. Elizabeth, Ada's next younger sister, was about to have her first baby after several years of trying. Naturally she'd want her mamm there.

"Maybe your aunt needs her for a little while," she suggested. "It would be wonderful kind of you to share Grossmammi with her, ain't so?"

"I guess," Sadie said, her voice filled with reluctance. She nuzzled against Naomi's coat. "But we need her more."

Naomi smiled, even as her heart winced. For sure, Ada's kinder needed her mamm. Emma

Miller had been the constant in their lives since Ada died.

"While she's away, you can write her a letter, and the postman will take it all the way to Aunt Elizabeth's house in Ohio," she said.

"But I can't write yet," Sadie protested, even as Joshua nodded at the idea.

"You can draw a picture for her," Naomi said. "I'll tell you what. While Grossmammi is away, I'll come over one day and help you make a picture and a letter to send her. All right?"

"Promise?" Joshua studied her face, as if measuring whether this grown-up could be trusted to do what she said.

"I promise." Naomi met his gaze.

Apparently satisfied, he smiled.

Warmed by that smile, Naomi put her free arm around him, hugging both children even as her heart hurt for their loss.

The door clicked behind them. Naomi looked up, to find Nathan watching her with an expression she couldn't interpret.

Chapter Two

Naomi had her arms around his children, and they leaned into her embrace. Nathan forced down a flicker of pain that it was Naomi, not Ada, who embraced them. This was a gut thing, he told himself firmly.

The idea that had taken shape in his mind when he was talking to Isaiah yesterday seemed even better today. Naomi could be the answer to his problems, and he could be the answer to hers. Why not grasp this solution?

Naomi was looking at him a bit apprehensively. He'd delayed too long in greeting her.

"Naomi, it's gut to see you. I see you got my message from Isaiah."

"Ja, he came over to tell me." She rose, pulling off her mittens. "The kinder were keeping me entertained."

"So I see." He held the door open. "You two go in to Grossmammi now."

"We want to go with you and Naomi," Sadie said, her pert tone an echo of her mother's voice.

"Not now." Nathan gestured to the kitchen. "Naomi and I have business to take care of. You can see her later."

Pouting a little, Sadie did as she was told, and Joshua followed her inside.

Once the door was closed, Nathan turned to Naomi. "I heard from Isaiah about your situation. I hope it is all right that he told me."

Naomi's smile was a bit rueful. "It will be all over the township by now, I should think."

He nodded, acknowledging the fact of life in Pleasant Valley—everyone knew everything, usually sooner rather than later. "So I understand why you have to find a place to put your beehives. Let's take a look around." He gestured toward her buggy. "If we take your buggy, we can cover more territory, ja?"

She nodded, walking quickly to the buggy. Naomi wasn't one to waste words, he'd noticed long ago. She'd been an odd choice of best friend for bubbling Ada, he'd always thought. But maybe that was why they were such close friends. They didn't compete with each other.

Naomi climbed to the buggy seat without waiting for him to help her. She slid across the seat and handed him the lines when he got up beside her. "You should drive, since you know where we are going."

It was a subtle reminder, he thought, that it was her buggy and her choice.

He took the lines and clucked to the horse. They moved off down the lane. "It won't be so easy to see the vegetation, now that everything has died back, but I'll show you what there is."

Like any farmer, he knew every inch of his land

as well as he knew his own body. But Naomi was the expert when it came to bees, and the decision would be hers.

Once they were behind the barn, he gestured off to the right. "This might be the best spot on my land for the hives. It's not far off the lane, so you could drive up close, but it's far enough from the house so the kinder won't be getting too close."

Naomi turned her head to gaze at the field, her bonnet brim cutting off his view of her face. Still, he didn't need to see her to know what Naomi looked like . . . he'd known her all his life, and she wasn't much different from the girl she'd been. Her hair was just as flax-colored as it had been when she was a child, drawn back severely from a center part and confined under her kapp.

Ada had usually had a strand or two of brown hair escaping to curl against her cheek, but Naomi's hair was as contained as her temperament, and that, everyone knew, was quiet, controlled, and serene, even in the midst of raising her four younger siblings and managing her difficult father. He didn't think he'd ever seen Naomi's blue eyes flash with anger. Small wonder the family had been shocked when Naomi refused to go along with her daad's decision for her life.

"What about clover?" Naomi asked, clearly thinking about her bees while he'd been wool-gathering.

"This field has plenty of clover. So does the

one on the other side of the lane. I suppose you mainly want clover honey." He snapped the reins, telling the mare to step up. "We'll go back a bit farther toward the woods."

The ground rose in a slow, gentle slope, then lifted more abruptly to the nearest of the rolling ridges that marked off Pleasant Valley. The woods were a mix of hemlock, pine, and maples.

He drew up where the lane widened enough to turn around before it petered out to a narrow track. "Right along there at the edge of the pasture you'll find a nice growth of alfalfa, and that field running up to the woods is filled with wild-flowers in summer."

"Really?" The face she turned to Nathan was animated. Apparently there was something that could excite her—the bees. "I've always wanted to try alfalfa and wildflower honey. You can get such different flavors by providing a variety of vegetation the bees like. Daad's fields have mostly red clover. It makes a nice, mild honey, but I'd love to have other flavors."

He nodded, not knowing much about it but enjoying seeing her pleasure. That boded well for her response to his offer, he'd think.

"There's something else I want to show you." He turned the mare, enjoying the ease with which the animal moved. One thing you had to give Sam Esch, for sure . . . he knew how to train a buggy horse.

"Right up here," he said, as they moved back up the lane toward the house and outbuildings. He could sense the interest simmering in Naomi. So far, so gut.

He drew up at the outbuilding, and hopped down. He held up his hand to Naomi, but she was already jumping down as lightly as a girl.

He unlocked the door with the key that hung from a hook well out of reach of the kinder. "This was built for a chicken coop, but Daad decided the chickens did better on the other side of the barn. He used this place for storage, but we cleared it out last year."

He fell silent, giving her time to observe the wide-plank floor, swept clean, the windows at either end, the long rows of wooden counters on either wall where nesting boxes had once sat, and the rectangular wooden table he'd moved in.

"I thought this would be the kind of space you'd need for processing and packaging the honey," he said finally, when she didn't speak. "Will it do?"

She looked at him then, her eyes shining. Funny, but he'd never noticed how dark a blue her eyes were—almost navy in color. No one would describe Naomi as beautiful, but her eyes were, for sure.

"It is a hundred times better than what I have now," she said. "But are you sure? You might find some other need for this space—"

"I would not go back on our arrangement once we have a deal," he said. He shouldn't have to say the words. Surely she knew that about him.

"A deal," she repeated slowly, and he could almost see her calculating. "Well, with what I make at the bakery, I should be able to pay a reasonable rent. But I don't know where I'm going to live yet, and that might—"

"I'm not wanting to take money from you, Naomi," he broke in, wondering if it was guilt he was feeling for manipulating her this way. "You see, with Emma being gone for three weeks or more helping Elizabeth, I need someone to watch the kinder. So I'm offering a trade: you get this for your honey yard in exchange for taking care of the kinder for me until Emma comes back. What do you say?"

He settled back, confident. Of course she would say yes. This was exactly what she needed for her bees, she already cared about the children, and everyone knew what a fine caregiver she was.

But Naomi didn't answer right away, and he felt a flicker of impatience with her.

Finally she spoke, not looking at him. "I . . . I would like to think on it for a day or two. Is that all right?"

Arguments sprang to his lips. He struggled, suppressing the words, sensing it would do no good. She was looking at him anxiously, and he managed to smile.

"Ja, of course. But I must know soon, because of Emma leaving."

She nodded, her gaze shielded. "Tomorrow. I will let you know tomorrow."

With that he had to be content.

"Am I being foolish?" Knowing she had to talk to someone she could trust to advise her, Naomi had sought out a quiet moment at the bakery in Pleasant Valley to talk with Paula Schatz and her niece, Hannah Brand, who ran the bakery together.

As Plain Mennonites, they understood her better than any Englisch employer ever could. Only the small print of their dresses and a slightly different kapp style marked them externally as different from the Amish, although they worshipped in churchhouses rather than in homes and had electricity and telephones in their houses.

"For sure you're not making a mistake in holding firm against your father's plans for you," Paula declared, the network of wrinkles around her eyes deepening. Paula had a reputation for being a bit outspoken, but she'd been a good friend to Naomi. "Your daad is . . . well, I won't say he's selfish, but he's overly fond of his own way."

"That's right," Hannah echoed loyally. "If he doesn't want you to live at home any longer after all that you've done for him, he shouldn't try to tell you what to do with the rest of your life."

"Ach, Daad is not so bad. He's just . . ." Naomi

let that fade away, because she couldn't think what to say. "Anyway, now that the shock has passed, I even feel a little excited. I thought the course of my life was set, but now it's wide open again. The trouble is that I don't know what to do with it."

Paula and Hannah exchanged glances in the way of communicating silently that they did. Hannah gave a slight nod.

Paula reached across the small round table to squeeze Naomi's hand. "Well, I know one thing you can do right now. With Hannah married and living in her own house, I'm feeling a bit lonesome in that apartment upstairs on my own. So Hannah's old room is yours for as long as you want it."

Naomi could only stare at her for a moment. Her brothers and sisters had invited her to move in with them, of course. That was only natural and to be expected in an Amish family. But for Paula to offer was different, and no one who knew Paula would believe the part about her being lonely.

"I . . . That is wonderful generous of you. But I should not intrude—"

"Ach, who is talking about intruding? You work here, you are our friend. What could be more natural? Besides, it is only for as long as you want. If you make other plans, it will not hurt my feelings."

"Say yes, Naomi," Hannah said, adding her

urging. "It would make us happy to be able to help you."

Relief swept through Naomi. Staying with Paula would ease her trip in getting to work, that was sure. She could even help Paula with the baking in the evening, which would give Hannah a break. And she'd have the time she desperately needed to think about her future without pressure, something she wouldn't have if she stayed with any of her siblings.

"Denke, Paula. Hannah. I would be ser pleased to accept your invitation."

"Gut, gut, that's settled then." Paula patted her hand. "You chust bring your things in anytime. Today, if you want. I would think the sooner you're out of your father's house, the better."

"I think you are right." She felt a little disloyal saying that about the place that had been her home all her life, but it was true. "I'll pack a few things tonight and bring them when I come to work tomorrow."

"Gut." Paula gave a satisfied nod.

"What will you do about the offer from Nathan?" Hannah said, her tone gentle. After many years away, Hannah had returned to the Mennonites of Pleasant Valley only earlier this year, but now she was happily married to William Brand, raising her small son, and as settled as if she'd never left. "If the situation is as good as you say for your beehives . . ."

"I know." Naomi could talk about it with Hannah, who was a loyal friend despite the differences between them. "I just . . . I feel as if all anyone values in me is my ability to take care of other people's children." She shook her head ruefully. "It sounds so selfish when I put it that way."

"You are gifted with children," Hannah said gently. "Look how my Jamie attached to you. But there's nothing wrong with wanting something else for yourself as a way of working. What about your bees?"

Naomi blinked. "What about them?"

"You know how everyone loves your honey. You could be packaging it and selling it yourself, making a nice business of it."

"Ja, for sure." Paula, ever the businesswoman, jumped in immediately. "All you need is to label the jars and decide on a price. We could put a display right on the counter and folks would snap it up."

"That's right." Hannah's eyes sparkled. "I know you give away most of your honey, but people would be glad to pay for it. You could even expand your business—get more hives, process more honey."

"I could." The idea took hold and would not be dismissed. Naomi couldn't have done it while living at home and taking care of all the gardening, the house, and the canning and preserving, but she could now. Betty was taking over all those tasks. "But that brings me back to where I'm going to put the hives. How could I take care of Nathan's children when I've refused my own brother?"

"That's entirely different," Hannah said. "This is only for a few weeks, not for life. And think of the rewards."

"But my work at the bakery—"

"We can handle that if we need to," Paula said. "It doesn't change anything."

Everything they said made sense, and Naomi discovered she couldn't find any good reason to keep arguing.

Any good reason except the one she couldn't speak—that each time she got too close to Nathan King, she felt again like that sixteen-year-old who had to say no to the things she wanted most in the world.

By late afternoon the next day, Naomi had begun to feel as if she'd been swept up by a tornado and put down in a totally different world. She stood behind the counter at the bakery, stacking fresh loaves of cinnamon bread in the wire basket, something she had done a hundred times before, but still, it was completely different today.

She had spent the morning checking on various farms where she might be able to put her hives. Several folks had offered her the space, apparently willing to risk her daad's disapproval, but none had been so good a situation as the one Nathan offered.

This afternoon she had moved a few of her belongings into the spare bedroom in the apartment over the bakery, settling her buggy horse in the stable behind Katie and Caleb Brand's shops just down the street. It was an obvious outward sign of her new life, and she'd half expected a clap of thunder to admonish her at her open flouting of her father's wishes.

Nothing had happened, and doing the familiar work was steadying. Still, she couldn't quite relax.

Her choices had narrowed when it came to the bees, and she'd promised Nathan an answer today. She must get over her foolishness, it seemed, and say yes to his offer. He was asking little enough from her. It certainly wasn't his fault that he reminded her of things better left in the past. Certainly Nathan would have long since forgotten the incident that loomed in her mind as a symbol of all she'd given up in her life. She must, as well.

As for Ada's kinder—well, they needed her, far more than any of her nieces and nephews did. And if it hurt her to grow to love them and then turn them over to someone else, she would smile and do it. After all, as Hannah said, it was only for a few weeks.

"Naomi?" Hannah's voice interrupted her

thoughts. "The bus has just pulled out, and I see Nathan and the children coming toward the shop. Could his mother-in-law have left for her daughter's already?"

Naomi turned, a loaf warm in her hands. Sure enough, Nathan walked right toward the bakery, holding hands with Joshua and Sadie in that protective way he had. If Emma had indeed left Pleasant Valley on the bus, Naomi had no time for wavering about her decision.

Nathan approached the door, his face determined under the brim of his black hat. She put the loaf in its proper place and smoothed down the white apron she wore in the bakery. Something fluttered in her stomach, gentle as a butterfly's wings. Time to stop dithering and give Nathan his answer.

The bell above the door jingled. Joshua and Sadie let go of Nathan's hands and came toward the counter in a rush, jostling each other in their haste.

"Grossmammi had to leave already," Joshua said, beating his small sister.

"She rode on a big, big bus," Sadie said. "I want to do that, too."

"I'm sure you will ride on a bus someday," Naomi told her. She looked up into Nathan's face, the butterfly flapping its wings faster. "So soon?" she said quietly, trying not to sound apprehensive in front of the kinder.

Nathan nodded, frowning a little. "There was a message on the answering machine in the phone shanty." He glanced at Joshua and Sadie, their faces pressed to the display cabinet, obviously not wanting to say more in front of them.

"I have a treat for two such good children," Hannah said, coming to the rescue. She slid the cabinet door open. "What will it be? Whoopie pies? Molasses cookies? Or a cupcake?"

The children looked up at her, eyes wide. "For us?" Joshua said.

"For you," Hannah said, smiling, her hand poised over the tray. "What do you like?"

Deciding took a few minutes, but finally Hannah led the children off to one of the round tables with a whoopie pie for Joshua and a chocolate cupcake for Sadie. Naomi could then let the concern show in her face.

"Is there a problem?"

Nathan shrugged. "I do not know more than that, but for sure Emma wanted to go at once."

Naomi nodded. Naturally Emma would do what she must, just as Naomi would. She opened her lips to say so, but Nathan spoke before she could.

"I have talked to my sister. She is ser busy with that big family of hers, but she will be glad to have Joshua and Sadie on any days that you need to be at the bakery. I hoped that would ease your mind a little."

"That is wonderful kind of Sarah. I would not

want to leave Paula and Hannah without any help."

"So, what do you say, Naomi? Shall we start moving your beehives?" Nathan smiled at her . . . the smile that was so seldom seen on his face in recent years.

Unfortunately, the smile increased her nervousness, and his mention of the beehives reminded her of something she should say to him . . . something that might change his mind about the whole thing.

"About the hives . . . I have been thinking that I might want to expand my operation and sell my honey." She watched his face closely, alert for any sign of disapproval. "That would mean more hives, more honey, more packaging."

He didn't look disapproving, only a bit puzzled. "That seems like a fine business for you, Naomi. You ought to have something to rely on."

Since she had no prospects of having a husband and kinder of her own. She finished what he was undoubtedly thinking, her heart wincing. But she would not let that hurt show on her face.

"That would not bother you? I would not want you to think that I am taking advantage of your offer."

He looked at her in what seemed honest surprise. "I could never think such a thing of you, Naomi. You were Ada's dearest friend, my friend, too, I hope. Have as many hives as you want. Now, do you have an answer for me?"

Still she hesitated, feeling as if the next step she took could change her life in ways she couldn't imagine. But she didn't really have a choice any longer. God had led her to this point. She would just have to trust that He controlled the future.

She sucked in a breath and looked at Nathan. "Ja, denke, Nathan. I accept your offer."

Chapter Three

By the next day, Nathan felt there was no time to waste. The sooner he got Naomi's precious beehives moved, the sooner he could stop worrying about who was watching the children.

At the moment, that someone was Libby Esch, Isaiah's wife, but she had her own work to do, and he didn't like to impose on her. So he'd picked up Naomi the first thing this morning with the spring wagon, and they were already nearing the lane to the Esch farm.

Naomi seemed to grow more tense the closer they got. He could sense her on the seat next to him, her body as tight as a coiled spring.

Was she regretting her decision already? Maybe he'd been wrong in pushing her into this agreement. There were other women he could have approached about taking care of Joshua and

Sadie while Emma was away, but none who were as uniquely suited to the job as Naomi was. Her close relationship with Ada, though it gave rise to grieving memories for him, was the very thing that endeared her to his children.

By the time he turned into the lane, he couldn't take the tension any longer. "Was ist letz, Naomi? Are you changing your mind about our agreement already?"

She turned a startled face to him. "No, of course I'm not regretting it."

"Then why are you clutching the seat so hard your fingers are like to break?"

"I . . . I'm not." She let go of the seat, rubbing her palms together. "I'm just concerned about moving the hives, that's all."

"We will be ser careful," he said. "And the mare is as steady as can be. She won't do anything unexpected."

"Ach, I know. I just . . ." Naomi let that trail off, as if unable to think of anything convincing to say.

"Komm." He tried to hold on to his patience. Was it possible Naomi wasn't as steady and serene as he'd always assumed? "Tell me what is really bothering you."

Naomi pressed her lips together for a moment. Then she shrugged. "I am worried about my daad. I would not want him to make a fuss about my decision in front of you." Her lips trembled a bit on the words.

His annoyance vanished. He should be ashamed of himself. Everyone knew how difficult Sam Esch could be, and everyone knew, as well, that he was displeased with his daughter's decision. Small wonder Naomi was feeling upset.

"Ach, I wouldn't worry about your daad." He tried to sound confident. "Most likely he won't even notice we're here."

That was hardly likely, but he couldn't think what else to say. He wasn't eager to have hard feelings directed toward him by a brother in the church. He could only hope Sam felt the same way.

Once the spring wagon had moved past the farmhouse without incident, Naomi seemed to relax a little. She pointed to the field beyond the barn. "The hives are there. I would think it best to turn around first, before we load them."

Naomi was pulling on long gloves as she spoke, and he felt a faint twinge of apprehension. He knew the dairy business inside out, but bee-keeping was a mystery to him. He could only trust to Naomi's experience.

"The bees are fairly dormant now, even though they don't actually hibernate." Naomi seemed to catch his thoughts as if he'd spoken. "Unless we jostle the hives and make them think we are a threat, they should stay quiet right through the move to their new home."

"Believe me, the last thing I want to do is

disturb them." He drew up next to the hives.

She smiled at his comment, as he'd intended. "Don't worry, then." She slid down before he could move to help her. "You'll turn the wagon while I check the hives to be sure all is well, ja?"

He nodded, hands tightening on the lines. He was used to being in charge on his own farm, but in this situation, he was just the helper.

When the wagon was properly positioned to allow them to move straight down the lane once they were loaded, he ground-tied the horse and went between the hives toward Naomi, careful not to startle her.

She was bending over one of the white, three-tiered hives, her face calm, her gaze intent. He waited, schooling himself to patience. Clearly he was going to need that quality when it came to Naomi and her bees.

Finally she looked up and nodded. "We will start with this one," she said.

He didn't question the decision. "What do you want me to do?"

"Luckily each hive is set on a board that can be lifted. That was Isaiah's idea." There was a trace of pleasure in her voice at her younger brother's cleverness. "At the time, I didn't think it would be needed, but now I'm glad of it."

She would never have anticipated moving them or leaving this place, in other words. But life had a way of taking sudden turns, as Nathan well knew. All you could do was try to hold on and accept the changes as God's will. That was easy to say but not so easy to do.

"You should put your gloves on now," Naomi prompted.

He nodded, pulling on the work gloves she'd told him to bring. "What now?"

"Grasp the board by the corners," she said. "Don't lift until I say."

A little amused at Naomi's bossiness, he obeyed. Holding the edges of the board, he waited for her signal, and they lifted the entire hive smoothly.

It was heavier than he'd expected. Was Naomi really going to be able to handle this? Maybe he should have brought Isaiah along to help.

But she didn't seem to strain at the weight. "I had best count our steps so that we move together," she said. "The ground is a bit rough. "Ready?"

"Ja." He held his breath, taking each step as she called it, matching the length of his strides to hers. Almost before he could speculate on what would happen if one of them tripped and dropped the hive, they'd reached the wagon.

"Let it rest on the tailgate until I climb in," he said. "Then we can slide it into place."

"Ja." Naomi smiled up at him once he stood above her on the wagon. "You are gut with the bees, Nathan. They need someone who is quiet and steady. I'm glad you are helping me."

He ducked his head, the characteristic humble response to praise, surprised by how pleased he was at Naomi's good opinion. "What would you do if you ever had to move a hive by yourself?"

"It happens sometimes," she said. "The hives are in three pieces, so I would just lift off one at a time. But this is a better way of doing it, I think. It's less likely to upset the bees."

Over the next half hour they worked together smoothly, transferring one hive after another to the wagon without incident. Naomi's cheeks grew rosy from the cold air. She must be tired, lifting the heavy hives and carrying them, but her serenity never faltered. Maybe that patience and caring served her equally well whether she was dealing with children or bees. The idea intrigued him.

"Bees are like kinder, ja?" He took his position at the side of one of the few remaining hives.

Naomi's smooth forehead wrinkled with puzzlement for a moment, but then she nodded, catching his meaning. "Ja, I guess they are. Both of them need a lot of loving attention in order to do their best."

That wasn't quite what he'd been thinking, but it was typical of Naomi's humility. Following her lead, he lifted the hive and began walking backward to the wagon. They were nearly there when Naomi's attention faltered, she missed a step, and the hive tilted.

Nathan reacted instantly, taking the full weight of the hive, leveling it. A dangerous buzzing issued from the hive, and he held his breath, imagining a swarm of angry bees coming after them.

"I'm sorry." Naomi's voice was soft. "That was my fault, for sure. I will keep talking, because they know my voice and it may calm them. Some people would say that I am foolish to think they know me, but I am sure. Just as the dairy cows know you, ja? So the bees know me and trust me and understand that I will not let anything bad happen." Her voice had grown slower and softer as she talked, and he realized that the hive was silent now, save for a low, even hum.

Naomi waited another moment, perfectly still even though he knew her muscles must be straining. Then she nodded, and they crossed the few feet to the wagon and transferred the hive.

Nathan held his breath as he slid it into place. Then he climbed back down, careful not to jostle the wagon with his movement.

"That was . . ." His words died out as he realized what it was that had caused Naomi to stumble. Sam Esch stood not ten feet away, staring at them.

"So." Sam's tone was a harsh contrast to Naomi's soft, comforting voice. "You are really going through with this foolishness."

The comment was clearly directed at Naomi, but Nathan found himself stiffening anyway.

"Nathan has kindly offered to have the hives on his farm." No trace of annoyance showed in Naomi's manner. "We will move them today, so that Betty need not worry any longer about being stung."

"That is not the point, as you well know." Sam's face reddened. "The plans I made were for the best. I never thought to say this about you, Naomi, but you are being disrespectful and disobedient. Scripture directs children to obey their parents."

"Naomi is not a child any longer." Nathan spoke before thinking and immediately regretted it. He could only make things worse, not better.

But the look of gratitude that Naomi sent his way almost made it worthwhile. Almost. He had no wish to be at odds with Sam Esch. Sam was well-known for hanging on to a grudge, despite the church's teaching on forgiveness.

Sure enough, Sam's face turned an alarming shade of purple. "Naomi is my child. She will do as I say." He turned the force of his personality on her. "Since you have the hives loaded, you can take them right to Dick Holder's farm and accept payment. Then you will move to your brother's without any more foolishness."

Nathan expected Naomi to wilt under the force of Sam's wrath. Surprisingly, her expression didn't change, whatever turmoil she was feeling inside.

"I am sorry to inconvenience you, Daadi. But I

have made my own arrangements. You do not need to worry about me any longer. I wish you and Betty every happiness in your new lives."

Sam's hands clenched into fists at this calm, open defiance. "No daughter of mine—"

"Sam?" A voice caroled through the frosty air. "Sam, please komm. I must speak with you." Betty stood at the edge of the yard, a shawl wrapped around her shoulders.

Sam's angry glare seemed to wilt. He turned toward the yard. "In a moment, Betty. I just—"

"But I need you now, Sam. Komm." She shivered elaborately. "Don't make me stand here in the cold. And you know I dare not be any closer to the beehives."

Sam glanced back at his daughter. Nathan could almost see the angry words trembling on his lips. Then, as if compelled by a force stronger than anger, he turned and walked toward Betty. She took his arm firmly in hers. Talking, smiling at him, she led him toward the house.

All the breath seemed to go out of Naomi. She sagged, and Nathan reached out quickly to steady her.

"It's all right now," he said. "Betty will keep him busy, and we can load the last few hives and be out of here quick as can be."

Naomi swallowed so hard he could see the muscles work in her throat. "I am sorry. I did not want to expose you to Daad's anger."

He wasn't sure how to respond. She was making too much of it, it seemed to him. But it was clearly important to her.

"I have seen and heard far worse than Sam," he said finally, keeping his tone light. "He will get over this, you'll see."

"I hope so." Her expression was so troubled that his heart hurt for her.

"I know so." He smiled, inviting her to see the light side. "Anyway, if she has half a chance, Betty will keep him occupied, ja?"

She was silent for so long that he thought he'd failed to lift her spirits. Then, finally, she smiled. "Love makes people do funny things, I guess."

Feeling ridiculously pleased at having made her smile, he nodded.

Naomi felt she couldn't draw an easy breath until the bees were safely settled in their new home. That confrontation with Daad had been more upsetting than she'd wanted Nathan to see. After all, Daad wasn't his problem, and she didn't want him to face any repercussions in the community for helping her.

But Nathan seemed to take everything in stride. When they'd arrived at his farm, Isaiah and Nathan's father had hurried to help, and they'd had the bees settled quickly and without incident. The men had gone off to the barn, talking of this and that, with no mention made of Daad's scene.

Relieved, tired, and a bit apprehensive all at the same time, Naomi headed for the house, prepared for the next challenge . . . convincing Nathan's children that she was an adequate substitute for their grandmother for the next few weeks.

She went into the kitchen, only realizing how chilled she'd been when she felt its warmth, quickly followed by the equally warm hug from her young sister-in-law Libby.

"You feel half-frozen," Libby chided. "You must warm up. I made hot chocolate for the kinder. You'd like some, ja?"

"That sounds wonderful gut." Naomi slipped her heavy jacket off, smiling at Libby's cheerful greeting. Libby and Isaiah had been married just a year, and Libby still seemed much more like a teenager than a married woman, with her rosy cheeks, sparkling dark eyes, and the enthusiastic way she had of greeting every new challenge. And it was certain-sure that the upheaval in her husband's family presented a challenge.

Libby put a steaming mug on the table, so Naomi sat down. She smiled at Joshua and Sadie, who had identical cocoa mustaches on their upper lips.

"Hot chocolate is sure a treat on a cold day, ain't so?"

Joshua nodded, but Sadie pouted. "It doesn't taste like Grossmammi's," she said.

Naomi caught the flicker of hurt in Libby's face.

Libby was still young enough to be bothered by such a comment.

"Of course not," Naomi said. "Hot chocolate is supposed to taste different, according to the person who made it." She took a sip of Libby's cocoa. "Hmm, I think Libby's tastes like pretty smiles. What does your grossmammi's taste like?"

Sadie's mood changed, quick as the flicker of a firefly. "Hugs," she said promptly. "Grossmammi's tastes like hugs."

"Gut answer, Sadie," she said, exchanging glances with Libby. "If Grossmammi was here right now, I'll bet she'd give you a big hug."

"If you make it, what does yours taste like?" Joshua asked, his little face serious.

"Ach, you'll have to taste it and tell me. The person who makes it can never say."

He nodded, as if satisfied with her answer, but didn't say anything else, lifting his mug to his lips instead.

Naomi watched him, wishing she knew what went on in Joshua's thoughts. Sadie's emotions seemed all on the surface for anyone to read, but Joshua, like his father, didn't give himself away so easily.

"Ach, I must get home to fix Isaiah's lunch." Libby reached for her jacket, her eyes lighting up at the thought of her husband. "There's beef stew simmering on the stove, and I brought two loaves of bread when I came this morning." She nodded toward the bread board on the counter.

"Denke, Libby. That is ser kind of you." Libby's efforts had saved her the trouble of rushing to get lunch fixed. Her arrangement with Nathan was that she would fix lunch and supper, but she'd have to leave quickly after that to get back to Paula's before it was too dark.

"No problem at all." Libby gave her another quick hug and whirled toward the door. "I'm ser glad you're here, Naomi. And you know you're wilkom to move in with us anytime. We wish you would."

"Ach, wouldn't that be a fine thing, to move in on a pair of newlyweds," Naomi said, smiling. "Get on with you, before Isaiah comes home and finds the kitchen cold."

Dimpling, Libby waved to the children and hurried out, the door closing on the wave of chilled air.

Still smiling, Naomi turned back to the children, to find them surveying her solemnly. A wave of uneasiness swept through her. Ada's children had suffered an enormous loss when their mother died. Now their grandmother, the person they relied on most, was gone. A few weeks no doubt felt like an eternity at their age. How could she possibly meet their needs?

Nonsense. She gave herself a mental shake. They were just children. They needed to feel as if they belonged, to feel useful, to feel loved. She could meet those needs, surely.

A half hour later, Naomi wasn't so convinced. Joshua and Sadie resisted every effort to get close to them, Sadie with her constantly reiterated refrain that Grossmammi didn't do it that way while Joshua, outwardly obedient, kept his every thought and feeling locked up inside.

Time, she reminded herself. It takes time.

Meanwhile, Nathan and his father would be coming in soon for lunch.

She checked on the beef stew, stirring to be sure it wasn't sticking, and then found a knife to cut the bread.

She glanced at Sadie, who stood behind her, holding a rag doll by one foot. "Sadie, will you set the table for middaagesse, please?"

Sadie responded with a pout. "Let Joshua do it."

Naomi gave her the look she always used on her younger siblings when sassiness occurred. "I'm sure Joshua has his own chores to do."

"No, he doesn't," Sadie said.

Naomi ignored the comment. "I'll get the plates down from the cabinet and you put them around."

For a moment the issue hung in the balance. Then Joshua spoke.

"I'll help you, Sadie. We'll do it together, ja?"

"That is ser kind of you, Joshua." Naomi set the plates on the table, then turned back to the stove, showing her assumption that they'd do as they should.

For a moment there was silence behind her. Then she heard the plunk of plates being placed around the table.

Allowing herself a slight smile, she took a handful of flatware from the drawer. "Can you figure out what each person needs to eat with?"

"For sure," Sadie said, her moodiness dispelled. "I know."

Naomi warmed some applesauce, adding a sprinkle of cinnamon. Sadie's comment teased at the back of her mind. How could Joshua not have chores? He was six, an age at which every Amish child accepted responsibility as a matter of course. Even a three-year-old could toddle around the table, putting spoons in place. Perhaps Sadie had just been exaggerating, as Ada used to when she wanted to make Naomi laugh.

Nathan and his father came in a few minutes later, causing her to shrug off her perplexed thoughts.

"I set the table, Daadi," Sadie announced.

"Gut, gut," Nathan said, hanging up his coat.

"I helped, too," Joshua said.

Naomi set the tureen of beef stew on the table. "I thought perhaps he had his own outside chores to do, but he wanted to help his sister."

"That was kind," Nathan's father said, ruffling Joshua's hair. "Everyone helps, and then no one has to do too much."

For some reason Naomi didn't understand, that comment seemed to annoy Nathan, to judge by the look he cast his father.

"There will be plenty of time for outside chores when the boy is older," he said, his tone gruff. "Let us sit down, before Naomi's fine meal is cold."

"It's mostly Libby's fine meal," Naomi said. "She had everything cooked before we returned."

Did Nathan see the disappointment on Joshua's face at his comment about waiting until he was older? Why wouldn't he be training Joshua in work around the farm, something that surely was natural? Her brothers had been helping Daad at his age, just as her sisters had been helping her. That was how kinder learned.

She slipped into a seat at the side of the table and found that Ezra King, Nathan's father, was surveying her with something like approval. Perplexed, she bowed her head for the silent prayer before the meal. Usually at this point she mentally recited the Lord's Prayer. Today she found other words filling her mind.

Guide me to understand this family and their needs, Father. Lead me to put aside my own selfish concerns and see how to help them.

She finished just as Nathan raised his head, the silent prayer ended.

Over the meal the conversation was mostly about the beehives. Mainly it was Ezra who seemed interested, plying her with questions, which she willingly answered. It was nice to find someone who wanted to know about bee-keeping. Her own family, other than Isaiah, usually thought of it as Naomi's rather odd hobby, even though they cheerfully ate the honey.

By the time Nathan and Ezra went back out to work, Joshua and Sadie had picked up on their grossdaadi's interest.

"We want to see the beehives, Naomi." Sadie carried her plate to the sink without being asked. "Please can we see them?"

"Ja, please," Joshua added. "We never saw a beehive up close before."

Much as she welcomed their interest, Naomi hesitated. "Suppose we wait until tomorrow to visit the bees," she said.

Sadie's face puckered, and she looked ready to make a fuss.

"You see, moving is very hard on bees," Naomi added quickly. "They like to have their hives in the same place, year after year after year. Imagine how hard it would be for them to wake up and find they're in a different place." She could see Sadie's quick imagination working on that image. "If we wait until tomorrow to visit them," she continued, "they'll have a chance to get settled down. Then they won't be bothered by our visit. All right?"

They nodded.

"But what will we do this afternoon?" Sadie added. "I want to do something."

"We'll make a letter to send to your gross-mammi," she said, remembering the promise she'd made before she'd realized that she'd be taking care of them. "Joshua can print the words, and Sadie, you can make a picture."

Sadie's pout wasn't quite gone. "I don't know what to make a picture of."

"What about the beehives? You saw them when your daadi and I went past in the wagon, didn't you?"

Sadie's face lit up, making her look so like Ada that it grabbed Naomi's heart. "I'll get the paper and crayons," she said, and scurried from the room, to return a moment later waving paper and clutching a box of crayons.

Joshua slid into a chair. "You'll have to help me with the words," he said. "I'm not in school yet."

She'd intended to wash the dishes while they worked on their letter, but the dishes could wait. "I will be happy to do that with you, Joshua."

Sadie was already busy with her picture, the tip of her tongue showing between her lips as she concentrated. Naomi had never seen a purple hive, but she didn't intend to discourage the child.

Joshua, a sheet of lined paper in front of him, studied all the crayons before picking up a red one. "What should I say?"

"Suppose you start with 'Dear Grossmammi,'" she said.

He nodded and bent to the paper. To her surprise, he didn't need as much help as she'd expected, given that he wasn't in school yet.

He had turned six in September. Nathan certain-sure could have started him in school if he'd wanted. Apparently he hadn't wanted.

She spelled a word here and there, helped Sadie decide on the colors for the trees she was drawing, showed Joshua how to spell *hive.* It was very peaceful in the warm kitchen, and she began to relax, just as the children did. Her fears had been silly, maybe. For sure she would miss Joshua and Sadie when their time together was over, but this was a unique chance to get to know Ada's children better. She shouldn't let her own private grief affect that fact.

The door opened and she looked up, startled, not expecting Nathan to return so soon. But it wasn't Nathan, and her stomach clutched. Jessie Miller, Ada's youngest sister, stood there, door open behind her, letting a blast of cold air into the kitchen and sending the children's papers fluttering to the floor.

That was Jessie, for sure. She always had to make people look at her. Though she must be over twenty by now, she acted much of the time like a thirteen-year-old, causing her mamm, Emma, endless worry. As the Plain People said delicately, Jessie was a touch odd.

"Jessie, how nice to see you. Shut the door,

please. You're letting the cold air in." Naomi had found, over the years, that addressing Jessie as calmly as if she were about ten worked as well as anything.

Jessie shut the door with a decided slam. "You can leave now, Naomi," she announced. "I'm going to take care of my sister's children."

Chapter Four

Nathan stopped on his way into the barn, his attention caught by the buggy pulled up by the back door of the house. He knew it, for sure. It belonged to Ada's mother. And since Emma was off in Ohio already, it could only be Jessie, her youngest daughter, who'd driven it here.

Concern flicked at him like a pesky gnat, and he tried to wave it away. It was natural enough for Jessie to stop by, wasn't it? With her mamm away, she was probably lonesome.

Still . . . without pausing to analyze his reaction, he headed for the house. Emma had talked about taking Jessie with her when she went to help her other daughter, but for whatever reason, it had come to nothing.

Maybe he should have offered to keep track of Jessie while Emma was away. Concern turned to guilt. Emma did so much for him and the kinder —that was the least he could have done. But he couldn't help cringing at the thought of trying to watch over her.

He opened the back door and stepped through the mud room to the kitchen, not bothering to take his jacket off. He didn't think to be inside that long.

Papers and crayons were scattered across the kitchen table. It looked as if Naomi and the children had been working on a project when Jessie came in. At the moment Joshua and Sadie were watch-ing their aunt with a bit of wariness.

Jessie swung to face him, and as always, he was forcibly reminded of Ada—same rosy cheeks, same curling brown hair and sparkling eyes. But what had been pertness in Ada was something sharper in Jessie. She was as impetuous as a child, he sometimes thought.

"Jessie, I did not think to see you today. Is there any word from your mamm?"

"I told Naomi she could go." Jessie ignored his question, intent on her own plans, whatever they might be. "But she won't. You tell her, Nathan."

His heart sank. Jessie could be unreasonable when she set her mind to it. "Why would I tell Naomi to leave?" He kept his voice calm, as if he spoke to a shying horse. "She is here to help with the kinder while your mamm is away."

"You don't need her." Jessie sent a flashing look at Naomi, and he realized that even Naomi's serenity seemed a bit disturbed. "I can take care of my own niece and nephew without anybody else around."

Warning lights flashed in his thoughts. Ada had never allowed Jessie to watch the children alone, and Ada had certain-sure known her own sister.

"Is that what your mamm said?" he asked, knowing full well it wasn't.

Jessie pouted. "Mamm thinks I can't do anything, but I can. I can!" Her voice rose on the words.

Harassed, he looked at Naomi, wishing he could tell her to take the children out without saying the words and upsetting Jessie even more.

Naomi took Joshua and Sadie by the hand. "The kinder were just going to show me their pony," she said quietly. "We'll leave you to talk."

It seemed he didn't need words for Naomi to understand. Jessie reached out a detaining hand, but Naomi had already led the children past her.

"Gut idea." He ushered the little ones into the mud room where their jackets hung. "Jessie, I see there is some coffee still in the pot. Would you like a cup to warm you before you drive back home?"

"I told you. I'm not going home. I'm staying here to watch Joshua and Sadie. In fact, I should move in while Mamm is away. I'm your own sister-in-law, not like Naomi. She isn't anything to you."

The door closed, and he could only hope Naomi

hadn't heard that last comment. "Komm, now, Jessie. You know that wouldn't be fitting, for you to stay here. Besides, I already made arrangements with Naomi."

"I don't care—"

"Soon you'll have a new niece or nephew." He kept talking, hoping to distract her. "I'm sure you'll be going out to Ohio to visit your sister and the new little one, won't you?"

"I guess." The topic of a trip to Ohio seemed to distract her. "I don't know why Mamm didn't take me this time. I could help."

"I'm sure you could." He kept his tone soothing, relieved that the storm seemed to be passing. Ada had always said that Jessie's tempers would come less frequently as she grew older. He hoped she'd been right. "But right now, your mamm trusts you to take care of things at home, ain't so?"

"There's nothing to take care of but the horses and chickens, and anyone can do that."

"But not as well as you can," he said, praying for calm. "Your mamm is counting on you, ain't so?"

"I guess so." She began to button her coat.

"I'll walk out to the buggy with you," he said. "Maybe when you get home, your mamm will have sent a message about the new boppli."

"Maybe so." Jessie's steps quickened, and they crossed the porch and approached her buggy.

Relieved, he began to think about getting back

to his work. But Jessie grabbed his arm, her fingers digging in. She was looking past him, to the paddock where Naomi stood with the children, admiring the black pony nuzzling Joshua's hand.

"You have to be careful," Jessie said, lowering her voice as if afraid someone would hear.

Nathan's patience was waning. "I'm always careful of the kinder."

"Not the kinder. It's Naomi you have to be careful of. She wants to take Ada's place."

The idea was so ludicrous he nearly laughed, but he caught himself in time. Nothing offended Jessie more than thinking someone was laughing at her.

"I'm sure Naomi has no such idea," he said. "But I promise, I'll be careful."

That seemed to soothe Jessie, and she got into the buggy and drove off down the lane without another word.

For a moment he stood looking after her, feeling the worry nagging at him. Shouldn't Jessie be outgrowing these odd humors of hers? Sometimes she acted as if she were thirteen instead of twenty-one.

He shook his head, trying to shake off the worry. Now he had to go and say something to Naomi, he supposed. Women certainly complicated a man's life.

When he reached the paddock, his daad had joined the children, giving them bits of apple to feed Coal, the black pony. Naomi rested her hands on the top bar of the fence, watching them with a smile. Nathan came to stand next to her.

"If they feed that pony much more, she'll be too fat to pull the pony cart," he said.

"I don't blame them. Coalie's a sweet-tempered creature, ain't so?"

He nodded, wondering what he could say to put the incident with Jessie in its proper place. He studied Naomi's face. She was her usual contained self again, and the hint of distress he'd seen when he first came in the house was banished. She hadn't bothered to put a bonnet on just to come out to the paddock, and the chill breeze tossed the strings of her kapp.

"It was gut of you to bring the kinder out," he said finally. "Jessie is not so temperamental when Emma is here." Was that an explanation or an apology? Maybe a little of each.

"I understand," Naomi said. "I just was not sure what to do when Jessie said what she did. I knew that Ada did not leave her alone with the kinder, but I didn't know if that had changed."

"No." He found himself wanting to say more— to pour out what worried him about Ada's little sister. But that seemed disloyal, and really was none of Naomi's business.

Well, that wasn't quite true. Naomi had charge of Joshua and Sadie when he wasn't there, so she had a right to be concerned.

"No," he repeated. "I think it best not to rely on Jessie to watch them. Emma says she is young for her age, and not responsible enough yet." He realized how ferhoodled that sounded as soon as he said it and found himself resenting the fact that Naomi had made it necessary.

Naomi was regarding him with a grave expression. "Maybe Jessie could use a little help. There is a clinic over in Mifflin County—"

"Nonsense," he said sharply. He knew the clinic she meant. It was run by Mennonites, and it served people from the Plain communities who needed help with mental problems. "Jessie's family is perfectly able to deal with any problems she has."

And it's none of your business. He didn't add the words, but he might as well have.

Supper was ready, keeping warm on the stove while Naomi waited for Nathan to come in the house so that she could leave for town. She'd already seen Isaiah walking across the stubble of the cornfield toward the house he and Libby rented, and a few minutes ago Ezra King's buggy had passed the house as he headed back to his daughter's place.

When Nathan did come in, she'd leave quickly. She'd already been embarrassed enough for one day over his implication that she'd been gossiping about Jessie.

Her cheeks burned just thinking about it. Nobody would accuse her of being a blabbermaul. It wasn't in her nature. Anyway, she'd just been expressing her concern for Ada's little sister. Most likely none of her family wanted to admit it, but pretending Jessie would outgrow her problems didn't seem to be helping at all.

Sadie, who had been building a house with blocks in the corner of the kitchen, skipped across the room to grasp Naomi's apron. "Can I have a snack, please, Naomi? I'm awful hungry."

"You are, are you? Well, supper is ready when your daadi comes in. In the meantime, what about a carrot stick?" She offered the saucer of carrot and celery sticks she'd cleaned for supper.

Sadie tilted her head to one side. "I'd rather have a cookie."

"Cookies are for dessert. You can have some carrots and celery now."

Sadie looked for a moment as if she'd protest, but when Joshua left his game behind to grab a handful of carrots, she changed her mind and snatched a few.

"Denke," Joshua said, mindful of his manners. "Are you going to have supper with us, Naomi?"

"I'm afraid not. I have to drive into town to the bakery, and if I stay any longer, it will be dark by the time I get there."

"I wish you could stay and put us to bed," Sadie said. "Daadi isn't so gut at that as

Grossmammi. She likes to snuggle and tell stories."

"Maybe you should tell Daadi that's what you like," she suggested. "Sometimes daadis don't think of things like that." She put an arm around Sadie and hugged her, then tickled her until she giggled.

What she'd said was true enough—men didn't seem to take naturally to hugs and snuggles as women did with young ones. But she would think Nathan would make an extra effort in that way, just because Ada was no longer here.

"I don't see why it has to get dark so early," Sadie said, with a quicksilver change of subject. "I wish it stayed light so we could play outside after supper." She climbed on a chair so that she could see out the window, making a face at the gathering dusk.

"It's the change of seasons," Joshua said. "Everyone knows that, silly."

"I'm not silly," Sadie retorted. "We could have fall and winter and still have it be light out, couldn't we?"

"I'm afraid not." Naomi suppressed a smile at the child's reasoning. "You see, God made the earth to turn so that each part of it would get springtime and harvest time and even winter, when the plants sleep and get ready to come back again in the spring. Every one of God's creatures needs a rest time, rabbits and raspberries and even little girls."

Joshua nodded. "That's why Daadi and Grossdaadi and Isaiah cut all the corn and the hay, so that we would have enough to feed the animals all winter long." He spoke with the lofty assurance of the older brother. "Maybe next year I can help, Grossdaadi says."

Naomi bit back a comment about how her brothers had helped when they were his age. Nathan obviously didn't want his son involved with the farm work, and that was his decision.

"You know what I like about winter?" Sadie seemed to think she'd been out of the spotlight long enough.

"Sled riding? Building a snowman?" Naomi guessed.

"No, silly." Sadie hopped down from the chair and launched herself against Naomi's knees.

Naomi caught her, spinning her around and making her laugh. "What then? Icicles?"

"Christmas," Sadie crowed. "I love Christmas. I want to make a present for Daadi, and one for Grossdaadi, and for Grossmammi—" She paused for breath.

"I wish we could make presents," Joshua said. "I remember when Mammi helped me make a bowl out of clay for Daadi."

The sorrow in his voice cut Naomi to the heart. "We can work on presents," she said. "I will help you, and if we haven't finished when your Grossmammi comes back, I'm sure she will help you." It was probably just as well to remind them and herself that she was here temporarily.

Sadie threw her arms around Naomi in another massive hug, and even Joshua smiled. Naomi's heart warmed. They were dear to her already, these children of Ada's. How could she help but love them, just as she'd loved their mother?

The clop of hooves sounded from outside, and Naomi glanced at the window. "Your daadi is bringing my buggy. It's time for me to go, but I will see you first thing tomorrow, ja?"

"Will we start on the presents tomorrow?" Sadie said, not to be diverted from the subject of Christmas now that it had come up.

"I will give some thought to what you could make, and we'll talk about it tomorrow, all right? I'll have to get the materials you need for the presents, so we need to decide what you're going to make first."

"Shh." Sadie put her finger to her lips as the back door opened. "It's a secret."

"What is a secret?" Nathan said, coming into the kitchen.

"We can't tell you, Daadi," Sadie said.

"Or it wouldn't be a secret," Joshua added.

Judging by the sparkle in Sadie's eyes, Naomi doubted that she'd be able to keep a secret for more than a few minutes, but there was no harm in that.

"There is meat loaf ready for your supper, with

potatoes and carrots. Also applesauce and gelatin salad and fresh rolls."

"Sounds great," Nathan said. He was looking at the stove, not at her, as if perhaps he was no more eager to look at her than she was to look at him. "You don't need to go to so much trouble."

"No trouble," she said, taking her jacket from the hook and slipping it on. "Maybe you can make a list of things you and the kinder like, so I'm sure to have them." She turned to the little ones. "I will see you tomorrow. Have sweet dreams."

Their voices echoed in her ears as she tied her bonnet in place and went outside. To her surprise, Nathan came out with her, and she found herself tensing. Was he going to say something else about Jessie?

He took her elbow to help her up to the buggy seat and then paused, holding her arm. "Naomi, I am sorry I spoke sharp about Jessie earlier. I should not have."

She might be able to think of something to say if not for the firm clasp of his hand, warm even through layers of dress and jacket. "It's all right," she said after what she felt was too long a time. "Ada used to talk to me about her worries over Jessie, that's why I spoke. But I would never say anything to anyone else."

"I know you're not a blabbermaul, Naomi." He gave her one of his rare smiles. "I will see you tomorrow then."

He handed her up into the buggy. She drove off down the lane, her arm still tingling.

"The kinder are dear little ones." Naomi paused in kneading the cinnamon raisin loaf long enough to answer Paula's question about how the day had gone. "I can't take their grossmammi's place, for sure, but maybe I can keep them happy while she's away."

"Ach, you know full well that if anyone can, it's you." Paula had a sprinkling of flour on her glasses, as usual, and maybe even a bit in her gray hair. She was engrossed in making the rye loaves that folks loved so dearly. "It's not being prideful to accept that God gave you certain gifts."

"One of your gifts is making your rye bread, that's certain-sure," Naomi said. "The customers can't get enough of it."

"It's the orange rind I put in," she said, apparently serious although Naomi doubted it was just a matter of orange rind. "And speaking of things folks love, when are you going to bring me some jars of your honey that I can put up for sale?"

"Goodness, I haven't even thought about it. I would need to put some kind of labels on the jars. And what would we charge? Besides, all of this year's honey is in the storage cellar at Daad's. I don't know what he'd think if I wanted to take it away."

"It's yours, after all." Paula's tone was practical, as always. "The honey came from your bees. You bought the hives, you took care of the bees, and you packaged the honey. It's up to you what you do with it. Besides, the two of them certain-sure can't eat that much honey."

True enough, but Naomi still quailed at the thought of going to Daad's house and removing the jars of honey. "I'll think on it," she said evasively.

Somewhat to her surprise, Paula didn't pursue the subject. They worked on opposite sides of the long table in the bakery kitchen. Darkness pressed against the windowpanes, but inside was the glow of the lights and the warmth of the ovens.

It was peaceful, being here with Paula, kneading the bread and shaping it into loaves that would nourish others. The rhythm of kneading was soothing, and it made Naomi happy to think that she was giving Hannah this evening to spend with her husband and son. It made a long day, for sure, but it was worthwhile, and that was a good feeling.

Finishing the loaves and setting them aside under clean tea towels for a second rising, Naomi began shaping the walnut coffee ring. Slicing partially through the roll of filled dough, she turned each slice so that the rich filling showed. They would bake the rings tonight, and then Paula could finish them off quickly with a bit of powdered sugar drizzle in time for the morning coffee rush.

"Are you sure it's not a problem for me to be gone so many days at Nathan's?" Paula was so kind to her that Naomi felt a twinge of guilt each day she took off.

"Now, we've been through all that," Paula said with mock severity. "I'd be selfish for sure if I begrudged that time to help a neighbor. Anyway, with Hannah partnering with me now, things are running smoothly. You don't need to worry."

That raised another troubling thought. Paula had always said she could use Naomi for as many hours as she could work, but that was before her niece, Hannah, had come back to Pleasant Valley and gone into partnership with her. Maybe . . .

A sharp knock at the back door interrupted Naomi's train of thought. She exchanged startled glances with Paula and then reached for a towel to wipe her hands off.

"I'll go."

"Look before you unlock the door," Paula cautioned, and she nodded.

There'd been a time when no one in Pleasant Valley would even think of locking their doors, but times had changed, even here.

She drew aside the curtain on the window to find that the late-evening caller was her brother Elijah. Her heart jolted with unpleasant speculations, and she hurried to unlock the door and yank it open.

"Elijah, was ist letz? Is one of the kinder sick? Or something wrong with Daad?"

"No, no, nothing like that." Removing his hat, he nodded politely to Paula. "I am sorry to disturb you when you are working, but this is the only chance I had. Naomi, I must talk with you."

He sounded solemn. With the sense of some new disaster about to befall her, Naomi led him into the shop.

Chapter Five

Naomi switched on the low lamps in the section of the bakery where there were tables and chairs for customers. She gestured Elijah to a seat and stood for a moment, hand on the back of a chair.

This was the first opportunity she'd had to talk with Elijah alone about her situation with Daad. As the oldest son, even though he was younger than she by nearly three years, Elijah was the one Daad was most likely to listen to. If anyone could heal this breach in the family, surely it would be Elijah.

His coming here alone to talk was a good sign, wasn't it? She smiled at him as he removed his winter black felt hat and put it on the table.

"You'll have a cup of coffee, won't you? And there's some walnut streusel coffee cake, too."

He started to shake his head, and then he seemed to think better of it. "Ja, that would be a treat just now."

Elijah seemed tense, but perhaps he'd relax if she gave him a bit of time. Naomi fetched the coffee, setting a cream pitcher and sugar bowl next to the cup. Elijah doctored his coffee so much it was a wonder he could taste it at all. She cut a generous slab of the streusel coffee cake and put it in front of him before she sat down.

"Eat," she urged him. "We don't often have a chance to sit and talk by ourselves, ain't so?"

"Ja, that's what Lo—That's what I thought," he said.

So it was Lovina who had prompted this evening visit. Naomi's sister-in-law was a loving creature, but she had a firm core when she thought something needed done. She had more influence on Elijah than probably even he realized.

Elijah sipped the coffee, his ruddy cheeks flushing a little. Maybe he sensed Naomi watching him.

"Paula's made a gut little business for herself here, ja?" He glanced around the room as if he hadn't seen it dozens of times before.

Did he know that Naomi could read the signs only too well? He was still her little brother, when all was said and done, and she knew when he was stalling.

"Komm, Elijah." She kept her voice gentle. "You did not stop in to talk about Paula's bakery. Whatever it is, it's best just to speak out."

"Ach, I was trying to lead up to it." His face relaxed in the slightly shamefaced smile she remembered from his childhood. "The thing is, Lovina and I were talking. It seems like Daadi surprised us all so much with his news that we didn't have time to think things through. Lovina thinks . . . well, we both fear that it wasn't handled very well. It's up to Daad if he wants to remarry, for sure, but he might have given more thought to you."

Naomi was surprised and touched. "Denke, Elijah. Thank you for saying so." And she'd have to thank Lovina, too. She'd clearly been using her influence on Elijah, who was too ready to go off half-cocked at every new idea.

"Ja, well, Lovina and I want to be sure you know that we would be ser glad to have you live with us." He looked as if he were trying to remember all the things Lovina had said to him, reminding Naomi of the brother she'd helped memorize his spelling words years ago. "There's no denying it would be helpful to Lovina to have you there, and we wouldn't think of asking you to give up your bees. In fact, I'll be glad to pay the rent to Nathan."

Elijah sat back, looking like a man who'd done his duty and was relieved to have it over. With one hand he smoothed his beard—chestnut-colored, it persisted in curling no matter how he tried to stop it.

"I'm glad you came tonight, Elijah. It grieved me to think you might be angry with me."

"Not angry, for sure. Just worried, that's all." He was on surer ground now, waiting for her to say yes.

But she was going to disappoint him. "I thank you for your invitation, and my thanks go to Lovina, as well. But I am content with things the way they are."

It took Elijah a moment to realize what she was saying. His cheeks flushed. "You won't move in with us?"

"I think it's best for me to stay here. I have my work in the bakery, and my work with Nathan's kinder as well."

Elijah's eyes narrowed, and he looked more like Daad. "You are taking care of Nathan's kinder. How is that better than taking care of ours? How do you think it looks, that you would do that instead of coming to us?"

She would reply softly, because it was important to preserve her relationship with her brother. "I'm not concerned with what other people think of our business, Elijah. You surely know I love your kinder, but right now Nathan's little ones need me." She remembered what Paula had said. "I am only there for a short time, until their grossmammi comes back. Ada was my dearest friend. It's the least I can do for her kinder. That's different from moving in with you."

"Ja, it's different." His voice was clipped. "You're picking them over my young ones."

"Your kinder have two parents who are willing and able to take gut care of them, and you surely know I would drop everything to help you in time of trouble, don't you?"

Had he forgotten so easily all the years she'd devoted to him and the young ones? Maybe he really was just hurt that she seemed to have put someone else before him.

Elijah shook his head, his face set in stubborn lines. "You are being headstrong, Naomi. I never thought to see that in you. Don't you see that your behavior has folks already saying that you're hoping to catch Nathan for yourself?"

It was like a slap in the face. She stiffened, her mind reeling until she could get it under control. Were folks really saying such a thing? Or was that just Elijah, trying to bend her to his will?

She took a deep breath, steadying herself. "If there are blabbermauls in our community, I am sorry for them, saying such foolish things. And I am disappointed in you for repeating them."

His mouth set, Elijah rose. She stood with him, holding on to the edge of the table.

"Elijah, you are still the little bruder I love. I think it might be best if you go now before we both say more words we will regret."

He stared at her for a moment, angry and baffled, it seemed. Then, without a word, he turned and stalked out.

Naomi stood where she was, glad of the sturdy table beneath her hand, trying to deal with the pain and doubt he left behind.

The mist that clung to the valleys on November mornings had already vanished, chased away by the sun, when Nathan sent his buggy horse into the field behind the barn with a pat of the horse's rump. Coalie trotted up to greet the mare, then whisked around and broke into a canter across the frosty grass. Something about the nip in the air must have invigorated the horses, unlike the Herefords, whose placid dispositions never seemed to change.

Sometimes he wished people were as easy to deal with as animals. He leaned on the fence instead of rushing on to another chore. By November, with the corn harvested and plenty of hay in the loft, things eased up a bit even on a dairy farm, so he could spare a few minutes to look at the fields spreading out toward the woods and then the ridge in the distance.

He'd been relieved to see Naomi her usual serene self this morning. He'd been unhappy over his curtness with her about Jessie, even though he'd tried to make amends.

His fingers tightened on the rough plank fence.

Jessie couldn't be left alone with the children. Ada had been the first to admit that truth, and she'd certainly known her little sister as well as anyone. Emma had agreed, and as long as she was here, Jessie had never so much as shown an interest in watching them.

So what had caused her to get that bee in her bonnet about being the proper person to care for Joshua and Sadie while Emma was away? With Jessie, it was impossible to tell. She was a creature of whims, like a flighty horse that would take exception to a bit of paper blowing across the road.

Little though he'd relished hearing Naomi speak of Jessie, he had to admit that she had probably known Jessie as well as anyone other than family. Emma had worried about Jessie and coddled her, near as he could make out, while Ada had been kind but clear-sighted where Jessie was concerned. Elizabeth, the middle sister, always seemed to go her own way, paying little heed to what went on unless Jessie embarrassed her by some outburst. And as for Seth, the only boy—well, Seth had jumped the fence to the Englisch world at eighteen, leaving his family responsibilities behind for others. Emma heard from him now and then, and she'd once admitted that the checks he sent made a big difference after her husband died. Still, it wasn't like being there and helping.

Which brought Nathan full circle back to Naomi. If she were right that Jessie needed more help than any of them could give . . .

No, he wasn't going to think that way. He turned toward the barn, caught a flicker of movement, and realized it was Naomi and the children, walking along the lane toward the bee yard. Worry knotted his stomach, even though common sense told him it was needless. The bees were dormant now, and they were no danger. Still, it would be best if Joshua and Sadie didn't get the idea that it was all right to be around the hives.

He cut across the field toward them, stubble crackling under his work shoes. He'd just drop a word in Naomi's ear.

Despite Nathan's quick strides, Naomi and the children were already in the midst of the hives by the time he reached them. He slowed his steps, not wanting to look as if he were alarmed by the children's nearness to the bees.

"You can't hear them buzzing now because they're not moving around," Naomi said, apparently answering a question Joshua had asked.

"Can't you wake them up, Naomi?" Sadie, her cheeks rosy from the cold, looked up at her. Then Nathan's movement must have alerted the children, because they glanced at him—Joshua a little warily, as if he anticipated being sent back to the house.

That look gave him pause. He didn't want his son thinking of him as someone who always said no.

"Naomi is showing us where the bees live, Daadi," Sadie piped up. "I want her to wake them up so we can see them."

He glanced at Naomi, and she smiled. "It would be bad for the bees to be wakened now. They're all cozy in their home for the winter, snuggled up close together to stay warm. The bees all crowd closely around the queen, and they whir their little wings to help keep the hive warm for her. If we disturb them, they might get sick."

"I wouldn't want to make them sick." Sadie looked appropriately sad for an instant. "But when will they come out of their hive?"

"In the spring," Joshua said. "Lots of animals sleep in the cold weather. Remember the story Grossmammi read us about the bears?"

"That's right," Naomi said. "One warm day, you'll notice all sorts of creatures stirring. When the plants start growing, the bees will start coming out of the hive. I will put a branch outside the entrance to each hive, which makes them fly up higher and take a look around."

"Really?" Nathan couldn't help being interested himself.

Naomi nodded, smiling. "It's an old beekeeper's trick that my grossmammi taught me. When the hive is in a new location, you have to make the bees fly up higher, so they take in the larger landscape and find their way back to the hive."

"I'd forgotten it was your grossmammi who started you off with the bees." Naomi had been fairly young when her grossmammi passed, but she'd already been trained in how to care for the bees.

"Ja, that's the way of it. Mother to daughter to granddaughter in our family, all learning to care for the bees." She glanced at the children. "So, in the spring, the bees will fly up out of the hive, take a look around, and know it's time they got to work."

"Making honey for us," Sadie said.

"That's right. But they have other important jobs, too. If they don't carry the pollen from one plant to another, the crops won't grow properly."

"Bees are part of God's plan for the world, ain't so, Daadi?" Joshua looked to him for approval.

"That's right." His smile encompassed all of them, and he found he was in no hurry to deliver his message and rush back to work. "God lets us take care of the earth for Him."

He might not articulate it in words very often, but like most Amish, he felt that farming was a privilege. Other jobs were important to the community, for sure, but farming brought a person closer to God's earth.

"There aren't so many wild bees around as there used to be," Naomi said. "That makes our bees even more precious, and we must never do anything to disturb them. Even when they're awake and flying around, you must never go close to the hives unless Daadi or Grossdaadi or I bring you."

She smiled at Sadie, who looked ready to burst out with her inevitable *Why?*

"Because if you do, the bees might think you are not Sadie and Joshua but a bear, come to steal their honey. And if they think that, they'll sting." Forming her fingers into pincers, she nipped at the children, making them giggle.

Smiling as he watched, Nathan felt his worry subside. Naomi had warned the children, probably in a way they'd listen to better than if he'd just ordered them to stay away. Naomi was an unusual woman.

He studied her face as she began telling the children a story about the bees. Naomi had often faded into insignificance next to lively Ada, but her serenity had its own appeal. Knowing what her life had been like since her mamm died, he'd guess that serenity was hard-won.

"Now we will say good-bye to the bees," she concluded. "Families with bees know that you should tell them whenever something is happening in a family." She looked around her at the hives. "This is your home now, and I will always be here to take care of you. Joshua and Sadie live here, and they are your friends."

"Good-bye, bees," Sadie said promptly. Joshua, with a flicker of embarrassment, did the same.

"Off we go, now." Naomi began shepherding the children back toward the house. Nathan fell into step with her while Joshua and Sadie darted ahead.

Naomi sent a glance his way. "Were you checking up on me then, Nathan?"

"No, I . . ." He gave a reluctant grin, knowing she'd not believe a denial. "I just wanted to be sure the kinder were warned about getting too close to the bees. You did that better than I could."

"It's only common sense, after all," she said. "Most young ones raised on a farm learn how to behave around the animals, and bees are no different."

"They have stingers," he reminded her.

"Ja, and horses have teeth and hooves," she retorted. "But I'll bet you were working around them long before you went to school, ja?"

He shrugged, the question reminding him uncomfortably about his conversation with Daad about protecting the children. "I guess so." He watched Joshua, showing Sadie a tiny wildflower that had somehow managed to evade the frost.

"You got plenty of bumps and bruises, if you were like my brothers." Naomi shook her head. "I'll never forget the day Elijah ran into the field with that bad-tempered old bull we had, waving a tablecloth he'd snatched from Mamm's laundry.

Thought he was going to be a bullfighter, I guess." She smiled, shaking her head. "The bull gave him a boost over the fence, and then Daad gave him a hiding for being so foolish."

Nathan had to smile at that image of Elijah, who had turned a bit pompous once he'd married and started running the store in town. Still, his heart would surely stop if he ever saw Joshua doing such a thing.

"You are thinking you'd be more scared than angry," Naomi said, her gaze on his face. "Ja?"

He nodded. "Guess I am."

"So Daad was, too. I saw his face, and he was scared half out of his wits. But I guess he knew there were some lessons Elijah had to learn for himself."

Nathan stopped, and Naomi halted, too. She looked up at him, her deep blue eyes clear and untroubled.

"You are trying to say that I'm overprotective with my kinder, ja?"

Faint frown lines showed between her brows. "I did not say that, Nathan. They are your kinder, and you must raise them as you see fit. I just thought you might have forgotten some of the things you got up to when you were Joshua's age."

"I haven't forgotten. At least, I don't think so." Honesty compelled him to add the qualifier. "But that's not the point. I had two parents to look after me. Sadie and Joshua don't."

"I know." Pain flickered in her eyes, and he knew she was thinking of Ada, as well.

He closed his mind to the thought that she was grieving Ada. "Then you'll understand that I have to make the decisions where Joshua and Sadie are concerned." He said the words with finality. Naomi would either accept that or she would leave.

"Ja, of course," she said, bowing her head in agreement.

She understood then. Good. So why did she make him feel like such a bully?

Overall, it had been a good day, Naomi thought as she rolled out a piecrust late that afternoon. She'd found a basket of apples in the cold storage shed that would have to be used before a hard freeze, so apple pies seemed to be the answer.

Yes, a fairly good day. For the most part, Joshua and Sadie seemed to have adjusted to their grandmother's absence.

She glanced at the kitchen table. Joshua was still busy printing a story about the bees, but Sadie must have lost interest in the picture she was coloring, since she'd begun tossing crayons onto her brother's page.

"Sadie, would you like to roll out some piecrust with me?"

Sadie blinked, forgetting the pleasures of pestering her brother in an instant. "Can I?

Grossmammi always says I make too much mess."

"Well, messes are for cleaning up, ja? Komm, I'll let you make some little pies of your own."

Sadie scrambled down from her chair and pushed it over to the counter.

"Clean hands first," Naomi cautioned, and glanced at Joshua, head still bent over his printing. "Joshua, would you like to make a pie, too?"

Intent on the story, he didn't look up. "Denke, Naomi. I would like to finish my story first, ja?"

"That's fine. You will be a gut scholar when you start school." And at the rate he was going, the teacher would be hard-pressed to keep up with him.

"I'm ready," Sadie announced. She reached for the crust Naomi had been rolling, but Naomi shook her head.

"Not that one. I will give you some dough of your own to roll." She made a space next to her area, sprinkling the counter surface with flour and searching for a second rolling pin in the drawer. It would be an unlikely Amish kitchen that only had one, and sure enough, she found a second, smaller one, ideal for a child's hands.

"Now," she said, putting a ball of dough in front of Sadie. "You smooth some flour on your rolling pin, and then you begin to roll out the dough, like this." She demonstrated, and Sadie's fingers twitched with her desire to do it herself.

"I can do it," she declared, and Naomi put the rolling pin in front of Sadie.

The dough would no doubt be tough after the handling Sadie was sure to give it, but that was a first step in mastering pastry.

So they rolled and rerolled, Naomi managing to get two pies finished in between encouraging Sadie and showing her how to mound a few sliced apples, some sugar, and some cinnamon onto a round of dough and then pinch the dough together around the filling. Little purses, Naomi's mamm had called them, and that had been the first thing Naomi had learned to bake. For an instant she was back in that kitchen, standing on a chair next to Mamm and copying her movements.

The thought pierced her heart. She had had those precious years with her mother, while Sadie probably barely remembered Ada.

A half hour later they were taking the pies from the oven when the back door swung open. Naomi turned, expecting to see Nathan or his father, but it was Sarah Schultz, Nathan's married sister, along with three of her young ones—four, counting the babe she held in her arms.

"Aunt Sarah, I baked!" Sadie danced across the kitchen to tug eagerly on Sarah's cape while Sarah tried to remove jackets from her little ones.

"I see you did." Sarah's smiling gaze met Naomi's, and Naomi hurried to help her with the children.

"Sarah, it is wonderful gut to see you." She divested two-year-old Samuel of his jacket. "And the kinder."

"I thought I would stop to see how things are going, and then I'll pick up the older ones from school." With her lively brood, Sarah had her hands full, but she seemed to control them without effort. "Ja, Samuel, you can color, but not on Joshua's paper." She diverted her young son's attention to a picture of his own.

"Let me hold the boppli while you get your coat off, at least," Naomi said. "Will you have some pie or coffee cake? And there is coffee on the stove."

Sarah handed over the sleeping baby and stretched as she took off her jacket. "Ach, wouldn't you know little Matthew would fall asleep in the buggy?"

One-handed, Naomi began setting out a plate of oatmeal cookies for the children while she cradled the sleeping baby in her other arm. "The motion always puts them to sleep, ja? I remember when Isaiah used to fall asleep the minute we started to worship."

"And now he's married himself." Sarah poured a cup of coffee and helped herself to a slice of the coffee cake on the counter. With the children occupied at the table, she took one of the two rockers by the wood-burner. "Shall I take little Matt back?"

"I'll hold him." Naomi sat down in the other rocking chair, cradling the warm bundle against her. Would she ever stop feeling this longing for a babe of her own whenever she held one? Not likely, it seemed.

She'd been hoping for a chance to talk with Sarah. Things had happened so fast with Emma leaving that she hadn't had a chance to reassure herself that Sarah didn't mind her taking over here.

"Aaron, you share with your bruder." Sarah seemed to keep an eagle eye on her young ones. "I meant to stop by sooner than this, but yesterday was so busy . . . Well, I am here now. Are you settling all right with the kinder?"

"Ja, everything is fine." Naomi glanced at the children, satisfied that they were intent on what they were doing and not listening to the grown-ups. "I hope it is all right with you that I am watching them."

"All right?" Sarah echoed. "I couldn't be more pleased. Mind, I told Nathan I'd be happy to have his two at my house until Emma returns, but he thought they'd do better in their own home. And I can't deny he's probably right." She sighed. "Those poor kinder have been through enough in their young lives without being bounced around. As for you—I'm just thanking God you were able to fill in when Nathan needed you."

"Nathan is helping me, as well," Naomi said

quickly. "He's letting me have my beehives on his land."

"Ach, ja, I heard about the situation with your daad." She shook her head. "Foolish, I'd say, making such a change at his age, but there's no talking to men."

The last thing Naomi wanted to do was encourage any gossip. "I'm happy he and Betty found each other," she said, monitoring her tone. "And even though it was difficult to move the bees, this will be a better situation in the end, I think."

"That's how life works out sometimes, ain't so? The things we think are a disaster turn out to be God's way of putting us on a new path."

Naomi stared at her. She wouldn't have expected such an observation from Sarah, who seemed as busy and content with her life as one of the worker bees.

"I guess that's so," she said, not wanting to inquire into Sarah's reason for saying it.

Sarah darted another glance toward the children. The boys had deserted the coloring and were starting to build something with the wooden blocks from the toy box in the corner.

"At least with you here, there's no chance Jessie will be trying to take over." Sarah had lowered her voice, even though the children seemed well occupied. "That's what I was worried about most with Emma leaving."

Naomi shouldn't talk about Jessie with Sarah, but surely, since Sarah had brought it up, it would be appropriate to mention Jessie's effort.

"Jessie came by yesterday with just that thought in mind," she said. "But Nathan made it clear that I'd be watching the kinder."

"Gut." Sarah spoke firmly. "Sometimes I think he's too determined not to hurt Jessie's feelings, but she really can't be left with the kinder. I hope Jessie didn't make too much of a fuss."

Naomi wouldn't forget Jessie's shrill demands in a hurry. "Nathan handled it," she said.

"Gut," Sarah said again, and then she smiled, looking like the freckle-faced tomboy she'd once been. "Though Nathan probably didn't think it so gut. Men never want to deal with women's emotions."

Naomi just smiled, determined not to be drawn into that subject. "Joshua and Sadie are dears, and I'm wonderful glad to have this opportunity to know them better."

"They are gut kinder," Sarah said, watching as Sadie pointed out the apple purses she'd made to her smaller cousin. "Joshua should be in school this year, don't you think?"

Caught off-guard, Naomi nodded, then quickly backed up. "It's Nathan's decision. If he doesn't think the boy is ready—"

"Ach, Nathan can see for himself that Joshua is ready if he has eyes in his head." Sarah sounded frustrated. "I told him and told him Joshua should start to school this year, but he wouldn't listen, because he didn't want to hear. Nathan couldn't handle the thought of Joshua going off on his own." A shadow crossed her face, chasing away her exasperated look. "Nathan has been like that ever since Ada died, as if he can stop anything bad from happening to those kinder by keeping them close. The truth of it is that he's never gotten over losing Ada that way, and I fear he never will."

Chapter Six

So Emma's Elizabeth has a healthy baby girl, I understand," Paula said, working beside Naomi as they restocked the display case at the bakery. "Emma must be wonderful glad she could be there for the birthing."

"Ja, for sure." Naomi paused, holding a tray of fresh-baked pretzels, their aroma teasing her taste buds. "Elizabeth is naming her Ada."

"For her sister." Paula nodded. "It's natural Elizabeth should name the boppli for her sister, but I hope Nathan isn't upset."

Since Paula was looking at Naomi inquiringly, she obviously expected an answer.

"I'm sure he's fine." What else could she say? Nathan's face had been perfectly expressionless when he'd passed on the information from Emma.

The bell over the door jingled, heralding the latest in a long line of customers visiting the bakery on Saturday, and Paula moved off to attend to them while Naomi finished replenishing the case. This had been an unusually busy day in town, maybe because bright, sunny Saturdays were rare this late in November. The sunlight picked out the reds and browns of the last few leaves clinging to the trees along Main Street.

Naomi's life was as busy lately as the day had been, but she relished it. Even with going back and forth between caring for Nathan's children and working in the bakery, she seemed to have more energy than ever. Perhaps she had been getting stale, with little but Daadi and the bees to occupy her.

It was hard to believe one week of her time at Nathan's was finished already. Emma had said she might stay away as long as three weeks, if she was needed. And like Emma, Naomi would stay as long as necessary.

The bell jingled again, and this time Naomi broke into a smile when she saw who had come in. "Leah! It is wonderful gut to see you. You are so busy with the kinder these days that I seldom see you except for church."

Leah Glick came straight to the display case, holding her youngest, Rachel Anna, by the hand. Now there was a case of a late marriage with a widower working out. Leah had been the community's teacher, and no one had expected her to marry until Daniel Glick moved in next door with his three youngsters, and friendship had blossomed into love.

"The family does keep me busy, that's for sure." Leah smiled down at Rachel Anna, who was pressing her nose against the glass case, eyeing its contents. "I slipped out today to do some shopping." She nodded to her daughter. "She'll take her time in picking a treat," she said. "Long enough for you to tell me how you're enjoying working out at Nathan's place."

"The kinder miss their grossmammi, that's certain-sure, but we are getting along very well."

"Emma will be missing them, too, I guess," Leah said. "She'll be torn between staying with the new boppli and rushing back to Joshua and Sadie."

"I suppose so." The brightness of the day seemed dimmed, just for a moment. Surely Naomi wasn't mourning the end of her time with Nathan's children already, was she? She pinned a smile to her face. "I'm ser busy with the kinder and the bakery, that's certain-sure, but I don't know when I've been happier."

Leah's gaze lingered on her face. "You look happier than you have in a long time, Naomi. You won't take offense if I say I think the changes have been gut for you, will you?"

"Of course I won't." How could she? Leah was a friend, and a more good-hearted person she couldn't imagine. They'd known each other all their lives, and even though Leah was a few years older than she was, that hadn't made a difference to their friendship.

Leah was distracted by her daughter's tugging on her coat. Rachel Anna pointed a small finger at one of the pretzels Naomi had just put in that case.

"Is that the treat you want?" Naomi paused, her hand holding a square of waxed paper over the crisp, golden pretzel. Young ones were sometimes caught in an agony of indecision when faced with the bakery case.

But Rachel Anna seemed to have a mind of her own. She gave a brisk nod, her blue eyes shining.

Naomi lifted the pretzel and put it on a paper plate for the child, who took it with a shy smile. "You smile just like your mammi, did you know that, Rachel Anna?"

The child considered for a moment. Then she gave another sharp nod, making them both laugh.

"Ach, I'm nearly forgetting what I wanted to tell you," Leah said. "We finally have a date for our girls' Christmas party. It will be at my house on the fifteenth of December. You will be there, won't you?"

Naomi nodded. "I wouldn't miss it."

Their girls' Christmas party was one of many

such events that would be held from November right through January in Pleasant Valley, as groups large and small met to celebrate. Their particular girls' group was composed of women who had been in their rumspringa gang, as they called it. Not that Naomi had been able to participate much then, but Leah made sure she came to every Christmas party anyway.

"It'll be ser gut to have our friends together, and it's kind of you to have us at your house. Your poor husband will probably—"

The bell jingled again, and Naomi glanced automatically toward the door. Her breath caught, the words flying out of her head. It was her father, coming into the bakery on a Saturday, something that was unheard of. And Betty was with him— maybe their first appearance in town since their quiet wedding last week at Betty's church district.

Naomi wasn't the only one to lose the thread of the conversation, she realized. A hush had fallen over the room, with even their Englisch customers alerted by the sudden silence of the Amish.

Betty glanced around the shop with a tight smile, and conversation started again. Naomi tried to arrange her face in some expression other than shock. If Betty had actually gotten Daadi to bring her into the bakery for a snack, things had certainly changed at home.

Daadi stared at Naomi, but before he could come toward her, Betty tugged his arm and led him to a table. Paula headed toward them, but Naomi met her gaze and shook her head.

"I'd best wait on them," she said quietly, steeling herself for an unpleasant exchange. But surely Daad wasn't eager to make their disagreement public any more than she was.

Leah gave her a rueful smile. She took her little girl's hand, clucking a bit at the pretzel crumbs dusting her jacket, and straightened her bonnet, a miniature replica of Leah's own.

Naomi took a deep breath, planted a smile on her face, and approached her father and new stepmother. "Daad. Betty. It is ser gut to see you today. What may I get for you?"

"You may—" Daadi began explosively, but Betty put her hand on his arm, silencing him.

"I will have coffee, denke, Naomi. And maybe a piece of Paula's walnut streusel cake. Your daadi will have coffee, too, ja? And maybe some pie?" She looked at him.

He grunted. "Ja. Pumpkin, if Paula has it."

"Right away," Naomi said and moved quickly toward the counter, trying to keep a smile in place.

Leah leaned across the counter. "It looks as if Betty is having a softening effect on your daad." She kept her voice low, so that no one could hear over the clink of dishes and the murmur of conversation.

"I guess so." Naomi couldn't help the doubt in

her voice, but maybe Betty was able to manage him better than Naomi ever could.

She filled the order quickly and carried it back to the table, seeming to feel many pairs of eyes observing her actions. That was one thing you could be sure of in a small community like Pleasant Valley—everyone knew everyone else's business. She could remember saying that to each of her younger siblings as they entered their rumspringa years. *Don't ever think word won't get out about what you are doing. It will.*

Naomi put coffee and plates in front of them, holding her breath. "Would you like anything else?"

Daad shook his head. Then, at a look from Betty, he nodded toward an empty chair. "Can you sit with us and talk for a moment?"

With a quick glance around the shop to assure herself all was well, Naomi sat down, clasping her hands in her lap.

"I want to say—" Daad stopped and cleared his throat. Then he gestured toward Betty. "Betty has made me happy. I would like to see you make her wilkom in the family."

Naomi had never heard her father speak that way, and for an instant she was too stunned to answer. She collected her wits.

"Of course you are wilkom, Betty. It is wonderful gut that you and Daadi are happy together."

Now, if only Daadi would let her go her own way, as well . . .

"Denke, Naomi." Betty, her cheeks maybe a little rosier than usual, put her spoon very precisely next to her cup. "I was hoping you might stop by the house next week. We could do some sorting together. Combining two households is not an easy task."

"I'm sure that's so." Most of the family had helped move Betty's things into the farmhouse, but it had been on a day Naomi was working, giving her a good reason not to take part.

"And it is only fair for you to take a share of all the canning you did this year, ain't so?"

Naomi swallowed hard. Perhaps, in the midst of her disagreement with Daad, she had been unfair to Betty, who probably felt caught in the middle.

"That is wonderful kind of you, Betty. Denke. And I would be happy to do anything I can to make you feel comfortable in the house."

"Gut, gut, that's settled then." Daad rubbed his hands together. "You stop by anytime, and when you do, I'll leave you and Betty alone to visit, ja?"

Naomi nodded. Daad and Betty had clearly come to the bakery with this aim in mind. She felt a twinge of doubt and brushed it away, feeling ashamed. This was what she'd been praying for— Daad and Betty were trying to mend fences with her. The least she could do was cooperate.

Naomi had returned to the farm as usual on Monday morning, and it surprised Nathan how glad he was to see her.

Natural enough, he assured himself. Things ran so much more smoothly when she was there to look after the children.

Nathan slowed his steps to keep pace with his daad as they walked toward the house. The feeble sunshine of the morning had disappeared behind a thick bank of clouds. Daad pulled his knit gloves up under his sleeves and cast an experienced gaze at the sky.

"Looks like snow to me," Daad said. "Flurries, anyway. That will make the kinder happy."

"Ja, I heard them urging Naomi to go sledding with them once it snows. I doubt we'll get enough for that, though."

Daad shrugged, and Nathan wasn't sure whether he was expressing doubt over the amount of snow likely to fall or the possibility that Naomi would want to go sledding.

"Surely is nice when Naomi is here," Daad said. "She's wonderful gut with the young ones."

Nathan found himself stiffening. "Emma is wonderful gut with them, too, and their gross-mammi besides."

"I was not criticizing Emma," Daad said mildly. "Just pointing out that you are fortunate to have Naomi while Emma is away. And it is gut for the kinder to have someone take care of them who's more their mamm's age, ja?"

Nathan nodded, pressing his lips together, hoping he was not being so defensive because he'd just been thinking how glad he was for Naomi's presence.

Maybe it was natural to feel a tad guilty at that comparison. He owed Emma a great deal. She'd been constantly present for the children ever since Ada's death, and he could never forget his debt to her. She'd taken over the kinder and the house at a time when he'd been so dazed he could barely dress himself, let alone take care of his children.

He brushed his shoes on the mat at the back door and held the door for his father to go in. They stamped into the kitchen, most likely bringing a blast of cold air in with them.

Naomi stood at the stove, stirring something in a pot, and for an instant her slim figure reminded him so strongly of Ada that he couldn't catch his breath. Then he realized that Joshua and Sadie were standing on chairs on either side of her, close to the stove.

Too close. In a few quick strides he'd reached them and lifted both children down.

"That is too dangerous for you."

Sadie's face puckered on the verge of tears, and he knew he'd spoken too harshly.

It was Naomi's fault, he told himself.

"But, Daadi, we're making candy," Sadie wailed, and Joshua looked at him with reproach in his face. "Naomi is letting us help."

"Ja, and now you're going to help by putting

butter all over this platter for me to pour the candy on," Naomi said.

If she'd been taken aback at Nathan's abrupt action, she hid it well. She set a large meat platter on the table in front of them and then dropped a slice of butter at each end of it.

"Use your hands now. That's why we washed them, so you can work with your hands. Spread the butter all over the platter."

Easily distracted, Sadie instantly began to do as she was told, but Joshua gave Nathan a long look before turning to the work.

Daad bent over the pot, sniffing as Naomi beat its contents with a wooden spoon. "Ah, penuche. I haven't had that in—well, too many years to remember. We will enjoy that for sure."

"It is just about ready to pour." Naomi gave it a final stir and lifted the pot from the stove. "Everyone step back now, because the candy is very hot."

The children took several obedient steps away from the table, and Nathan found he was doing the same. Naomi poured the thick, caramel-colored candy onto the platter, getting the last of it with a wooden spoon. Sadie seemed to hold her breath until the candy was all transferred to the platter. Then she clapped.

"It's so pretty," she said. "Can we eat it now?"

"Not until it cools," Naomi said. "That hot sugar would burn your tongue for sure. Once it cools, we will cut it into pieces. You can eat a piece and give a piece to your daad and grossdaadi, ja?"

"And save a piece for Aunt Sarah the next time she stops by," Nathan added. "And Aunt Jessie, too."

If Nathan hadn't been looking directly at his son when he said the words, he'd have missed it. But at the mention of Jessie's name, Joshua stiffened, his small face growing wary, just for an instant.

Then he was smiling again, leaving Nathan unsettled, as if his son had seen something that had disturbed his balance.

"Ach, look at the window," Daad exclaimed. "It is snowing."

There was a flurry of excitement as the young ones rushed to the windows to stare eagerly at the first few lazy flakes that drifted toward the ground.

Sadie pressed her face to the pane and then swung toward Nathan. "Can we go outside and play in the snow? Please, Daadi?"

He had to smile at her enthusiasm. "That is up to Naomi," he said. "Grossdaadi and I just came in for coffee. She is still in charge."

Sadie dashed to Naomi, who was scoring the candy with a knife. Clutching her apron, Sadie looked up at her. "Please, Naomi. Please can we go out and play in the snow?"

"Hurry and get your jackets on." Naomi's smile

warmed her face. "We will go and see how much snow there is."

The kinder stampeded toward the hooks where their jackets hung, and Daad moved to help them, leaving Nathan alone next to Naomi for a moment. He looked at her, feeling awkward.

"I didn't mean to snap—about the stove, I mean."

Her blue eyes measured him coolly. "It was the kinder you spoke to." She moved past him, headed for the door, leaving him feeling as if she'd put him in the wrong.

Naomi hurried outside, feeling the cold air nip at her as she pulled her jacket on. She didn't want the children to see her disagree with their father. But she also didn't want Nathan to put up unnecessary barriers between himself and his young ones.

She frowned, going down the back steps. Didn't Nathan realize how often he was saying no to them? Sadie and Joshua had been in no danger. Of course they'd wanted to see the candy, but she'd been careful to keep them out of harm's way. Better to have children stand on chairs to watch than trying to reach for something on the stove, she'd always found.

Well, it was unlikely she could change Nathan's attitude in the limited time she had left here. So she'd best concentrate on what she could do.

Sadie was spinning around, as if she were dancing with the snowflakes that were coming faster and thicker now. Joshua surveyed the sky with anxious eyes. "Do you think there will be enough snow for sledding, Naomi?"

"Perhaps not this time," she said, trying to cushion his disappointment when the flurries stopped, and she thought they would. "But soon. How many snowflakes can you catch on your tongue?"

That distracted them, as she'd known it would. Sadie ran around dizzyingly, chasing after the places where she thought the most flakes were falling. Joshua, in contrast, stood very still, tongue extended, as if he hoped to catch a shy butterfly.

Nathan came outside, holding a mug of coffee in one hand. He stood for a moment, watching his children with a puzzled look on his face. "What are you doing?"

"We're seeing who can catch the most snowflakes, Daadi," Joshua explained. "I caught five so far on my tongue."

"I see." He glanced at Naomi, his expression cautiously amused, as if wondering if she were angry with him. "Sadie has an interesting method, that's certain-sure."

"I'm not sure whether it will catch her any snowflakes, but it's guaranteed to make her dizzy," Naomi said.

Sadie, spinning wildly, bumped into her father

and then grabbed his hand. "You play, too, Daadi. See how many you can catch."

Naomi thought for a moment that he'd surely make some excuse about getting back to work. But he put his cup down, picked Sadie up and swung her around. "You are a snowflake yourself, I think, Sadie-girl."

She flapped her arms as if she'd take off. It was the first time Naomi had seen Nathan spontaneously play with one of the children, and it warmed her heart. She glanced toward Nathan's father, who'd come out onto the porch and stood watching them. He wore a startled smile, as if this was new to him, as well.

"I am a snowflake, I am," Sadie cried. When Nathan set her down she spun around, dancing as a thicker flurry of snowflakes descended on her. "I'm a snowflake, see, Joshua?"

"Ten," Joshua said, snapping his mouth closed. "I caught ten snowflakes with my tongue, Naomi. That's gut, isn't it?"

"For sure it is," she said. "Don't you want your daad to swing you around like a snowflake, too?" She had a feeling solemn Joshua wouldn't ask on his own.

"Ja, will you, Daadi?"

In answer, Nathan picked him up, lifting him high in the air and spinning around. "Now Joshua is a snowflake. A bigger one," she said.

"Me again, me again," Sadie chanted. She

115

stepped into her father's path, narrowly missing Joshua's flying feet.

Naomi pulled her back, giving her a hug. "I think it would be fun to play tag in the snow." She tapped Sadie's nose. "You are It, Sadie. Can you catch me?"

She'd thought she could easily outdistance the child, but Sadie darted after her so quickly she had to scurry to avoid being tagged. Nathan put Joshua down, and in a moment all four of them were scampering around the yard, snow in their hair, trying to escape.

Laughing and exhilarated, Naomi slowed down enough so that Sadie could tag her, knowing Sadie would soon tire of the game if she had to be It all the time.

"I'm It now," she said. "Who shall I chase? Joshua?"

She raced after Joshua, who squeaked and darted behind his father, then peeked around Nathan's bulk to make a face.

"Can't catch me," he said.

Naomi chased after him, sending him racing across the yard and back again to circle his father. Finally, laughing and breathless, she tagged him, nearly knocking Nathan down in the process.

Nathan caught her arm to steady her, looking down at her, his face ruddy with the cold, his eyes laughing. "Who are the kinder here, Naomi? You look as if you are thirteen again."

116

She met his laughing gaze and her heart lurched, seeming to tumble in her chest. For a moment she couldn't seem to breathe.

Was it her imagination, or was Nathan having a similar problem? Snow frosted his hair, and his face went oddly still for an instant, as if he was seeing something he hadn't seen before.

Then Sadie bounced into them, squealing, and Naomi turned to grab her, thankful for the distraction. Her heart still seemed to thump erratically, and she fought to control it.

She could not have feelings for Nathan King. She could not. Maybe it was a very good thing that Emma would be back before long.

Chapter Seven

Naomi walked down Main Street toward Katie Brand's quilt shop late that afternoon. The snow flurries earlier had tapered off, as she'd expected, but even a brief flurry had made her think of Christmas and the gifts she hoped to find time to make in the busy days ahead.

Others in Pleasant Valley were certain-sure thinking about the approach of Christmas. The Englisch merchants had already decorated their shops, and while the Amish didn't use lights, that didn't mean she couldn't enjoy looking at what others had done.

The gift shop was beautifully decorated already, with swags of greenery twined with hundreds of tiny white twinkling lights. Even Mr. Wainwright at the bookstore had hung a wreath on his door to greet customers, though everyone in town knew he'd as soon be left alone to read as wait on anyone.

The window of Caleb Brand's handcrafted furniture shop, right next to Katie's quilt store, showcased a small wooden chest of drawers with a bowl on top filled with greens. That would be Katie's doing, no doubt. She'd transformed Caleb's shop, as well as his life, when she'd moved in next door.

Naomi reached for the quilt shop door, a list in her mind of what she needed. Making a doll for Sadie was on the top of her priorities, so she'd best get the materials for that project today.

She smiled, thinking of Sadie's and Joshua's enthusiasm for the presents they were making to give their daad and grossdaadi and grossmammi. They'd had fun working on those the past few days.

The bell jingled as she entered the shop. It had begun to get gray and chilly outside, but inside the shop was all color and warmth. Quilts were stacked on the display bed in the center of the room, with still more hung from the walls. Toward the rear of the shop, row after row of fabrics lured the visitor to finger and compare and probably start a new project.

Katie, as warm and welcoming as her shop, stood behind the counter waiting on an Englisch customer. Katie glanced toward her, smiling in welcome, and Naomi nodded. She'd enjoy chatting with Katie about her projects, but not while Katie was making a sale. She could go and browse in the fabric section, where she spotted Katie's sister, Rhoda, holding up a bolt of fabric for another customer.

Even as Naomi started to move toward the back, the Englisch woman headed for the door, nodding a pleasant greeting as she passed. Katie came out from behind the counter.

"Naomi, it is ser gut to see you. You've been busy lately, ain't so?"

"Just a little, what with working in the bakery and also minding Nathan King's kinder several days a week."

"Ja, I heard you were helping him out while Emma is away visiting her daughter and the boppli. Will Emma be back in Pleasant Valley soon?"

"In another week or two, I think." Naomi didn't know for sure, but she did know the time was passing quickly, too quickly. "I'll miss Joshua and Sadie, that's for sure."

Nathan's children had taken possession of her heart, as she'd known they must. The inevitable parting would be difficult.

Still, given that foolish longing she'd felt for Nathan, it was for the best. Once she wasn't seeing him so often, she'd quickly forget, and things would go back to normal between them.

"What can I help you with today? Or should I guess? Christmas gift making?" Katie's blue eyes twinkled, as if she'd had this conversation with a number of people.

"You've guessed right. I did start some things for my nephews months ago, but I still have a few quilted place mats and such to finish. But first I must get materials to make a doll for little Sadie."

Katie nodded. "She's about five, ain't so? That's a gut age for dolls for a little girl."

"Almost five," Naomi said.

Katie hadn't been in Pleasant Valley all that long—only since she'd come to help her cousin with a new baby back in the winter, but she'd gotten to know folks quickly. And now that she was married to Caleb Brand, she was probably related to half the valley through either his family or hers.

"I have just the thing." Katie knelt to pull a large box from under the table. She cleared a space for it. "This is my remnant box, and there are plenty of pieces of fabric that will be perfect for a small project like a doll. What colors were you thinking of for the dress and apron?"

That was really the only choice to be made, since otherwise Amish dolls were alike, down to the replica of Amish clothing and the lack of faces.

"I hadn't really decided. Let's have a look." Naomi appreciated Katie's enthusiasm, which extended from the most expensive quilt in the shop to the smallest project. She glanced at Katie's face as she bent over the box, sorting the fabric into piles on the counter. Katie's enthusiasm was one of the first things Naomi had noticed about her when she'd come to Pleasant Valley, and if anything, it had intensified since her marriage to Caleb.

"This is a pretty pink." Katie smoothed out a piece of fabric. "Or this blue shade."

Naomi nodded, fingering the material and envisioning it made up into the doll. "The blue, I think. Then I'll need the fabric for the doll's body, and a piece of black for a coat and bonnet."

"Very gut." Katie folded the pieces Naomi had chosen. "I'll just have to cut a piece from the bolt for the black. About half a yard?"

Naomi nodded. "That sounds like plenty."

The bell on the door jingled. Naomi's throat caught as Jessie Miller entered. She let out her breath slowly. *This is Ada's little sister that you have known since she was born,* she lectured herself.

Unfortunately, the memory of that last encounter with Jessie hadn't faded yet. But surely Jessie was sensible enough not to say anything foolish in a public place where others could hear.

"Jessie. Wie bist du heit?" Katie greeted her with a smile.

"And how is your new little niece?" Naomi asked quickly, hoping that Jessie would be deflected from dwelling on Nathan's refusal to let her watch the children.

"Mamm says they named her after Ada." A trace of discontent crossed Jessie's face and as quickly vanished. "Everyone is well, Mamm says, and John's mother is helping out, too."

Naturally both new grandmothers would want to have their time with the baby, but Naomi hoped Elizabeth was not feeling overwhelmed with help.

"Are you getting along all right with your mamm away?" Katie asked. "If you need any-thing—"

Jessie cut her off with a quick shake of her head. "I don't know why everyone keeps asking that same question." Her tone was pettish. "I can manage perfectly well on my own."

Naomi was embarrassed for Jessie, speaking so in front of Katie, who didn't know her as well as most people. "I'm sure the offers are kindly meant," she said.

The frown that marred Jessie's oval face, otherwise so like Ada's, seemed to say she didn't appreciate Naomi's comment. "It's not needed. Mamm wouldn't believe it, but I like having a bit of freedom now and then."

On the contrary, that was probably what worried Emma the most.

Katie had been putting the material into a bag while they talked, and she placed the bag on the counter in front of Naomi. "That will just be two dollars for the fabric I had to cut," she said. "There's no charge for the remnants. I hope little Sadie enjoys her doll."

"Doll?" Jessie pounced on the word, her eyes sharp on the package.

"A Christmas gift for Sadie." Naomi picked up the bag, hoping to make a quick retreat.

"You'll be gone from Nathan's long before Christmas." A triumphant note rang in Jessie's voice, and it was loud enough to turn heads in the store. "Mamm says she's so worried about them that she's coming home early. So you don't need to bother with making any gifts for them."

Coming home early? Naomi's heart twisted a bit at that comment, but perhaps Jessie was just making it up.

"I always give Joshua and Sadie a little remembrance for Christmas." Naomi pitched her voice low, hoping Jessie might follow suit. "I know I won't still be there at Christmas."

"But that's what you were hoping, ja?" Jessie's voice was still too loud for comfort. "You thought with Mamm away you could take Ada's place. That Nathan and the kinder would love you, but they won't." She emphasized the final word with a gesture that sent the package flying from Naomi's hand.

For an instant the entire shop and everyone in it seemed to freeze. Then Katie moved to take Jessie's arm, while Naomi bent to pick up the bag, trying to pretend it had fallen accidentally.

"I want to show you something, Jessie." Katie tugged gently, turning her away from Naomi. "I got some new fabric in that's such a pretty shade of pink. It would be perfect for a dress for you. Komm and see."

For the space of a heartbeat Jessie didn't respond. Then she turned toward the fabric section. "Ja, I'd like to see it," she said, as normally as if she hadn't been in a fury a moment before.

Katie caught Naomi's eye as she led Jessie toward the back. *Leave quickly.* Her gaze telegraphed the words as surely as if she'd spoken them.

Naomi stood, clutching the bag with fingers that weren't steady. Humiliation made her cheeks as hot as fire. She put two dollars on the counter and slipped toward the door.

Katie was right. With her out of sight, perhaps Jessie would behave herself. They could pretend the ugly scene hadn't happened.

But her rational mind insisted that too many people had overheard for this to go away. The story would be all over the Amish community before nightfall.

"Don't you want to guess the secret, Daadi?" Sadie wiggled her way under the covers after her bedtime prayers that night, her brown eyes alight with mischief, her long braids hanging down the back of her white nightgown.

Nathan tucked the quilt around her closely. Ada had made the quilt for her daughter, and when he settled Sadie under it, he fancied Ada was putting her arms around Sadie.

"If I guess right," he said, "that would spoil the secret, ain't so?"

Sadie pursed her lips. "Well, I s'pose. But I wouldn't have to tell you that you guessed right."

Joshua groaned from the other twin bed. "You are such a blabbermaul, Sadie. You will never keep the secret until Christmas. You'll spoil it by telling."

"She's not going to tell." Nathan tried to sound sure of that fact, even though he, like Joshua, didn't think Sadie was capable of keeping a secret.

"It's fun to make things for people," Sadie announced. "And to give presents."

"And to get presents, ja, little bug?"

Nathan tickled her, reducing her to giggles. He could almost hear Ada's voice in his mind, telling him not to rile the children up when they were supposed to be getting ready to sleep. He stroked Sadie's hair instead. "Ja, it is wonderful gut to make a gift for someone. And to keep it a secret."

When Ada was alive, the house had been filled with secrets and laughter this time of the year. Sadie probably remembered very little of those days.

"Close your eyes now." He bent to kiss her cheek. "The sooner you go to sleep, the sooner it will be a new day."

Sadie squeezed her eyes shut, making him smile and shake his head as he crossed the hooked rug to sit on Joshua's bed.

"You are having a gut time making things with Naomi, too, ja?"

Joshua nodded, but his thoughts seemed to be elsewhere.

That strange expression he'd caught on his son's face earlier when Jessie was mentioned—what had caused him to look that way? He longed to ask the boy, but he hesitated. Joshua was a deep thinker, and it wasn't easy to know what troubled him.

Nathan smoothed the quilt over his son's small body. "You had a fine day today, too?"

Joshua nodded, frowning a little. "I like having Naomi here." He paused for so long that Nathan thought he wouldn't say anything else. Then he looked up at Nathan, his hazel eyes very serious. "But I like for Grossmammi to be here, too. I wouldn't want her to think . . ." He let the sentence fade away, but his face was anxious.

Nathan breathed a prayer for the right words. "Grossmammi knows you love her very much. She would say that it is fine for you to love Naomi, too."

Joshua held his gaze for a long moment. Then he let out a little sigh and closed his eyes, relaxing against the pillow. "Denke, Daadi."

"Sleep well," Nathan said softly, bending to kiss Joshua's forehead. Every day he prayed that he was raising their children the way Ada would want. He felt sure he'd said what Ada would have, this time, at least.

Nathan went quietly out of the room, leaving the door ajar so that he could hear the children if they called. Or, more likely, if they started chattering instead of going to sleep.

But all was quiet by the time he reached the bottom of the stairs, and he headed into the kitchen. He'd no sooner lifted the coffeepot from the stove than he heard a soft knock at the back door, followed by footsteps. Isaiah poked his head into the kitchen and grinned.

"Sorry I walked in. I thought maybe you were in the middle of putting the kinder to bed."

"Just finished." He held up the pot. "Coffee? And there's some of your sister's apple pie left."

"I would never say no to a piece of Naomi's apple pie." He shrugged off his jacket, hanging it on the back of the chair.

Nathan poured two mugs of coffee and set the

pie and a couple of forks on the table. No sense making more dishes to wash.

Isaiah didn't seem to mind the sloppy serving method. He cut a wedge of pie, lifting it to his lips for a bite and catching with practiced ease the apple slice that slipped out. "Gut," he said thickly. "Don't tell my Libby I said this, but no one makes apple pie like my sister."

Nathan grinned, cutting his own generous piece. "What will you give me for keeping your secret?"

"How about your mail?" Isaiah stopped eating long enough to search under the jacket, coming up with a folded newspaper and an envelope. He tossed them to Nathan. "No, I guess you'd best have it. I saw you hadn't picked up your mail when I was getting ours, so I brought it along."

The two mailboxes were side by side out along the road. Nathan got so little mail he often didn't check the box for several days in a row.

"*The Budget.*" He unfolded the newspaper that kept Amish in various settlements in touch with each other. "I'll read that tonight. And a letter from Emma." He looked at the envelope, wondering why Emma would find it necessary to write to him. But maybe it was messages for the kinder.

Since Isaiah was absorbed in eating, Nathan didn't hesitate to rip the envelope open and scan the page.

"What does Emma have to say?" Isaiah asked around a bite of pie. "Everything all right?"

"Ja. The boppli is a little sweetheart, eating and sleeping just as she should. Elizabeth sends her love to the kinder." He read a little farther, frowning. "Emma says she is coming back on Monday, so she'll be here Tuesday."

"Ja? That's sooner than she thought to return. Trouble with the other grandmother?" Like most of the valley, Isaiah was well-informed on what everyone did, and he'd know that Elizabeth and John lived on his parents' farm out in Ohio.

"No, nothing of the kind." Nathan's frown deepened. "She is worried about Jessie, she says." He looked up at Isaiah. "You will not repeat that to anyone, ain't so?"

"For sure I won't." Isaiah's fresh, boyish face creased with concern. "Jessie can be a handful, I guess."

"Ja." He hoped that was all it was. He should have been keeping better track of the girl, he supposed, but he was stuck here on the farm, and there were plenty of folks in town who'd gladly look in on her.

Tuesday. He put the letter on the table. That meant Monday would be Naomi's last day here.

All he could think was that the time had gone by too fast. Like Joshua, he was torn. Naomi would move on. That was her wish, after all, and he'd be selfish to want anything else. Still, he had to admit he was going to miss her, maybe too much.

Scraps of fabric, paste, paper, and scissors covered the kitchen table the next afternoon as Naomi worked with the children on the Christmas gifts they were making. After hearing from Nathan this morning how soon Emma was returning, she'd thought they'd better move a bit faster on their projects.

Joshua and Sadie didn't know. Nathan had said he thought it best to wait and tell them Monday afternoon, trying not to make something big out of the news. Naturally she'd respect his wishes.

Unfortunately, it was already something big for her. She looked at Joshua, his face intent as he bent over the pincushion he was making for his grossmammi. He was so like Nathan that her heart twisted a little.

And Sadie. Naomi had to smile. Sadie was making a calendar for her daadi, with a different picture for each month. Right now a triangle of red paper stuck to her cheek, and her tongue peeked slightly between her lips as she concentrated.

Even as Naomi watched, Sadie put her crayon down fretfully. "My bird doesn't look right, Naomi." There was a faint edge of a whine in the words, which suggested Sadie was getting tired.

"Why don't you take a break for some milk and cookies? Let the bird rest for a bit, too."

Sadie's normal sunny expression returned. She patted the drawing. "You rest, little bird," she crooned, and headed for the cookie jar, which Naomi had refilled with snickerdoodles that morning.

Naomi rose to get the milk. "Joshua, do you want to stop for a snack?"

"Denke, Naomi. I want to finish this first," he said. She could have predicted that response. Joshua was persistent, again like his daadi.

She got the milk bottle from the refrigerator and poured a glass, listening to Sadie's chatter with half her attention. Nathan hadn't said anything about why Emma was returning so soon. The memory of Jessie's words at the quilt store slithered back into her thoughts. Was it possible that Emma was coming back because she was worried about the kinder?

Nonsense, Naomi assured herself. It was far more likely that Emma was worried about Jessie. She knew the children were well cared for, didn't she?

One thing about that nasty tongue of Jessie's— the things she said couldn't be entirely dismissed. Or at least, not by her. Maybe other people just shrugged them off and quickly forgot.

The sound of hooves in the lane brought her back from a futile line of thought. She leaned over the counter to peer out the window.

"Your daadi and grossdaadi are back from the farrier's," she said. "Better hurry and hide any presents that are for them, ja?"

Her cookies and milk forgotten, Sadie squealed and began pushing the calendar pieces together, jumbling them. Naomi helped her while Joshua worked steadily on. Unlike Sadie, who'd pulled out everything she was making, Joshua had only brought the pincushion from its hiding place.

"Hurry, Naomi, hurry." Sadie jammed the pieces into the shoe box Naomi had given her for storing the project.

"There, that's it." Naomi clapped the lid on the box and shoved it into Sadie's arms. "Run and hide it."

Sadie spun and rushed out, and Naomi heard her footsteps thundering on the stairs just as the back door opened and Nathan came through into the kitchen. Her smile faded when she saw his expression. Why was he looking so solemn?

Avoiding her gaze, Nathan glanced at his son. "Go upstairs with Sadie for a few minutes, Joshua. I will call you when to come back down." As if realizing that would sound like punishment to the child, he tempered the words with a smile. "I just have to talk to Naomi in private for a bit."

Joshua nodded, and it was impossible to tell whether he accepted his father's reasoning or not. He slid from his chair and left the room.

Naomi's thoughts spun as crazily as a snowflake caught in the wind. What was wrong? Why did Nathan look so serious, as if he had caught her in wrongdoing?

When Joshua's steps receded up the steps, Nathan turned to her. Naomi's heart faltered at his expression. "Was ist letz, Nathan? What's wrong?"

"What's wrong is that everyone at the farrier's was talking about you and Jessie quarreling at the quilt shop yesterday." He took a step toward her. "What's wrong is that I didn't hear it from you."

Chapter Eight

Nathan could read the shock in Naomi's face at his words. Maybe he shouldn't have spoken so harshly, but the idea that everyone in Pleasant Valley was talking about his family just couldn't be borne.

Naomi put one hand on the back of a chair, seeming to gather control for a moment. "That is not what happened, Nathan."

He took an impulsive step closer. "That is what everyone at the farrier's was saying."

Her lips pressed together, as if she were censoring what she wanted to say. "I don't suppose the folks at the farrier's were in Katie's shop yesterday afternoon."

He dismissed that response with a gesture. "Maybe not, but they heard it from folks who were there. Half the township is talking about my family."

"I am sorry that you were embarrassed." Naomi's calm seemed imperturbable.

While he might value that quality under normal circumstances, right now it just served to irritate him further. "It is not a question of embarrassment." He knew that was false the moment he said it, but he wouldn't go back. "I should have heard it from you, not from someone else. You know that is true, Naomi."

Those words seemed to finally disturb her calm. "Ja, maybe I should have spoken," she admitted. "But the last time I brought up something about Jessie, you didn't want to hear it."

Why did women always remind you of the thing you least wanted to think of whenever you argued with one of them?

"Maybe so, but this is different." He took a breath, trying to reclaim the balance he'd lost when he'd walked into the barn at the farrier's and heard several brothers talking about Jessie and Naomi. He put his hands on the back of a chair, mimicking Naomi's posture across the table. "Let's start over again. What happened with you and Jessie yesterday at the quilt shop?"

Naomi nodded, as if approving his effort to calm down and discuss the incident. "I had gone in to get some fabric for a doll I am making." She hesitated. "It's for Sadie. For Christmas. That's what Jessie objected to."

Knowing Jessie, he found it hard to predict what might upset her, but this seemed innocent enough. "She was in the shop as well, then."

"She came in while Katie was putting my fabric in a bag. Katie didn't realize, of course. She mentioned that I was making a doll for Sadie." She stopped, as if that was all that needed to be said.

Nathan blew out a breath, praying for patience. "Why would Jessie care? Was she also making a doll?" That might explain it, if Jessie imagined some competition for Sadie's affection.

Naomi looked startled. "No. I don't think so, anyway. She said that I didn't need to make a gift, because I wouldn't be here at Christmas. And that her mother was coming back early because she is worried about my caring for the children."

"There was more than that said, I think. Unless someone was making up the story completely." He kept his voice quiet, not wanting Naomi to feel she couldn't be open with him. He'd made that mistake already.

She shook her head, a slight frown furrowing her forehead. "It was nonsense," she said. "I'm sure even Jessie doesn't believe it. She was just wanting to hurt me . . ." She let that trail off, clearly not wanting to say more, maybe regretting she'd said as much as she had.

But he had an obligation to Ada's family to deal with this situation, no matter how much he'd rather run the other way. "What did she say?"

Naomi seemed to focus her gaze on the scraps of fabric on the table. "She said that I wanted to take Ada's place with you and the kinder."

"Nonsense." He said the word sharply. "As you said, that was just nonsense. Jessie is like a child, blurting out things she doesn't mean. She is probably sorry and embarrassed by this time."

Naomi looked as if she didn't quite accept that last part, but she nodded. "There were a couple of other women in the shop, and I'm afraid they overheard. But Katie distracted Jessie very quickly, and it was all over in a moment."

He smiled a bit wryly. "Even a moment was enough to get the gossips going. It will be wonderful gut when Emma gets back to look after her."

"Ja." Naomi's gaze clouded. "Jessie said something to Katie about liking her independence. That worried me a little. Jessie is . . . well, impetuous."

Impetuous was one word for it, he supposed. Naomi was being cautious in what she said, not wanting to upset him, most likely. "Emma is the only one who can handle her sometimes."

Naomi lifted her gaze then, meeting his eyes. "I am sorry, Nathan. I would have avoided Jessie if I could have. I'm sure she'll forget all about me as soon as her mamm comes back."

"Ja, I think you're right. When you leave next week—"

"Next week?" Sadie was suddenly there, rushing across the kitchen to throw her arms around her. "No, you are not going already. I don't want you to go, Naomi. How will I finish Daadi's present without you?"

Joshua followed his sister into the kitchen, looking at Nathan apprehensively. "I'm sorry, Daadi. I couldn't get her to wait."

"It's all right, son." Sooner or later he'd have to tell them Naomi would be leaving. He'd just have preferred later. "Sadie, stop the fussing. Your grossmammi is coming back on Tuesday. You'll be glad to see her, ain't so?"

"I want Naomi." His daughter shot him a mutinous look. "I don't want her to go away."

"Ach, I'm not going away, silly girl," Naomi said gently, smoothing Sadie's hair back with her palm. "I will be working at the bakery, but I will still come out to watch over the bees, ja?"

"You said you'd teach us more about the bees," Joshua said. "You won't forget, will you?"

"I would never forget something so important," Naomi said, her hand on Joshua's shoulder. "I am looking forward to showing you all about the bees. Now, I think we should make something special to welcome your grossmammi back. What should it be?"

Her tears forgotten, Sadie began talking eagerly, and Joshua joined in, both of them focused on Naomi as she smiled at them.

Nathan's heart seemed to cramp. He'd gotten used to having Naomi here so quickly. He wasn't sure he'd get used to her absence anywhere near as fast.

It wasn't until Saturday that Naomi found the time for her promised visit to Betty, her new step-mother. Sunny, her carriage horse, whickered when Naomi turned into the familiar lane, her ears pricking forward. The mare, at least, seemed to be anticipating this visit.

She probably should have come sooner, Naomi knew. She walked toward the back porch, pulling her jacket more tightly against the chill wind that was blowing. She wouldn't want Betty to think she didn't appreciate her efforts to make peace.

But to tell the truth, Naomi's nerves were stretched taut. Despite Daad's assertion that he'd just wanted her to get acquainted with Betty, she couldn't help expecting him to take the opportunity to try again to sway her to his plans for her future.

The back door opened, and Betty stood there, smiling in welcome. "Naomi, komm. You must be cold."

Naomi stepped inside, the warmth enveloping her, and surrendered her jacket to Betty. She tried to keep a smile on her face as Betty hung it from one of the hooks in the back hall as if Naomi were a guest. Which maybe she was, and she ought to accept that fact.

"There is coffee and pumpkin bread," Betty said, leading the way into the kitchen. "Would you like it now to warm up, or after we have finished our sorting?"

"That's wonderful kind of you, Betty. Let's work first, ja?" She suspected it would be easier to find something to say to Betty if they were both busy.

"That's fine," Betty said. "I have some linens laid out on the bed that I thought you could help me decide what to do with. It's not easy to combine two households. We have too much of one thing and not enough of another, it seems." She chuckled, as if she'd made a joke.

Naomi smiled dutifully as she followed Betty up the flight of stairs. Maybe this adjustment would be easier if Daadi had married someone the family already knew well. Betty had come from a church district that was a county away, and the family had met her only once in a while at a wedding or a funeral.

Or maybe it would have worked out all the same in any event.

"Komm, sit." Betty patted a space on the bed next to a stack of sheets and coverlets. "We can be comfortable while we sort." She paused for a moment. "Your daad has gone to the mill to see

139

about some feed, so I doubt he'll be back much before supper."

In other words, not until Naomi had left. She felt a rush of gratitude, sure that this was Betty's way of reassuring her.

"I think we can have everything sorted by then," Naomi said. "What were you thinking about these things?" She gestured toward the items laid out on the bed.

"They are the extras beyond what I need." Betty touched the pile of coverlets. "Probably your mamm made these, so you children should have them. You can pick out what you want and what you think should go to each of your brothers and sisters. You'll know what they'll like better than I would. Or your daad, for that matter. Men don't take much interest in such things."

"That's wonderful kind of you." And more thoughtful than Naomi might have expected. She had probably been misjudging Betty, and that wasn't fair. "Are you sure you have enough without these?"

"Ach, ja, a chest full of things. I was married for thirty years to my first husband, and things certain-sure accumulate in that time."

Naomi picked up a quilt that Mammi had made when she was expecting Sara. Sara should have this one. "You must have been very lonely after your husband died," Naomi said, starting a stack for her younger sister.

"Ja, I was." Betty sighed a little. "I didn't expect to be quite so lonely, with so many relatives and friends living nearby. But we had no children, you see, so in the evening, once things were quiet, it was just awful lonesome."

"I understand." Naomi did, to her surprise. Even staying with Paula now, she felt that loneliness sometimes, especially on the rare quiet evening. It came of having no one of her own, she thought.

"Well, now you have Daad for company. Just don't let him get so engrossed in the newspaper that he forgets you're there." She smiled, and Betty smiled back with a twinkle in her eye.

"You are right about that, Naomi." She reached out to pat Naomi's arm. "And you'll forgive me, won't you, if I make any mistakes with you or your brothers or sisters? I'm just not used to having such a big family."

"Don't worry about us." Acting on impulse, Naomi clasped Betty's hand. "Just make Daadi happy, and everything else will work out all right."

"Denke, Naomi." Betty squeezed her hand briefly. "I'll remember that advice."

The talk between them was easy during the rest of the sorting, and Naomi had the impression that Betty had said what she'd wanted to for this visit. Well, that was fine. They were both a little on edge, most likely, trying to make the best of the situation.

At the end of an hour, all of the linens had been

sorted, boxed, and marked for pickup, and Naomi had taken hers out to the buggy. All in all, it had turned into a fairly pleasant afternoon. She didn't suppose she and Betty would ever become close friends, but at least they could get along together. Surely harmony in the family was the most important thing to both of them.

Naomi carried some extra boxes she'd brought back into the house with her. "Shall we go ahead and sort out some canned goods now?"

She didn't really care that much about the vegetables and fruit she'd canned, but the honey was also stored in the basement, and she did intend to take that with her. Paula was eager to set up a display at the bakery and start selling jars of honey.

Betty led the way down the narrow cellar stairs and stopped at the bottom, lighting the overhead lamp. "Please, take whatever you can use."

Betty gestured toward the long shelves that lined one wall. Naomi had filled the jars over the summer and fall, as she always did, moving any older canned goods to the front to be used first.

"I don't really need much," she said, putting a few jars of applesauce in one of the boxes before moving on to the jams. "I'm just one person."

"But . . ." Betty shrugged. "Well, things might change," she said vaguely. "You can always pick up more jars later, if need be."

Taking a few jars of string beans, Naomi walked

to the shelves that contained her store of honey. She stood for a moment, looking with satisfaction at the rows of jars, the honey glowing amber. This was really the work of her hands, far more so than all the rows of canned vegetables. Reaching, she began to stack the jars of honey in the box.

Betty watched her in silence for a few minutes. Then she moved restlessly. "I thought you said you only needed a few."

Kneeling by the box, Naomi looked at her, a little confused. "That was of the fruits and vegetables. Don't worry. I'll leave plenty of the honey to get you and Daad through the winter."

"You are taking all the rest? You can surely store it here if you want. What will you do with so many jars?"

Naomi realized she was gaping and gathered her wits. She'd assumed Betty knew about her plan to market the honey. Certainly the word had gotten around the rest of the family, but perhaps Betty hadn't heard.

"Paula Schatz at the bakery has agreed to let me put up a display of the honey. I intend to start a little business, selling my honey to customers."

"But—" Betty's plump face crinkled in dismay. "Maybe you should talk to your daad about this idea. I'm not sure he would think it a gut plan."

Naomi tried not to clench her teeth. "Daad understands that the hives are mine. Certainly I respect his opinion, but I must decide this for myself." She tried to smile. "It's not so unusual for an Amish woman to have a little business, ain't so?"

Betty dismissed that with a wave of her hand. "You are an unmarried woman, Naomi. Surely you would do better to allow yourself to be guided by your father." Betty took a step closer. "You will say that this is not my business, but I only want what's best for everyone. Your father feels sure that once you move in with your brother—"

Naomi turned away, lifting the heavy box and carrying it to the stairs. Maybe Betty had invited her here today in order to get to know her better, but it seemed clear that her main aim had been to persuade Naomi to heed her father's wishes.

You can catch more flies with honey than with vinegar. The old saying flitted through her mind. Daad, angry and giving orders, had been the vinegar, and it seemed Betty was meant to supply the honey. Ironic, given that it was the honey Naomi would be taking out of here today.

"I thank you for your concern, Betty." She took the second box, filling it quickly with honey jars. "I am leaving some of the honey mixtures for you, as well as the plain clover honey. I know Daad likes the rhubarb and berry honeys. Just let me know if you run out of anything, and I'll try to replace it."

The second box filled, Naomi hefted it, her muscles straining. In her haste to be gone she'd put too much in the box, but she would manage. Without waiting for a response from Betty, she carried the box on up the stairs and out to the buggy.

When she came back for the other box, Betty seemed to have regained her composure. She watched without comment as Naomi carried it to the door.

"Naomi." Her voice stopped Naomi before she could get outside. "I hope you will not regret this action."

Naomi looked at her, arms straining from balancing the heavy box. "Denke, Betty. It was ser gut of you to invite me. I know my sisters and the boys will appreciate the quilts and coverlets you are sharing with them." If they could end on a civil note, at least, that might be a bit of goodwill salvaged from this visit.

"Your daad was right about your stubborn nature," Betty said, as if making a pronouncement from on high. "I hope you will think again before you persist on this path. If not, your father plans to speak about it to the bishop."

Stony-faced, Betty held the door open. Feeling as if she'd just taken a blow to the heart, Naomi walked out.

Betty's sharp words still rang in Naomi's head the next day at worship. She shifted a little on the bench where she sat in the midst of the unmarried women. About an hour and a half into the three-hour service, the benches started feeling rather hard, and she wasn't the only one to shift position a bit.

Head bowed, she let her gaze steal toward Bishop Mose, who sat in his accustomed place, seeming to listen with close attention to the minister who was giving the sermon today. Had there been some special attention in his glance her way when the ministers had entered the large basement room where worship was being held? Or was her imagination, or her guilt, prompting her to imagine it?

She fixed her gaze firmly on the preaching minister. She should not let her eyes or her mind wander during worship, but it was hard to concentrate when her thoughts bounced around so many different issues.

Behind her a baby whimpered for a moment and then was quiet again. No one would think badly of a mother who had to take a little one out during the service for feeding, but it seldom happened. She could remember Leah saying, when Rachel Anna was tiny, that she'd timed her feedings down to the minute in the hopes that she wouldn't have to go out.

Gradually, as the years went by and she grew older, Naomi had moved farther back in the rows of unmarried women. There came a time when a woman had to accept the fact that marriage wasn't for her.

A long time ago, she'd given up all hope of knowing what real motherhood was. So why was she thinking about babies now? If she couldn't concentrate on the sermon, she ought at least to be praying for peace between herself and Daad. The thought of speaking to Bishop Mose, kind as he was, filled her with dread.

That was not a subject that was any more likely to fill her with the peace of the Sabbath. And she knew, if she were honest with herself, why she had been thinking of mothering. It was because her time with Joshua and Sadie was coming to an end.

She had been kidding herself to think it wouldn't be difficult to give them up even after so short a time. It would hurt, but surely the hurt would pass quickly. She'd be busy at the bakery, and Paula's enthusiasm over the honey sales would help to distract her.

Besides, it wasn't as if she wouldn't see Joshua and Sadie again. She had spotted Nathan's tall figure when he'd arrived for worship, the children clinging to his hands, still looking a bit sleepy. She would see them at worship, at community events, and often when she went to the farm to tend the bees. Life would settle down to normal eventually.

She caught a glimpse of movement from the corner of her eye and tilted her head to look. Sadie was slipping across the aisle between the

147

men and women, as quiet as a little mouse. Now, what was she up to? Nathan usually kept the kinder close by his side during worship, sitting with his father and sister and her family.

Sadie reached the end of Naomi's row and began sliding in, climbing over legs and probably stepping on a few toes in her haste. The rustle of movement was surely obvious to anyone looking their way.

Sadie stopped at Naomi's knees. Giving her a drowsy smile, she climbed into Naomi's lap.

Naomi cradled the child in her arms, feeling Sadie's little body relax against her. Sadie patted the front of Naomi's cape, and she might just as well have reached in and patted her heart.

Naomi held her close. She'd been wrong. She wasn't going to stop missing Sadie and Joshua any time soon.

And Nathan? Her thoughts backed away from that topic. It was far better not to think of Nathan at all.

Chapter Nine

So this is Naomi's last day," Daad said, fastening his jacket against the cold as he and Nathan came out of the kitchen after lunch. "We will miss her, ain't so?"

Nathan decided to take that comment as if Daad meant the children. "The kinder will, but they will be excited to have their grossmammi back."

"Ja, I suppose. I think Naomi will miss us, as well." Daad went slowly down the steps. The flower beds on either side were barren, the few stalks that remained lying on the ground. Only the hardy oregano that Ada had planted near the porch still showed green.

Nathan shrugged. "She didn't look bothered by it being her last day." That had nettled him a little, Naomi seeming to show no regret at leaving them.

Daad gazed at him with reproach. "Naomi would not show her emotions in front of the kinder. She would not want to upset them."

His father's words made sense. Naomi hid her feelings behind her calm manner and serene face, but that didn't mean she didn't feel them.

He started to speak, but turned instead at the sound of the door opening behind them. Naomi stepped out on the porch, wrapping a thick black shawl around her shoulders.

"Nathan, can you spare a minute? There's something I wanted to speak with you about."

Nodding, he turned back toward the porch. "You'll be cold out here. We should go inside."

"I'm fine." She drew the shawl closer. "I didn't want to speak of this in front of the kinder."

He went back up the porch steps to stand beside her. "Feels like snow in the air."

She nodded, her thoughts obviously on something other than the weather. "Since this is my last day, I wanted to talk with you about paying rent for the use of your land and the shed. Did you want me to pay each month?"

Nathan was surprised by the strength of his feelings. "I don't want you to pay at all."

Naomi blinked, probably surprised in her turn. "But . . . we agreed, didn't we? I would watch the kinder in exchange for setting up here, but after that I would pay you."

"I don't think we ever spelled it out, did we? Anyway, you have more than repaid me for having the beehives here by your care of the kinder."

"That was easy. I love them."

There was a flash of emotion in Naomi's eyes as she said the words, a hint of something very deep, quickly hidden again behind her usual calm. But he'd seen the emotion, and it threw him off balance. All he could do was repeat himself.

"I don't want money from you, Naomi."

She stiffened, and he could sense her opposition strengthening. "This is a business arrangement. It's not right to mix business and friendship. I have to pay you rent if I am using your property."

Frustration had him gritting his teeth at her stubbornness. For someone so outwardly serene, Naomi had a core of strength that would not be moved when she thought she was right.

He'd have to find another way around this

barrier, but he certainly wasn't going to accept money from her.

He studied her face, wondering what she was thinking.

"What will you do if I refuse to take your money?" he asked, trying to measure the depth of her determination.

Her struggle showed itself in her shallow breath and clenched hands. "Then I would have to move my beehives again."

He shouldn't have pushed her so hard. It wasn't fair to make her admit she'd give up something she wanted so much. But what was he going to do with her?

The idea came so quickly that it must have been lurking in the back of his mind. "Ach, Naomi, what makes you such a stubborn woman?"

She smiled, maybe relieved to hear the light tone in his voice. Maybe assuming that meant he was giving in. "How would I have raised four siblings without it?"

"All right," he said. "Here's how I see it. You having the beehives on my land is the same as if I was leasing land to a tenant farmer, ain't so?"

She frowned a little, considering his words, and then she nodded. "I guess."

"Well, when I let Harvey Muller, my neighbor, put corn in the field adjoining his property, I didn't take money from him. I just took a share of the crop."

Her frown had intensified. "It's not the same thing. There's my using the shed, for one thing."

Had there ever been such a stubborn woman? He surprised himself with how much patience he was showing with her.

"A shed that would be sitting empty otherwise, so that I'd have to keep it clean and in repair," he pointed out. "I consider it a fair trade if you provide me with a share of the honey for my family."

"Nathan, you know full well that I am happy to do so anyway." Her tone was lightly scolding.

But this time he knew how to get around her. "Now who is mixing business and friendship, Naomi?"

It took a moment, but her expression dissolved into a smile. "All right. I give up. But it still seems to me that you are getting the short end of the deal."

His heart seemed to warm at her smile. "Maybe you are underestimating how much we enjoy honey," he said. "And now you must go back in the house and get warm." He touched her arm, turning her toward the door. "I don't want to be responsible for you getting a chill."

She stepped away and then turned to smile at him. "Denke, Nathan," she said, and went into the house.

A smile lingered on his lips as he walked toward the barn. It had taken all his ingenuity, but he had gotten an agreement from Naomi. She would not be paying him money for something he intended to do as a friend.

Friend. He repeated the word. He had always thought of Naomi as Ada's friend, but in the past couple of weeks that had changed. After seeing her nearly every day and talking with her about anything and everything, she was his friend, as well.

Their time together was coming quickly to an end. After today, she wouldn't be busy in the kitchen or with the children when he went in the house. Strange as it was to admit it, he was going to miss her.

Naomi poured oats into the feed bin in her mare's stall, gave her a final pat, and headed out of the small barn behind the quilt shop. It was kind of Caleb and Katie to let her stable the mare there. Unlike Nathan, Katie hadn't quarreled when Naomi had insisted on paying her. Maybe Katie, having much in common with her, understood Naomi's need to pay her own way.

She slid the door closed, latching it, and started toward the street. Dusk was drawing in, and a fine, misty rain had started falling when she was halfway back from Nathan's house. She'd be glad to get in where it was warm.

She wouldn't be driving back and forth to Nathan's nearly so often now that her work there had ended. As she'd promised Joshua and Sadie, she would be there to look after the bees. Did they realize that wouldn't be very often during the winter?

Probably not, and she hoped they wouldn't think she was letting them down. Most likely they'd be so excited to have their grandmother back that they wouldn't even notice.

She was getting what she'd wanted—a new life, work to do that didn't involve raising someone else's children, the freedom to make some decisions on her own. So why did she feel so low today?

Since she didn't have an answer for that question, maybe it was good that Katie, seeing her passing the front window, tapped on it. Smiling, she gestured for Naomi to come in.

Naomi was happy to step inside the bright, warm quilt shop for a moment. She rubbed her arms briskly.

"Do you have a few minutes before you go back to the bakery? There's something I wanted to show you, and you look as if you could stand to warm up a little."

"Ja to both of those," Naomi said. "Winter is coming on for sure. I just wish it would decide to snow and be done with it. I've had enough cold rain."

"Komm, let me have your jacket." Katie helped her out of the damp coat and hung it on the end of a quilt rack. "You'll have a mug of cocoa, won't you? Rhoda just made some."

"That sounds gut, but I don't want to put her to any trouble . . ."

"No trouble at all." Rhoda emerged from the back, holding a mug filled with foamy cocoa. "I heard you come in and poured it."

"Denke, Rhoda. That is wonderful kind of you." Naomi picked up the mug, enjoying the heat against her palms.

Rhoda nodded and glanced at her sister. "I'll finish cleaning up in back, ja? I don't think we'll have any more customers this afternoon."

"I think you're right." Katie glanced at the gray street. "That will be gut."

She turned to Naomi as her sister disappeared into the back room. "I had a quilting class this afternoon. Beginners, they were, and so there's a mess of scraps to be cleaned up."

"Your sister has turned into a wonderful gut helper to you, I think." Naomi knew that teenaged Rhoda had had some difficulty adjusting to life here in Pleasant Valley when she'd come to live with her sister, but now it seemed she'd found her place.

"I don't know what I'd do without her," Katie admitted. "It's funny how things turn out sometimes, isn't it? When Rhoda first came, I was dismayed at the very idea of taking charge of her. Now I think it's the best thing that could have happened to me. Best after meeting Caleb, of course."

Naomi smiled. Everyone in the valley knew how in love those two were. "You said you wanted to show me something?" she reminded Katie.

"Ja, I've been thinking of this ever since I saw the display of your jars of honey at the bakery this morning. And bought one, too," she added, smiling.

It was on the tip of Naomi's tongue to say she'd be happy to give some to Katie, but she managed to restrain herself. If she were to make any profit from the honey, she couldn't give it away to everyone.

It wondered her why Katie had been thinking of something in regard to her display, though. "Was there something wrong about the honey?" she asked.

"The honey was delicious," Katie exclaimed. "No, what I was thinking was a Christmas gift idea I saw in one of the craft magazines. It seemed to me that it would be simple to do, and it might encourage people, especially Englisch customers, to buy some jars for little gifts." Katie stooped behind the counter, reaching for something. "So I made one up, just to show you how it would look." She set a jar on the counter.

Naomi picked it up. Sure enough, it was one of her jars of honey. But the top had been decorated with a bit of red and green fabric and tied with a red ribbon.

"You see, it's just a circle of bright fabric, cut with pinking shears so that it won't fray." Katie's cheeks flushed with her typical enthusiasm. "I put a little piece of quilt batting on top to make it puffy, and then I put the fabric over it and tied it with a ribbon. What do you think?"

"It's pretty." Naomi turned the jar in her hand, considering. "Do you really think this would make folks want to buy it for a Christmas gift?"

Katie smiled. "It seems foolish, I know, but you'd be surprised at what makes folks buy something this time of year. You could try it and see, ain't so?"

Naomi nodded. "Denke, Katie. It was kind of you to think of it. I will try it. Do you have more of the fabric?"

"Plenty, and the ribbon, as well. Just take a little to try, and then if you need more, I'll put some back for you."

Katie began measuring fabric and ribbon, her hands moving surely.

"I see what makes your shop such a success," Naomi said. "You're so enthusiastic that everyone who walks in probably wants to make something."

"I love what I do," Katie said. "This shop is what I always wanted." She was quiet for a moment, pulling ribbon from a spool. "You know, in the beginning my mother was very opposed to my coming here and starting my shop." Her gaze met Naomi's. "I know about your troubles with your daad," she said. "I didn't want you to think that you are the only one."

That startled and touched Naomi. It was inevitable that Katie would know about the situation with Daad. Probably most in the valley knew.

"The shop is such a big job. How did you manage if you didn't have support?" Her jars of honey seemed minuscule in comparison.

"My daad interceded for me. Usually he lets Mamm have her way where the girls are concerned, but not this time."

"Unfortunately, my daad is the problem. And my mother isn't here to step in."

Katie nodded. "Maybe your stepmother . . ." She let that thought trail off.

"I hoped that might be the case." Naomi's throat tightened at the memory of how she'd parted with Betty. "But she just wants Daad to have his way."

"That's a shame, for sure." Katie's gaze met Naomi's, and her eyes were filled with understanding. "I just wanted you to know you aren't alone. If you want to talk about it anytime, I'm here."

"Denke, Katie." She blinked, afraid she'd embarrass herself with tears. "I just pray I'm doing the right thing. If Daad goes to the bishop about me—"

"Surely he wouldn't do such a thing," Katie said.

"I hope not, but Betty said he was thinking about it." Her worry probably showed in her voice, but she couldn't seem to help it.

"Bishop Mose is always fair," Katie said. "I'll never forget how he supported me when we had that trouble with vandals. You know, maybe you ought to talk to him first. I'm sure he'd give you gut advice."

"I . . . I'll think about it." She would, but she shrank from being the one to bring their family troubles to the bishop's notice. And what if Bishop Mose said she should do what Daad said?

She made an effort to push that possibility from her mind. "You said your mamm opposed your coming here and opening the shop. How does she feel now that the shop is such a success?"

Katie grinned, handing her the bag of materials. "She's happy now. To hear her tell it, the whole thing was her idea. But it's not because of the shop. It's because I finally got married."

Naomi smiled, as she knew Katie had intended. "I don't think I can count on that to solve my problems with Daad."

"You never can tell. I thought marriage was out of the question for me, too," Katie said. "But I've learned that sometimes God has surprises in store for us."

Nathan nailed a replacement fence board into place, satisfied that the barrier along the road would last another year, at least. With cars and the milk tanker going by regularly, this fence had to be secure.

He stood, stretching a little, and glanced back toward the house and barn. Now that Emma was back from her trip, life was returning to normal. Joshua and Sadie missed Naomi, but they'd been happy to see their grossmammi this morning and hear all about their new little cousin.

Normal, he thought again. Only the rectangular white boxes of the beehives reminded him of the past few weeks.

It wasn't that he was ungrateful to Naomi. She'd been a blessing when he'd needed someone to care for the children. But Emma knew and understood his ways. Besides—

A high voice cut through the cold air, and Nathan swung toward the sound. It was Joshua . . . running toward him along the road, calling out to him.

Nathan dropped his hammer and headed for the boy, his heart pumping. Something must be wrong. Joshua shouldn't be out on the road.

Even as he thought it, a car rounded the bend coming toward him. Coming toward Joshua.

"Joshua, get back!"

His son didn't give any sign of hearing him, but fortunately he was well off the side of the road. The car whizzed harmlessly past.

Nathan rushed to Joshua, grabbing his shoulders.

"Was ist letz? What are you doing out here? The road is dangerous."

Joshua gasped for breath. "Grossmammi." He stammered the word, his face white. "Komm, schnell."

Snatching his son up in his arms, Nathan ran toward the house. "What happened?" He got the words out over the pounding of his heart.

"She fell." Joshua buried his face in Nathan's neck, and Nathan felt a hot tear against his skin. "She fell down, and she can't get back up again."

"It will be all right." Maybe that wasn't true, but it was all he could say.

He pounded up the lane toward the house as Daad rushed from the barn. He must have heard Joshua shouting.

They reached the porch at the same time. Nathan pushed Joshua toward his grandfather and hurried inside.

Emma lay on the kitchen floor, an overturned chair next to her. Someone had brought a blanket and pillow to her, and Sadie sat on the floor beside her, holding her hand.

Emma looked up at him and tried to smile despite the pain that ravaged her face. "Ach, I'm causing so much trouble."

"Never mind." Nathan knelt next to her, relieved that at least Emma was conscious and seemed in her right mind. "What happened?"

"Foolish, so foolish." She moved her hand in a

161

feeble gesture toward the chair. "Thought I'd get a platter from the top shelf."

Foolish, for sure, but nobody ever thought an accident would happen to them. He clasped her free hand in his. "Tell me where you are hurt. I must call the paramedics, and they will want to know."

"My hip, but maybe it's not so bad. Joshua and Sadie have been taking care of me." She tried to move and gasped in pain.

"Just lie still, Emma," Daad said. "We'll stay with you while Nathan calls for help." He moved to take Nathan's place, letting Joshua sit beside him.

Nathan nodded, moving carefully away from Emma so that he didn't jostle her by accident. "I'll be right back."

The phone shanty was by the barn, and he ran across the yard toward it, his mind moving faster than his feet. Call 911 first, that was the important thing. Someone would have to tell Jessie, and he dreaded the thought of how upset she might be.

Jerking the door open, he grabbed the phone and pushed the buttons, quickly giving the information to the dispatcher. Luckily the firehouse wasn't far, and the Pleasant Valley emergency teams prided themselves on their fast response.

Once he'd hung up, he turned toward the door and then stopped. He'd have to go to the hospital with Emma. Daad couldn't manage the children and take care of the milking as well. And there was a phone at the bakery.

In a moment he heard Naomi's voice on the other end of the line.

"Nathan? Is something wrong?"

"Emma has fallen. I must go to the hospital with her. The children . . ."

"Don't worry about them. I will be there soon." He heard her saying something to someone else and then she was back on the line. "Paula will drive me, and she says she'll take you on to the hospital."

She disconnected before he could stammer out his thanks.

Not that she or any of the Plain People of the valley would be waiting around for thanks. Soon the word would spread, and there would be plenty of people showing up to help.

He hurried back to the house, dread seizing him as he opened the door. If Emma had taken a turn for the worse . . .

Foolishness, he knew. Emma still lay where she was, making an effort to talk normally to the children. But her gaze fastened on him, and he read the fear in it.

"It will be all right. The paramedics are on their way, and I will go to the hospital with you."

"But the kinder," she protested. "And how—"

"It's all taken care of," he said, hoping the words

would soothe her. "Naomi is on her way also, with Paula driving her, and Paula will take me to the hospital. Don't worry. Just rest, and soon you'll be back on your feet."

Even as he said the words, he heard the faint wail of a siren in the distance, getting louder. The emergency team must have beaten their best record to get here so soon.

In a few minutes the kitchen was crowded with people and equipment. Daad took Sadie and Joshua by the hand and led them into the living room, hushing their protests.

"We must leave the rescue people room to do their work," he said.

Nathan could breathe easier once the children were out of the way. He didn't want them to see their grandmother in pain, and no matter how gentle the EMTs were, it would be difficult to get Emma onto a stretcher and into the ambulance.

His stomach churned as he watched. This must have been what it was like when they came for Ada. If he'd been here . . . But if he'd been here, it would never have happened.

Emma bit her lip as she was moved to a stretcher, a moan escaping her. In the other room he heard Sadie start to cry, and his heart twisted. He wanted to protect his children from everything that might hurt them, but he couldn't.

He hastened to hold the door open as the paramedics moved the stretcher. They were lowering it down the steps when a car pulled in, swinging around the ambulance. Paula Schatz's car, the offending chrome painted black. The doors swung open, and Naomi was hurrying toward him.

One little piece of his tension slipped away. Naomi was here, and she'd take over. The children were safe with her.

Chapter Ten

Praying silently for Emma, Naomi hurried into the house, pausing only long enough to hang up her jacket. She couldn't do anything for Emma but pray, but there was certainly something she could do for the children.

Sadie's sobs reached her as she crossed the kitchen and went into the living room. Ezra, Nathan's father, sat on the sofa with Sadie in his lap and Joshua next to him. He patted Sadie's back and looked up at Naomi with relief plainly written on his face.

"I told Sadie that Emma would be all right, but . . ." He let that sentence trail off, shrugging a little.

"Sadie." Naomi reached out to take the little girl, and Sadie clung to her, wrapping her arms around Naomi's neck. "Komm. Stop the crying.

Your grossmammi might hear you. Think how bad it would make her feel."

Sadie pulled back, sniffling. "It would?"

"Ja, of course it would. She loves you."

"She said you and Joshua took gut care of her," Ezra said, rising and motioning for Naomi to take his place. "That made her happy."

"You did?" Naomi sat down, putting her arm around Joshua and seating Sadie on her lap. "That was wonderful smart of you."

Sadie nodded and then glanced at her brother. "It was Joshua," she whispered. "He told me what to do."

"So you both helped your grossmammi." She snuggled them close.

Sadie relaxed against her, but Joshua sat with his shoulders squared, as if he had to carry a burden. What was going through his mind? Was he blaming himself for Emma's accident?

"Do you want to tell me about it?" Surely it was best for them to talk rather than to keep it inside and worry. She met Ezra's gaze. He nodded and slipped out to the kitchen.

"I heard Grossmammi fall," Sadie announced. "I was playing with my dolly." She nodded toward a plastic baby doll that lay under the rocking chair.

"What about you, Joshua? Did you hear her fall?"

He nodded. "I went to the basement to get a jar

of applesauce for her. She was going to make an applesauce cake. When she fell . . ." He stopped, his eyes dark with misery. "I could have held the chair for her."

"Ja, you could have," she said, keeping her voice calm. Like his daadi, he was quick to take responsibility. "But you were doing something else for her. You couldn't have known she would fall." She smoothed his hair back from his face. "Whenever there's an accident, we always think there was something we should have done. I'd guess your grossmammi is thinking that right now."

Some of the stiffness went out of Joshua, and he nodded. "That's what she said. After she fell. She said she should have known better."

"Ja, we always think so, don't we? That's what makes it an accident. Nobody's fault—it just happened. And you certain-sure did the right things for Grossmammi afterward."

"We got a pillow," Sadie said. "And a blanket. And then Joshua ran to get Daadi while I held Grossmammi's hand."

"You both did exactly the right thing," Naomi said. "Now, suppose we straighten up the kitchen before Daadi gets back. Maybe we could bake something."

"Not applesauce cake," Joshua said quickly.

"How about snickerdoodles? We can pack some up to take to your grossmammi if she has to stay in the hospital."

"I love snickerdoodles." Sadie slid from Naomi's lap. "I like to push them down with a fork."

"That is the fun part, isn't it?" She ushered the children toward the kitchen. They would be upset over Emma's fall for a bit, but the busier she kept them, the better. They'd be more likely to mention anything that was bothering them while she was working with them.

Especially Joshua. She studied his face, noticing the wariness in his eyes. Sadie would get her bounce back quickly, but it would take Joshua a bit longer, maybe because he was older and remembered more about Ada's accident.

She closed her eyes for an instant, murmuring a silent prayer for him. And for herself, that she would know how best to help these children.

By the time they reached the third sheet of cookies, someone was knocking at the back door. Naomi wiped her hands on a tea towel and went to answer it. News spread fast, and the neighbors would have seen the ambulance pull in.

"Naomi, I thought you'd be here." It was Leah, along with Barbara Beiler, her sister-in-law. They both carried baskets. "Is there any news of Emma?"

"Not yet." Naomi gestured them on into the kitchen, where it was warmer. "It's gut of you to stop."

"We saw the ambulance go by," Barbara said,

putting her basket on the counter and lifting out a casserole dish. Plump and rosy, Barbara was as noted for her cooking as she was for being something of a blabbermaul. "I had beef stew on the stove already, so I brought it for your dinner."

"Denke, Barbara. That's ser kind of you. I'll be able to heat some up for Nathan when he gets back."

Barbara clucked. "Who knows how long that will be? It must have been pretty serious, for them to carry Emma away on a stretcher."

Leah glanced at the children and then gave her sister-in-law a meaningful look. "I'm sure the paramedics were just being extra careful," she said repressively. She set her basket down. "Elizabeth and I made cinnamon raisin bread this morning, so I brought a couple of loaves."

Elizabeth was Leah's teenage stepdaughter, and a sweet, responsible girl.

"Denke. And be sure to tell Elizabeth how much it is appreciated." Naomi ruffled Joshua's hair. "Joshua loves raisin bread."

"And you are making snickerdoodles, I see." Leah leaned over the table, where Sadie was busy pressing the tines of a fork on the rounds of dough. "They look like little waffles, don't they, Sadie?"

Sadie nodded. "I like to make them."

"And eat them, if you're like my kinder," Leah said, smiling.

As a former teacher, Leah had a nice way with the young ones, Naomi thought. She glanced toward Barbara, to find her eyes bright with curiosity.

"How did you get here so quickly?" she asked, not troubling to hide her desire to know everything that was going on.

"Nathan called the bakery, and Paula drove me. Then she drove Nathan on to the hospital, so that he could be there with Emma." She paused, wondering what it would take to satisfy Barbara's curiosity. "Paula's a gut friend. She's always willing to help with her car in an emergency."

"Well, if the accident had to happen, it's gut that Nathan could call on someone the kinder already know, like you." Barbara tucked a pot holder back into her basket. "Poor Nathan, going back to the hospital again. The memories that must bring back." She sighed, shaking her head.

Naomi realized that she was gripping the edge of the counter and forced herself to relax. Barbara had a warm heart, but she also had a gift for saying things she shouldn't.

"Why did you say my daadi is poor?" Sadie stared at Barbara, looking as if she'd burst into tears again at any moment.

"That's not what she meant," Naomi said quickly. "Just that it's a shame Grossmammi had an accident."

Barbara opened her mouth, but at a look from

170

Leah she closed it again. "Ja," she said finally. "That's what I was thinking."

"We're going to save some of the snicker-doodles to take to Emma if she has to stay in the hospital," Naomi said, keeping her voice light with an effort. She knew only too well what Barbara had meant by her comment. She was comparing Emma's accident with Ada's, saying that Nathan would be doubly upset to be heading to the hospital again, as he'd done the day Ada died.

And she was probably right, even though she'd have done better not to say it. Nathan would be reminded, but there was nothing anyone could do about it.

Darkness came on early in December, and Nathan still hadn't returned. Naomi was just tucking the children into bed when she heard the sound of a car coming up the lane.

"That is probably your daadi." She forestalled Sadie's attempt to rush downstairs in her bare feet. "Stay in bed where it's warm. I'll go and get him for you."

When she reached the top of the stairs, Nathan was already on his way up, shedding his jacket as he came. "The kinder are still awake?"

"Ja, they're waiting for you." She couldn't read anything in his face, so she followed him into the bedroom.

"Daadi, Daadi," Sadie clamored, while Joshua watched him with apprehension.

"Hush, now." He sat down on Sadie's bed, pulling the quilt over her, and reached out to Joshua, who came quickly to lean against him.

"How is Grossmammi?" Joshua's shoulders were stiff again, as if he were bracing himself to hear bad news, and Naomi's heart ached for him.

"She is doing well," Nathan said quickly, his arm snugging his son against him. "I stayed until she was in her own room at the hospital. She was sleepy, but she said to tell you she loves you and she'll see you again soon."

Joshua relaxed visibly, and Naomi felt herself do the same. *Denke, Father,* she said silently.

"Will she be here tomorrow?" Sadie asked.

"No, not tomorrow. It will take her a little time to get back to normal, so we must be patient." Nathan looked at Naomi, and she knew what he was asking without his saying a word.

"I will be here tomorrow, ja?" She bent to hug Sadie and then Joshua. "Now I should probably . . ." She paused, looking questioningly at Nathan. "Did Paula bring you home?"

"I did not want to keep her away from the bakery for so long. I hired Ben Miller to drive me back. He'll take you home, too."

Ben was a retired Englischer who enjoyed serving as a taxi driver for the Amish and the horse-and-buggy Mennonites when they needed to go someplace too distant to take a buggy.

"I should go then." She started for the door.

Nathan rose and came after her. "I must go down and speak to Naomi before she leaves," he told the children. "I'll be back up to say good night."

Naomi went on down the steps, aware of his sturdy figure behind her. Obviously she would come tomorrow. But what about the next day, and the next? There was more to be said about Emma's condition than Nathan had told the children.

When they reached the kitchen, safely out of earshot of the children's room, she turned to Nathan. "How bad is Emma's injury?"

"It's a broken hip." He passed a hand over his forehead, as if he longed to wipe away the events of the day. "She is back in her room and resting."

Poor Emma. A broken hip was serious, for sure, at her age. "Is someone with her?"

Nathan nodded. "Emma is cousins with Lizzie Taubner, and Lizzie is sitting with her tonight. Jessie was there, but she was so upset it seemed best to send her home."

That fact probably didn't need a comment. "I'm sorry. For Emma and for you."

"Denke." He ran his hand through his hair and gripped the back of his neck, his face drawn with fatigue and worry. "It is wonderful kind of you to come today. And tomorrow."

"What else would I do?" She managed a smile, trying not to think of her own concerns. "You have enough to do without worrying about who is taking care of the kinder."

"I shouldn't have expected Emma to watch them. If she hadn't been trying to do too much, this never would have happened."

Of course Nathan would try to take responsibility. "I do not think you could have prevented Emma from taking care of her grandchildren," she said, her voice mild.

Nathan shook his head, probably not cheered much by her words, true though they were. "I never even questioned Emma's taking over after Ada died. Maybe I was too shocked then to think it through, but that doesn't excuse me from taking her for granted since then."

"Nathan, Emma wanted to care for Joshua and Sadie. She loves them."

Naomi longed to comfort him and wasn't sure how. True, Emma was getting on in years and in other circumstances would have been happy to settle into a quieter role, but after Ada's death, she had done what she had to. That was all anyone could do in the face of such tragedy.

"I talked with the doctor," he said abruptly. "Emma will be in the hospital for a few days, and then she will be moved to the rehab unit. They will help her learn to walk again." He hesitated. Then he turned to her with a look of decision on his face. "I can't expect that Emma will ever be able to take on complete care of two young ones again."

She sensed what he was about to ask her and a wave of panic rippled through her. "You can't be sure—" she began.

He cut that off with a sharp gesture. "Joshua and Sadie have lost so much in their lives already. Now their grossmammi. They need a woman they can count on." He looked at her, waiting.

She wanted to help him, longed to soothe the pain and worry from his face. But that very longing set up warning signals in her heart. Caring for Nathan's children seemed coupled with caring about Nathan. She couldn't let that happen—it was a sure recipe for heartache. But she couldn't desert the children, either.

"I will take over the kinder for the next few days," she said carefully. "By then you will know better what the future holds."

"I know now." His jaw was tight as he ground out the words. "And I know that spending your life taking care of my children is not what you planned."

Naomi pressed her fingers to her forehead. "Nathan, I must have time to think. Please, don't ask me to decide something this big all in a minute." The panic intensified as she felt the situation spinning out of her control.

Something of her panic must have communicated itself to Nathan. He took a step back, seeming to force himself to relax. "You're right. I'm sorry. Just promise me that you'll think about it."

The wonder would be if she could think about anything else. "Ja. I will." She went quickly to get her coat before he could think of anything else to say to convince her.

But he didn't even try. He held the door for her. "Ben will pick you up in the morning and take you home tomorrow night, so you don't have to worry about driving the buggy when it's getting dark."

"Denke," she murmured. "I will be praying for Emma." She escaped, going quickly toward the waiting car.

It was too bad she couldn't escape her thoughts so easily. Doing as Nathan wanted meant changing the course of her life once again, when she'd barely begun to get used to the aftermath of Daad's remarriage.

And if she did say yes, where would she live? She couldn't stay with Paula if she wasn't working at the bakery.

A month ago she'd thought she had no choices at all about her future. Now she had too many.

Nathan tossed the final bale of straw down to Isaiah the next afternoon. "That will do it, I think." He swung himself onto the ladder and climbed down from the loft.

Isaiah was already putting fresh straw in the last stall. Daad, coming in the barn just then, shook his head.

"You boys have finished the cleaning without me? I told you I would help."

"You help with plenty," Nathan said. "Besides, Isaiah and I were seeing who could work the fastest."

Isaiah grinned. "I'm younger, so I'm faster."

Nathan tossed a flake of straw at him. "You're dreaming," he retorted.

"You are in a gut mood," Daad said. "Is there news from the hospital?"

Nathan nodded, knowing full well that wasn't the cause of his raised spirits. "The nurse I spoke to said Emma had a restless night, but she was smiling and talking today."

"Gut, gut." Daad gave him a knowing look. "And Naomi is here with the kinder again. She will keep their minds off what happened yesterday."

"Last time I looked in, they were making Christmas cards," Isaiah said. "I remember Naomi doing that with me."

"I expect you wanted to join them," Daad teased, gathering up the binder twine from the bale.

Isaiah grinned. "Well, it did look like fun—all that colored paper and crayons and paste." He turned to Nathan. "Do you want me to get that harness ready to go for mending?"

Nathan nodded. "Ja, that would be gut. I'll try to drop it off tomorrow at Bishop Mose's harness shop."

Isaiah headed for the tack room, but Daad stood where he was, looking at Nathan with a question in his eyes. "You are going to ask Naomi to stay for gut, ain't so?"

"I already did, last night. It's the best solution I can see." He just hoped by this time Naomi was ready to admit it was.

"What did she say?" Daad leaned against a stall, shifting his weight as if tired of standing.

"She wanted time to think about it." He couldn't help clenching his jaw. "I don't have time. I'm going to talk to her again this afternoon. I thought maybe you could bring the kinder outside so we can have a word in private. I wouldn't want them to hear."

"I will," Daad said. "But . . ."

"But what?" He didn't want to sound impatient with his father, but he felt driven to have this settled.

Daad's gaze was steady, and he frowned a little. "It is not fair to push Naomi into taking over the kinder if it's not what she wants. She might have reasons you don't know about for wishing her life otherwise."

Nathan took a deep breath and let it out slowly, calming himself. "I can't pretend it's not impor- tant to me, because it is. But I will try not to push."

"And try to listen, as well. Naomi is not one to blurt out everything that's on her mind. You must give her a chance to talk and not rush her."

Much as it exasperated him, he had a sneaking suspicion Daad was right. He'd spent the night coming up with answers for every objection he thought Naomi might raise. Was that pushing? Well, maybe so.

"I promise I'll be patient and listen," he said. He nodded toward the house. "Maybe we'd best do it now, before I get impatient again."

Daad nodded, and they started toward the house side by side. Nathan rehearsed what he would say, hoping he had the right words to persuade Naomi. Her answer was too important to leave to chance.

Joshua and Sadie looked up from the table when the door opened.

"Who wants to go and give the horses a carrot?" Daad said.

"Me, me." Sadie slid off her chair first, but Joshua beat her to the coat hooks.

"I can get my coat on faster," he said, and promptly got it turned the wrong way around.

Laughing, Naomi came to his aid and then helped Sadie into her jacket. "Don't forget your mittens. I'll get some carrots for you."

In a moment Daad and the young ones were out the door, with Sadie still chattering a mile a minute. Naomi turned to Nathan, and the smile slowly faded from her face.

"I guess you want an answer from me."

Reminding himself of Daad's words, Nathan tried to relax. He pulled out a chair at the table, pushing the children's cards to one side. "I thought it would be better to talk about it when the kinder aren't around. We couldn't really discuss it much last night."

Moving slowly, Naomi took the seat across from him. It reminded him of the countless times he'd seen her sit with Ada in this same spot, talking and laughing with cups of tea cooling in front of them. He'd asked Ada once what they found to talk about for so long.

You always find things to say to an old friend, she'd responded. *Even if I can guess what Naomi would say, I like to hear it from her.*

He pressed his palms on the table, willing away the sound of Ada's voice. He'd best think about what Daad had said, instead.

"Daad is afraid I'm trying to push you into saying yes," he said, surprising himself. He hadn't intended to tell her.

But she smiled a little, and he was glad he had said it. "And aren't you?"

She knew him too well. "Maybe," he admitted. "But it is your decision."

"Ja," she said softly. She looked down at her hands.

He couldn't see her eyes, and that bothered him. He might be able to tell what she was thinking if he could look into her clear eyes.

"I know you love the kinder," he said. "So it's not that which makes you hesitate. Tell me what it is, and maybe we can solve it together."

She glanced up at him, and he thought she seemed flustered at being pinned down so. "Well, there's my honey business, to start with. It will take a lot of time when warm weather comes. I don't want to give that up."

"I don't want you to give it up. It's important to you. But there are enough extra hands here with me and Daad and Isaiah to help you out. I'll take it to the stores myself if you want." He had a momentary image of himself selling honey along with the milk.

Naomi's face warmed, and he thought she was seeing that same picture. "That wouldn't be necessary. But there's the bakery. Paula and Hannah have been wonderful kind to me. I wouldn't want to leave them shorthanded. And besides, I can't stay with Paula if I'm not working for her. That wouldn't be fair."

Her hands were gripping each other tightly, and he resisted the urge to place his hand over hers.

"Just talk to Paula and Hannah. See what they say. You can do that much, can't you?"

She nodded. "But—"

"Ja, a place to live is more serious. I don't like the idea of you driving back and forth all the

181

time anyway, especially in bad weather. If you were here—"

"I couldn't," she said quickly, her face filled with something like panic. "Nathan, you know that wouldn't be suitable."

"Not here in the house, no." Surely she knew he wouldn't suggest such a thing. "But Isaiah and Libby live right here on the property."

"I don't want to move in with them. Newlyweds don't need an older sister sharing the same roof."

"Not the same roof, either." His own patience surprised him. But this was important, and he had to get it right. "But the grossdaadi house where my daad's aunt used to live is right across the lane from Isaiah's place. We've kept it in gut shape, and we'd just have to move some furniture in." He could see that the notion appealed to Naomi, and he leaned forward. "You'd be right next to your brother and his wife. I'd think that would make your daad happy."

She lifted an eyebrow. "I don't know if I'd go that far, but it would stop the mouths of the gossips, at least."

That startled him. "You believe folks would gossip because you're here taking care of my kinder? Why?"

She looked at him as if he were about Joshua's age. "Folks always gossip. I'm too close to you in age, and Ada's friend besides. They would—" She stopped, her cheeks growing pink.

They would say she was trying to catch him. He filled in the rest of the sentence for her. He should have thought of that possibility, but it had never entered his mind.

He kept himself from saying it was ridiculous. "At least if you were living next to family, that would discourage talk."

Naomi let out a sigh, seeming to relax a little. "You have an answer for everything. Except for one thing. What if Emma doesn't agree that she can't come back full-time?"

Why did women always have to make things so difficult? Emma surely would see common sense about the situation.

Or would she?

"I think," he said slowly, "that Emma will realize it herself when she sees that her recovery takes a long time. By then, Joshua and Sadie will be settled happily with you. She'll see that having you here is best for them."

When Naomi didn't answer, he clasped her hands in his, gripping them firmly so that she raised a startled gaze to his. "The kinder can't be left feeling that everything in their life is temporary."

His voice cracked on the words, and he was ashamed at himself for showing so much emotion. But Naomi returned the pressure of his hands with warm, quick sympathy.

"All right," she said. "I will work it out with

Paula and Hannah somehow. It will be fine."

He was suddenly very aware of the warmth of her touch, of her fingers pressing his. He let go and shoved his chair back to stand.

"Gut," he said, wondering where all this confusion he felt had come from. "Gut."

Chapter Eleven

"Are you sure you don't mind?" Naomi looked from the jars of honey she was stacking on the counter to Paula, busy cleaning the bakery case at the end of the day.

"Ach, how many times must I tell you?" Paula was mock scolding. "I'm not saying we won't miss you around here, because we surely will. But you must go in the direction you feel led."

"I hope I am being led to the right thing." Doubts had crept in, of course, once she was away from the farm and had time to think. "I feel as if my life is being turned upside down yet again. And what if Emma does recover enough to come back to the children?"

Paula paused, frowning a little. The sleeves of her print Mennonite dress had been pushed up, and she was enveloped in the white apron she wore in the bakery.

"I try to put myself in Emma's place," she

said. "We are about the same age, ain't so?"

Naomi nodded. Paula was certainly still very active. She'd resent it if anyone tried to take over for her, although she was giving her niece more and more responsibility.

"A broken hip is serious business," Paula said. "It will take time for her to recover, and by then, she may have gotten accustomed to your watching the kinder."

"That's what Nathan thinks." It was reassuring to hear Paula echo his thought, since Paula wasn't trying to persuade her to do something.

"We never know just how things are going to turn out, do we?" Paula shook her head. "We just have to do what seems right at the time. And certainly it's right to take care of those mother-less kinder. Who will do it better than their mother's dearest friend?"

"I hope so. It's a big responsibility."

"About that, I don't have any doubts," Paula declared. "You can give the kinder the home life they need."

"Aunt Paula is right." Hannah, finished cleaning the small round tables, came to the counter. Her attention was caught by the jars of honey. "You did some more of the Christmas ones. They look so pretty." She touched the bright red fabric. "They've been selling very quickly."

"I noticed." Naomi had been surprised today to see how many jars had gone from the bakery.

"I'll try to do some more in the next few days." Struck by a sudden thought, she looked at Paula. "That is, if you still want to sell them since I won't be working here any longer."

"For sure I want to sell them," Paula declared. "And there's no need to rush out of your room, either. You should wait until everything is fixed up the way you want it in the grossdaadi house."

"Denke, Paula. That will be Saturday, I think. Isaiah and Libby have been helping, and Lovina says she'll have Elijah bring some furniture over that day. And Nathan's father also brought some things he doesn't have room for since he moved in with his daughter. So they'll all be helping on Saturday."

"I wish it wasn't such a busy day for the bakery, so that we could come and help, too," Hannah said. She reached up to tuck a strand of brown hair back under her kapp. "We'll stop out to see your place soon, though." She hesitated. "Is there any furniture from . . . from your childhood that will be coming?"

She shook her head, her throat tight. "Daad has not been talking to me. I guess that's better than being scolded all the time, but I wish . . ."

"I know." Paula reached across the counter to clasp her hand, her normally cheerful face serious for a moment. "You don't want to be on bad terms with your own daad. But you must give him time. He'll come around."

That was what she'd been praying, but she hadn't seen any sign of it yet.

Paula put some leftover cookies and cupcakes into a bag. "You must take these to Joshua and Sadie tomorrow." Her tone was brisk as ever. "They'll like a treat."

"Every child likes a treat," she said. "And some grown-ups, too." She put the cookies and cupcakes into the basket in which she'd carried the honey jars.

Hannah took off the extra apron she wore in the shop, smoothing down her dress as she prepared to go home. Her son, Jamie, who had been playing with blocks in the corner since the last customer left, came over to tug at her skirt.

Naomi smiled. "I think Jamie knows when it is time to go home."

Jamie smiled back at her. He took his finger out of his mouth and said, "William."

"Daadi," Hannah corrected. "William is Daadi now."

"Daadi," Jamie said, seeming contented.

It was gut to see that the little boy was adjusting to William Brand as his daad. William was wonderful gut with children, of course, and Jamie had been too young even to remember his own father.

"What are you thinking?" Hannah asked. She had a gift for discerning when a person was holding something back. "Are you still concerned about raising someone else's kinder?"

"Not exactly." That opinion of hers seemed something long ago and far away now. "It's not like caring for my brother's young ones, where they'd always be turning to their mammi. Joshua and Sadie don't have a woman in their lives all the time without their grossmammi."

"They need you," Hannah said. "But something is bothering you."

She nodded. She could say things to Hannah and Paula that she couldn't tell to her own family. "I'm afraid that people are going to talk. Nathan doesn't seem worried about it, but I hate the thought."

Paula planted her elbows on the counter. "Ja, well, there's no doubt that folks do too much talking about their neighbors' business. So long as you know you're doing the right thing, you can only ignore them."

"That's not so easy," Hannah said, echoing Naomi's thoughts. She smiled slightly. "I know what it was like to be talked about when I started working with William on his stammering."

Hannah, who had gone to college for speech therapy before she married, had helped William immeasurably.

"Well," Naomi said, "if folks talked about you and William, you had the last laugh, because you fell in love. That's not going to happen in my situation."

Hannah's eyebrows lifted. "How can you be

sure? Once he is seeing you every day, Nathan may begin to have feelings for you. And you already do for him, don't you?"

Flustered by the direct question, Naomi ducked her head, knowing her cheeks were flushing. "I don't. And anyway, even if I did, it would be useless." She stared right at the truth that stood in front of her like a barricade. "Nathan cannot love anyone else, because he is still in love with Ada."

"I will be moving in, so I will be close to you every day. You don't need to worry about who is taking care of you."

Naomi might have been saying those words to the kinder, but at the moment she was addressing the bees. She was so used to talking to the bees when she worked around the hives that she seldom thought about how it must sound to anyone else. Now that the hives were here at Nathan's, she might have to be a bit more careful in what she said, though.

Still, no one was around right now. Libby had kindly come over to watch the children while Naomi wrapped the hives for the winter, since Naomi knew Nathan wouldn't want them coming out here with her. And the men were off taking care of a broken fence in one of the pastures, she thought.

She unrolled the black coverings that went

around the hives to provide some needed insulation for the cold weather. The pieces were already cut to fit, and they just had to be stapled in place. Normally Isaiah helped her with this job, but she'd determined to do it herself. No need for Nathan to think that both Esch family members he employed were off doing something other than their work.

Not that Nathan would care, but still, she felt as if she ought to be a bit cautious as they all figured out their places now that Naomi was here for good.

Naomi picked up the first piece of insulation, trying to hold it in place with one hand while she got the stapler out with the other. "Now, don't be alarmed at the sound of the staple," she said. "I will be finished soon, and you will like having the hive a bit warmer, ain't so?"

"I'm sure they will." The voice spoke behind her, and she jerked, losing her grasp on the insulation, which promptly rolled up around her arm.

"Ach, look what you have made me do," she scolded, trying to hide her blush. "Nathan, you must not creep up on someone who is working with bees."

"I wasn't creeping." His voice was mild as he unwrapped the insulation from her sleeve. "You were so busy talking to the bees that you didn't hear me."

She looked up at him, smiling a bit ruefully. "True enough. I was just telling myself that I should be more careful in what I say to the bees, just in case anyone was around. I wouldn't want you to think I'm crazy."

"I could never think that of you." Nathan returned her smile. The cold had made his cheeks rosy, and she could see the laughter lurking in his eyes.

Ach, well, she didn't mind Nathan laughing at her if it brought him a little pleasure.

"It looks as if you need a bit of help." He held up the strip of insulation. "Do you want me to hold or staple?"

"Neither, denke. I can manage this myself." She tried to take the strip from him, but he held on easily.

"Naomi, I am certain-sure you can manage anything you set out to, but it will be faster and easier to do this job with two people instead of one."

Perhaps she needed a little lesson in humility about now. "You are right. Denke, Nathan. Suppose I hold and you staple, since I know how the pieces fit on the hives."

He nodded, picking up the stapler she had dropped. "I have seen the hives with their black coverings in the winter, but I never looked very closely. Do you just wrap the insulation around them?"

"Ja, that's it."

Moving quickly because her hands were getting cold, she wrapped the insulation around the first hive, and was relieved to see that it fit perfectly with no torn edges. Sometimes the winter was hard on the insulation, or it ripped when she took it off.

She overlapped the edges and held them. "Now you can staple it along the seam."

"I'll try not to get your fingers." He bent over to run a neat row of staples down the edges.

That didn't surprise her. No matter what he was doing, Nathan seemed to work both neatly and quickly. Like most farmers, he could turn his hand to almost any job of carpentry or mending. She liked the way he understood what had to be done without any fuss or needless explanations.

"Will you hold this at the bottom? It's slipping a bit."

She stooped down, their arms entangling as she tried to hold the insulation at such an awkward angle. Her breath caught, and she was suddenly aware of Nathan's cheek next to hers, of the ruddiness of his skin and the fine wrinkles around his eyes.

She had to say something before Nathan realized she wasn't breathing. "Is that okay?" She managed to make the question sound fairly normal, she thought.

"Ja, that's it." Nathan straightened. Was it her

imagination, or was his breathing a bit out of rhythm as well?

Banishing the thought, she bent to pick up the next piece of insulation. Unfortunately, he did the same, and they cracked heads. Since hers was protected by her bonnet, she feared he'd gotten the worst of it.

"Ach, Nathan, I'm so sorry."

"No problem." He straightened, chuckling a little, his eyes warming as he looked at her. "I was just trying to save you a bit of work. Never mind. We'll soon get into the rhythm of working together, ja?"

"Ja, of course." She had to keep smiling, had to treat the moment as lightly as he did.

But the truth was that her heart seemed to be taking a beating in the past few minutes. Maybe it needed insulation more than the beehives did.

Nathan double-checked the row of wooden pegs in the bedroom of the grossdaadi house, making sure they were level. The past few days had been hectic, but he was determined that the place would be ready for Naomi to move into on Saturday.

And once in, she would stay. That was the heart of the matter for him. Naomi needed to be so satisfied with this situation that she wouldn't think of leaving. So whatever he needed to do to make that happen, he would.

Daad crossed the small landing at the top of the

stairs from the other bedroom. "Almost finished here?"

"Almost. Will you hold this steady while I screw it in?"

Nodding, Daad put his hands on the strip of wooden molding that held the pegs for clothing. "Your great-aunt never used this small bedroom much, that I remember. Are you thinking Naomi will have folks to stay?"

"She might." Nathan checked the level again and began putting in the final screws. "Her nieces and nephews maybe, or her sisters when they are here visiting." He voiced the thought that had been in his mind. "If Naomi feels this is her home, she'll want to stay."

Daad eyed him. "You think the house will make the difference?"

"Maybe not. But it is something I can make sure is right." He glanced at his father. What was in Daad's mind?

Daad caught the look. His weathered face creased in a smile. "Ach, Nathan, you were always the same. Deciding on doing something and then going after it with all your strength. Maybe that comes of being the oldest and the only boy in the family."

"Maybe it comes of the gut example my daad set for me."

They exchanged places, and he began setting the screws on the opposite end.

"Maybe," Daad said, but there was a trace of doubt in his voice. "It is a gut quality, to be persistent when you want something. But . . ."

"But what?" Nathan's shoulders tensed. Surely Daad didn't think he was wrong to want Naomi to care for the children.

"But we are only human. We can't always control how things turn out."

His throat tightened. He knew that better than most people. He'd wanted Ada, he'd wanted a family, and he'd wanted a gut life for them. But he hadn't been able to control the lightning that hit the barn, or the fact that in his absence Ada had been the one to go into the barn to try to save the horses.

"Having the right woman to care for the kinder is too important to Joshua and Sadie to leave to chance," he said, turning the screwdriver so hard that it was a wonder the board didn't split.

"I know. But are you sure this is the way to go about it?"

Nathan dropped the screwdriver into his toolbox and faced his father. "Naomi is the best person for the job. Don't you agree?"

"Ach, ja." Daad ran his hand along the molding. "But there is more to it, ain't so? What if someday you want to marry? What happens to Naomi then? It would be like this business with her daad all over again."

The prospect startled Nathan so that for a

195

moment he was speechless. Then he found his tongue. "I will never remarry." His tone was flat and final. He could not share his life with another woman.

Daad's gaze was intent on his face. "We don't know what the future holds. But what about Naomi, then? What if she should want to marry? Would you deny her that happiness?"

The depth of his surprise at the thought showed Nathan that he had accepted the attitude of Naomi's family, their calm assumption that marriage wasn't for her.

He would sacrifice a great deal for his children, but Naomi's future wasn't his to sacrifice.

"If that should happen, I wouldn't stand in Naomi's way." He knew he sounded stiff, unnatural even. "Are you thinking that I am being selfish?"

"Not selfish, no." Daad patted his shoulder. "Just very focused on your own needs."

He opened his mouth to say that it was the children's needs, not his own, but he could hear footsteps on the stairs and picked up his toolbox and held his peace.

"Here you are." Isaiah poked his head into the room and glanced around. "Looks gut. Libby wants to know can she start putting some things in the kitchen cupboards. Some of the sisters have brought dishes and such."

"Ja, I think the shelves are all cleared out.

There's one latch that's not working right."

"Just needs some oil," Daad said. "I'll go and do it."

Isaiah stepped aside to let Daad by. The house was small enough that two men more than filled the tiny landing.

"This room is nice," Isaiah said, glancing around the small bedroom with its sloping ceiling. "Are you thinking we'll put the pair of twin beds in here?"

Nathan nodded. "We should have that finished before folks come to help with the moving in tomorrow." He hesitated, Daad's words still hovering in his mind. Maybe he hadn't been thinking enough about Naomi. "Your family—will they be coming?"

Isaiah looked down at the toes of his work shoes, his fair skin flushing a little. Not even the beard kept him from looking like the boy he'd been. "I don't know. I'm not sure."

Nathan's conscience gave him a kick. "I didn't want to come between Naomi and her family."

"Ach, well, they'll get over it." Isaiah shrugged. "There's talk, I guess, over why Naomi is willing to take on your kinder when she didn't want to move in with Lige and Lovina and do the same." He used the childhood nickname that annoyed Elijah for some reason. "I told them that she'd probably rather be working for someone else and going to her own house at night." He grinned.

"Lige didn't like that very much, but Lovina said she could understand."

"Is Naomi upset about the way they are acting?"

Isaiah shrugged again. "You know Naomi. If she is, she doesn't show it. Anyway, I think if Lovina has her way, they'll be here tomorrow. And Lovina usually does, my Libby says."

Nathan nodded. The women probably understood each other more easily than a man could. "What about your daad?"

"Well, we can't count on him being here. You know how stubborn he is. Anyway, I wouldn't worry about it." Isaiah stepped back onto the landing. "I'd best go help Libby bring the dishes over."

Nathan nodded, following him down the stairs. He'd been determined to make Naomi so settled here that she wouldn't think of anything else. Had he let his own needs blind him to what was best for her?

Chapter Twelve

The small grossdaadi house seemed full to bursting on Saturday with the people who kept streaming in to help. Naomi's heart swelled with gratitude at the sight of Leah Glick and several other friends from their running-around group arriving early, all of them laden down with baskets and bags. She hurried to the door to greet them.

"Leah, Rachel, it is wonderful gut of you to be here. And Mary Ann and Elizabeth, as well." All of them were married now, of course. All of them had families except for her, but that didn't make a difference today.

"We have brought some kitchen things," Leah said. "And some groceries, too. I know you'll be cooking over at the farmhouse, but you'll still want your own kitchen and pantry to be well-stocked."

"That's for sure." Rachel carried a box filled with what looked to be canned food. "Point me to the pantry, and I will start organizing these things."

"Right over here." Naomi showed her into the small pantry that adjoined the kitchen, its shelves freshly painted. One section was already filled with her own jars of honey and the few things she'd brought from Daad's house. "But you didn't need to bring so much."

Rachel set down the bag and gave Naomi a quick hug. "Everyone wants to make you feel happy in your new home."

"It is ser gut of you." This was almost like setting up a house for a newlywed couple. Maybe it was a different sort of announcement. Perhaps they felt her move was declaring her singleness.

She chased that thought away. Her friends were

199

being kind, that was all, just as they would for anyone moving into a new house.

She went quickly back into the kitchen, leaving Rachel happily organizing the pantry. There she found Leah arranging dishes in the cabinets.

"Where did the others go?" She started unpacking glasses, removing their newspaper wrapping.

"Putting linens away," Leah said. "And indulging their curiosity, I think. They wanted to see the rest of the house."

"It's a nice little place, isn't it?" Naomi glanced around the kitchen, already beginning to feel as if it were hers. "Just two rooms down, plus the pantry and the laundry. And two bedrooms and bath upstairs. Plenty of space for me."

Leah nodded. "I can vaguely remember, I think, when Nathan's great-aunt lived here. He's kept it in gut shape since then."

"Ja, for sure." She began putting glasses in the cabinet to the right of the sink.

"Nice and close to Isaiah and Libby, too." Leah glanced out the kitchen window, to where Naomi's brother's place stood just across the lane. "They'll like having you so close."

"I hope so." Naomi glanced at the house as well. "They didn't exactly have a choice about it, since both properties belong to Nathan."

"Ach, you get along fine with those two," Leah said. She paused, blue eyes questioning. "Is it any better with the rest of the family?"

Naomi's throat tightened. "Not really. I had hoped that today . . ." She let that trail off. No sense in hoping for the impossible. Daadi did not forgive easily, and maybe Elijah had decided to follow Daad's lead.

Leah clasped her hand for a moment. "It will get better," she said. "Things will settle down to normal soon."

Naomi nodded. There wasn't really anything else to say, and it was hardly fair to grieve over those who hadn't come today. She must just be thankful for those dear friends who had.

Libby came in the door, her cheeks flushed from the cold, saying something back over her shoulder to Isaiah. The box she carried must have been heavy, because she set it down with a thump on the table.

"Goodness, what have you brought?" Sliding the last glass in the cabinet, Naomi closed the door and went to greet her young sister-in-law. Excitement was sparkling in Libby's eyes, and maybe it was that feeling, rather than the nip in the air, that had brought the flush to her cheeks.

"This came yesterday to the house. Isaiah said I should wait until today to bring it and surprise you. It's from Anna and Sara."

"So your sisters didn't forget you," Leah said, smiling. "They might be too far to drop in easily, but they wanted to join us."

"I didn't open it, much as I wanted to," Libby

201

said. "But hurry, Naomi." She darted to the counter and came back with a pair of scissors. "Let's see what they sent."

Smiling at Libby's enthusiasm, Naomi slit the tape and pulled the box lid open. She drew back the tissue paper to reveal the vibrant colors of a quilt.

"How lovely," Leah said. "A bear paw design." She stroked the patches. "It must be from Anna, for sure. She always was so artistic."

Since Leah had been Anna's teacher in school, she would remember. Naomi lifted the quilt out. Sure enough, a note from Anna was tucked inside.

For your new home. Love from Anna.

She stood still for a moment, holding the quilt against her, almost feeling her little sister's arms around her neck.

Libby, not waiting for sentiment, was diving into the box, pulling out a stack of tea towels, pot holders, and quilted place mats. "These are from Sara," she said, glancing at the note before passing it over to Leah. "I remember her telling me she didn't have the patience to make a whole quilt."

"Ach, but it was so sweet of her to do these." Naomi looked at each place mat and pot holder. Her family had not all lined up with Daadi, it seemed.

Leah raised her eyebrows, as if she knew what

Naomi was thinking. "You see, your family is happy for you."

"Of course we are," Libby said, immediately indignant. "Just because . . . well, never mind." She censored herself. "And I will have my favorite sister-in-law right next door to me." Her eyes danced. "Don't tell the others."

Leah laughed. "I won't."

Nathan and the children came in the back door just then, and the small kitchen was suddenly very crowded. Before she had time to do more than greet Joshua and Sadie, Naomi was swept away to make decisions about where the various pieces of furniture were to be placed, and whether she wanted the rocking chair in the living room or the bedroom.

The next hour passed in a haze of activity. If she ever figured out where everything was that someone else had put away, it was going to be a miracle.

She was setting a box of books on top of a bookcase to be sorted through later when she realized Nathan was standing next to her. She straightened. "Do you need me for something?"

"Not really. We're going to set up the big bedroom next, but you may as well stay out of the way until the bed is put together." He hesitated. "I just wanted to be sure everything is all right with you. That I didn't rush you into something you are regretting."

The concern in his eyes caught at her heart. "Denke, Nathan. But I have no regrets."

"Not even about your family?" He'd lowered his voice, although there was no one else in the living room to hear.

She sighed, feeling not so much sad as rueful. "Those regrets were there already," she said. "They don't really have anything to do with you."

His straight eyebrows drew down a little. "Are you sure? I can't help but see that Elijah didn't come today. If he's resentful—"

"If he's resentful of my decision, I am sorry. I love him dearly, but I must do what is right for me."

"Naomi—" Whatever Nathan was about to say was lost when Isaiah thudded down the stairs.

"We're ready to set up the bed, Nathan. Are you helping?"

"Coming," he called, and hurried toward the stairs without another word.

Naomi stood where she was for a moment, lost in thought. Nathan had seemed almost tentative, which was unusual in someone who was always so sure of himself. All in all, it was turning out to be a day filled with surprises.

And apparently the surprises weren't finished, because when she returned to the kitchen, Elijah and Lovina were just coming in the door.

"I'm sorry we weren't here earlier," Lovina said, setting the basket she was carrying on the counter and lifting the lid to reveal steam coming gently from a casserole dish inside. "Elijah had to be sure the morning rush was over and he had enough help."

"Saturday morning is always busy," Elijah said. He took off his gloves and slapped them together. "You know that about the store."

If his voice and his posture were a bit stiff, Lovina more than made up for it with a cheerful smile and a warm hug.

"Well, we are here now." Lovina was brisk. "Elijah, I hear hammering upstairs. Why don't you go and help?"

He nodded curtly and headed toward the stairs. Lovina's gaze met Naomi's.

"He'll get used to it," she said. "Don't let it worry you. Now, komm, let's get to work."

The rest of the morning passed with much coming and going. Naomi didn't have time to think about her brother's attitude, and maybe that was just as well. At least he was here. She could simply be happy for his presence.

A flurry of snowflakes in the early afternoon caused a sudden exodus, as people realized the snow might turn into something more than flurries. Naomi was kept busy saying good-bye and thanking folks, only to suddenly realize that the house was almost empty.

No, not quite. She could hear voices upstairs. She moved toward the steps. It was Lovina and

Elijah. Maybe they hadn't noticed the snow.

She'd better tell them so they didn't get caught on slippery roads. She took a few quiet steps up the stairs.

". . . stop being so prickly about Naomi watching Nathan's kinder instead of ours," Lovina said.

"You'd think her own kin would come first." Elijah's voice was a discontented rumble.

"Don't you realize what caring for Nathan's kinder might lead to? I think it's very likely that Nathan will end up marrying her."

Silence for a moment. Naomi pressed her hand against her lips, trying to keep from exclaiming.

Elijah burst out laughing. "Marry Naomi? Impossible."

Holding her breath, Naomi backed soundlessly down the steps. She had to get away. She couldn't let them know she had heard. That would be the worst humiliation.

She made it to the kitchen and stood leaning against the sink, gripping it with both hands. She couldn't get their voices out of her ears, and she wasn't sure which of them had hurt her most.

"Let's try to get the paste on the paper, not on yourself." Naomi wiped away a blob of paste that Sadie had managed to get on the end of her nose. The children were busy working on their Christmas cards at the kitchen table.

"Can we mail them as soon as we are done?"

Joshua was finishing a card covered with stars that was intended for his grossmammi.

"If the mailman hasn't gone yet, we can walk out to the mailbox and send them." Naomi glanced out the window. The red flag was still up on the mailbox by the road.

Looking the other way, across the pasture, she could see both Isaiah's place and hers. Hers. Wasn't it odd that the small grossdaadi house felt so much like home after such a few days?

Maybe not so odd when she compared it with the time spent at Paula's apartment. As welcoming as Paula had been, Naomi had still felt like a guest there.

But comparing it to the house in which she'd grown up—that surely was strange. Still, even though it belonged to Nathan, the little house was hers in a way that Daad's place had never been. She could sit up all night and read if she wanted, with no one to tell her it was time for bed. Not that she would, when she had to be up early with the children, but it was nice to have the freedom, even if she didn't use it.

"How does this look, Naomi?" Sadie held up a card decorated with the angel Naomi had helped her cut out. "Will Grossmammi like it?"

The angel was more than a little crooked, and some globs of paste had escaped around its edges, but that would hardly matter to Emma.

"She will love it," Naomi said, bending over to

drop a kiss on Sadie's hair. "Now print your name here at the bottom, the way I showed you. Then she'll know it's from you."

Joshua darted a quick look at the card, and she suspected he was thinking that Grossmammi would know even without the wobbly letters Sadie was printing. But he didn't say it.

Naomi had noticed that quality in him any number of times. Unlike most slightly older brothers, Joshua rarely teased his little sister. He seemed to have a naturally tender heart.

She rounded the table to look at his card. *Merry Christmas from Joshua.* The printing was even, the English words spelled correctly. Joshua's work was the equal of any first grader's, she felt sure.

And he wanted to learn. He'd blossomed under even the small efforts she'd made to teach him, and his curiosity knew no bounds.

Joshua should be in school. The difficulty would be in convincing Nathan.

The door opened, letting a blast of cold air into the back hall and kitchen. Nathan closed it quickly, stripping off his gloves.

"Brrr." Sadie gave a dramatic shiver. "It's awful cold. Do you think the bees are all right? Don't they get cold in the winter?"

"They're safe in their hives," Nathan said, heading for the coffee that was kept warm on the stove.

"But they're outside," Sadie protested, sliding

down from her chair, holding sticky hands away from her dress.

Naomi caught Sadie and wiped her hands with a damp cloth. "In the cold weather, the bees all cluster close around the queen. They're snuggled up tightly, and they move a little all the time to keep the hive warm. If you listen very closely, you can hear them."

"And the hives are wrapped in their winter blankets," Nathan said, smiling at her. "Remember when Naomi and I put the black coverings around the hives? That's to keep them warm."

"I still think they'd like it better in the house."

That was too much for Joshua. "Silly. It would be so warm in the house they'd think it was spring, and they'd all come swarming out of the hive to sting you." He wiggled his fingers, buzzing to imitate the bees, and dived at his sister. Sadie ran, shrieking, and he followed her.

Shaking her head, Naomi smiled back at Nathan. "And I was just thinking about how gut he was, not teasing his sister like Elijah used to tease the smaller ones."

"He is a gut boy." Nathan looked toward the living room, maybe thinking he should intervene, but the shrieks had turned to giggles.

"Very gut." Naomi picked up the cards the children had made. "Look what a wonderful neat job he did on this card for his grossmammi. Such fine printing," she added.

She was tempted to speak directly to Nathan about putting Joshua in school, but the memory of his earlier reaction stopped her. Maybe this was a time when a roundabout way to the goal was better.

Nathan's face softened as he looked at the cards. "Emma will be cheered up by these, ain't so?"

"I know she will. I'll just get them in envelopes, and we will take a walk to the mailbox."

She went to the drawer to fetch an envelope. When she turned back, Nathan was looking at the materials for her Christmas honey jars, still in the basket in which she'd brought them that morning.

"You shouldn't be entertaining the kinder all the time," he said. "You have your own work to do." He held up a jar. "You should be getting these ready to go on sale."

"I'll work on the jars this afternoon." She was a bit surprised. Some employers might think that she should be working on the honey jars on her own time, not his. Like Daad, for instance, who could always find work for what he considered idle hands.

Nathan touched one of the fabric circles. "Does the trimming really make them sell better? I would think folks would buy because they want honey, not because of what the jar looks like."

"Just because something's useful, that doesn't mean it can't be pretty, as well. And Paula says that she can sell them about as fast as I can make them. To Englischers, mainly, who give them as little Christmas gifts."

"Women, probably," Nathan said with a smile. "A man would not think of such a thing."

"What? A gift, or the decoration?" They were talking easily, and she was grateful. So often in the time since Ada's death their conversation seemed overlaid with sorrow.

"Both, probably," he admitted. "And that reminds me, if you think of anything Sadie or Joshua might like for Christmas, will you tell me? Ada always took care of Christmas presents, and I don't have an idea in my head, I fear."

Naomi nodded, glad that there hadn't been a shadow in his face at the mention of Ada. "I'll think on it." She slid one of the cards into an envelope. "I will want to go to the Christmas program at the school on Friday. May I take Joshua and Sadie?"

He shrugged. "Guess I hadn't heard much about it. Ja, take them, if you want."

"Denke." She tried to keep her smile to herself. Nathan might not have heard much about the school's Christmas program yet, but she suspected attending would whet Joshua's appetite, so Nathan would soon be hearing more than he wanted to about school.

Nathan went through the doors at the hospital entrance, his stomach tightening almost as automatically as the doors. Foolish. He should be over this reaction to the hospital by now, after several visits to Emma.

Still, he hadn't been in a hospital at all before the night he'd rushed here after Ada's accident. Nor since, until Emma's fall. Maybe it wasn't so odd that the very sounds and smells of the place made him want to run the other way.

Clutching the tin of snickerdoodles the children had helped make, he got on the elevator. It whisked him to the third floor almost before he could get his face composed in a smile.

Remember, be cheerful, Daad had cautioned him as he'd gone out to the waiting car for the trip to the hospital. Daad must have thought he'd needed the reminder.

He pushed open the door, wondering how many of the community's women he'd find there today. Emma had had a steady stream of visitors since word had got out—mostly Amish, but a few of her Englisch neighbors, as well.

But the hospital room wasn't crowded today. Jessie was there, of course, and Katie Brand from the quilt shop. His gaze went to the Englischer standing next to the bed. A doctor, he supposed.

The man turned, and a jolt of recognition hit Nathan hard enough almost to make him gasp. It was Seth—Seth Miller, Ada's older brother, who had jumped the fence to the Englisch world when he was just eighteen and never looked back.

"Nathan." Seth eyed him warily. Waiting for a reaction? Or maybe having a negative one of his own for his sister's widower?

"Seth. This is a surprise." He probably should say a wonderful-gut surprise, but he wasn't so sure.

Seth shook his head slightly. "I'm afraid I lost the dialect years ago," he said. "You'll have to speak English if you want me to keep up."

That merely served to emphasize the difference between the boy Nathan remembered and the man who stood before him.

"No problem," he said in English. "Emma." He bent over the bed to kiss her cheek. "You are feeling better today, ain't so? You have some color in your face."

She nodded, her faded blue eyes shimmering with what were probably happy tears.

"Seth is here," Jessie said. "My big brother has komm, so Mamm is glad."

Nathan gave Jessie a cautious look, wondering how glad she was to see this brother she probably barely remembered. She seemed . . . He sought for the word. *Reserved,* that was the word. For someone who normally wore her emotions on her sleeve, that was unusual.

"Well, here is something else to make you happy." He handed Emma the cookie tin. "Naomi and the kinder made snickerdoodles. They sent them to you with their love."

"Naomi?" Seth made the name a question.

"Naomi Esch," Emma said. "You remember her, Seth. She was two years younger than you and Ada's best friend all their growing up years."

"Yes, Naomi. Hard to believe she's all grown up now." Seth glanced at Nathan. "Are you and she . . ." He gestured in a way that seemed to link Nathan with Naomi.

"Ach, no," Emma replied before he could answer. "Naomi has just been taking care of Joshua and Sadie since my accident."

"That's all," Jessie added, with what seemed like unnecessary emphasis.

"You haven't told me yet how your accident happened." Seth drew a chair close to the bed and sat down, his hand on Emma's.

"Foolishness, that's how," Emma declared.

Her tale of climbing on a chair to reach the top shelf gave Nathan a moment to wonder what on earth Seth Miller was doing here. When he'd left, folks had thought that he'd be like so many young men, running off for a few months of adventure before coming home, chastened, to take their place in the community again.

But Seth had been the exception. He'd left the area, and the family had seldom heard from him. The occasional rumor had reached Nathan's ears: that Seth was working out west, that he'd gotten an education, that he'd done well for himself, or what the world would call well, in any event.

Seth hadn't returned for his sisters' weddings or his father's funeral. Or for Ada's funeral. He'd left all his responsibilities to other people. And now he was here.

Seth favored his father, or at least what Nathan remembered of him. Seth's hair had been light as corn-silk when he was a kid, but now it was more the color of wheat, cut short in what Nathan supposed was the latest style. His clothing was casual, like what the Englisch around here would wear—tan pants and a blue shirt. He looked smart and prosperous and as different as possible from the boy who'd run off. Why are you back? he thought again.

Jessie had drawn close to Nathan, and she seemed to be studying her brother with a certain degree of caution.

"Did you know he was coming?" he asked under the flow of talk.

Jessie shook her head. "He just walked in. I didn't even know Mamm had been in touch with him." Her face settled into discontented lines. "She should have told me."

"I'm sure she would have, if she'd known he was coming," he said, hoping to soothe her. No point in letting Jessie get upset and make her mother uncomfortable.

"Ja, well, why didn't you bring the kinder?" Jessie's sudden switch to English and to annoyance with him took Nathan off guard, and she

215

said it loudly enough to draw the attention of Emma and Seth, who looked at him questioningly.

"Well, I . . . I wanted to be sure Emma was ready to see them before I brought the two of them tramping into a hospital room. You know how rambunctious Sadie can be when she's excited."

"I'm glad you waited," Emma said. "Not that I'm not eager to see them, but I want to be up and looking more myself when they come. No sense in scaring them. They had enough of that with seeing me lying on the kitchen floor."

Nathan nodded, grateful. That was how he felt, as well. "You tell me when, and I will bring them. Or Naomi will, if I can't."

"They are moving me over to the rehab building tomorrow," Emma said. "It will be more pleasant for the kinder to come there, ja? And it will be wonderful gut for Joshua and Sadie to see their onkel." She clasped Seth's hand.

Nathan wasn't so sure it was all that wonderful, but he nodded. Not much else he could do. Seth wasn't under the bann, since he'd left before being baptized into the church, and there was no reason to keep his sister's kinder from him.

"How long will you be staying?" Nathan tried to keep his doubts from showing.x

"I'll be here through the weekend, I guess. I was in New York on business when I got the message from Mamm, so I took some time off.

I flew into Harrisburg and rented a car there."

Seth had explained more than he'd asked. Maybe he felt the need to justify his presence. Or his absence.

Jessie caught Nathan's arm in a quick, impulsive movement. "So you bring the kinder in by then," she said. "Not Naomi."

There was an edge to her voice when she said Naomi's name, but a glance from her mother seemed to keep her from saying more.

"I'll try." He patted her hand. He wasn't imagining her antagonism toward Naomi, but he suspected anything he tried to do about it would only make it worse. Maybe the excitement of having her big brother around would distract her from whatever bee she had in her bonnet about Naomi.

Jessie's antagonism. Seth's return. Nathan shrugged his shoulders, as if he could shrug off how uncomfortable it all made him.

Chapter Thirteen

It was very seldom that Amish children had an opportunity to perform in front of an audience. Naomi had never thought much about why, but it was probably because Amish children were taught to be humble, not drawing attention to themselves. That humility was an attitude that would serve them well their entire lives.

But the standard was suspended for the Amish school's Christmas program, and the community joined in support of the young scholars. Although Naomi had brought the children early, the lane going back to the white one-room schoolhouse was already lined with buggies.

"Hurry, hurry, Naomi." Sadie bounced on the seat next to her. "I want to see everything."

"So you will," she said, pulling into the next open space. "We are in plenty of time, for sure."

One of the older boys came running to tend the mare. It was obviously one of his jobs for the day.

"Denke." She slid down, handing him the horse blanket for Sunny. Sadie and Joshua followed her quickly.

"Komm." She took their hands, and they walked toward the school. Joshua's eyes were big with contained excitement while Sadie danced along, her feet seeming to skim the ground.

Naomi slowed as they reached the steps to the porch. "Once the program starts, you must sit still," she cautioned. Joshua didn't need to hear it, but Sadie did. "It would not be polite to talk or move around then, ain't so?"

"Ja, Naomi," Joshua said, and Sadie nodded.

"Like in worship," she said.

"That's right," Naomi said, smiling. "Let's go in and find seats."

That was easier said than done. The room was already crowded, and even with extra folding chairs set up, Naomi began to think they might have to stand.

"Look, Naomi." Sadie, wide-eyed, was staring at the chalkboard. It was decorated with a snow scene, filled with children sliding on a hill. "I can't wait to sled ride."

"That will be fun." Naomi trusted that Nathan's protectiveness didn't extend to keeping the children from enjoying the snow. "See the stars?" Strands of yarn reached across the room, bearing cut-out angels and many-pointed Moravian paper stars. That was something she could make with Sadie and Joshua. Talking about the symbols was a good way of teaching the children the meaning of Christmas.

She spotted Leah Glick motioning to her from across the room, indicating a chair next to her. Clutching the children's hands, Naomi began working her way through the crowd. Was she imagining it, or did conversation cease momentarily as folks saw her before resuming again?

By the time she reached Leah, she feared her cheeks were burning. She slid into the chair and then realized she had displaced Leah's step-daughter.

"Ach, I don't want to take Elizabeth's seat—"

"Not at all. She wants to sit with the little ones," Leah said, and indeed, Elizabeth seemed perfectly happy to gather Joshua and Sadie next to her along with Rachel Anna, Leah's youngest, and Gracie, Leah's little niece.

Anna Fisher, Leah's younger sister, was sitting in the next chair. She smiled a welcome, pulling a diaper bag over to give Naomi more space. She held her baby son on her lap, and it was her little Gracie who sat with Elizabeth.

"Anna, how your little David has grown." She had seen them at worship, of course, but it still amazed her how babies seemed to change to toddlers in the blink of an eye.

"Eight months old now, and crawling enough to get into things," Anna said, her blue eyes shining as she looked down at her son. He was reaching out as if to grab one of the stars that hung over his head.

"He's going to keep you running, for sure, with Gracie, too."

When Naomi leaned back again, she found Leah regarding her with what had to be sympathy on her face.

"I guess I'm giving the sisters plenty to talk about," she murmured, knowing Leah would understand what she meant about the attention she'd garnered when she'd entered with Joshua and Sadie.

"Pleasant Valley is a small place," Leah said. "Everybody knows everything."

"And what they don't know they make up."

There was a little bite to Anna's voice, and she patted Naomi's arm. "I understand. I haven't forgotten the talk that went around when I came home."

True, that had been a wonder to the valley when Anna Beiler came home after three years in the Englisch world, and with little Gracie, too. Tongues had flapped for sure.

"They mean well, for the most part," Leah said, her voice soft under the chatter of the children. "It'll be forgotten soon enough."

"Are they more interested in my disagreement with my daad or in my taking on Nathan's kinder?" She imagined both topics were exercising folks' tongues.

Leah shrugged. "A little of each. You mustn't let it trouble you. Everyone will soon be too busy with Christmas to think of anything else."

"I hope so." She glanced at the children. Maybe it hadn't been such a good idea to bring them, if it led to their hearing something they shouldn't.

Well, it was too late to change her mind about it now. She glanced toward the front of the room where a cluster of young scholars had gathered around the teacher, probably getting some last-minute instructions. The program would start soon, and Leah was right. Afterward, people would be so busy talking about it that they surely wouldn't have a thought to spare for her.

"I know you're happy with the family, but do

you ever miss teaching?" She gestured toward the front of the classroom, looking at Leah.

"I don't miss the stress of coming up with a new Christmas program each year. Ach, I can remember I'd start working on it in July." Leah smiled at the children in front of them. "Now the family takes up all my time and energy, and all I have to do is enjoy the program."

"Kinder have a way of doing that, don't they?" Naomi said. Even when they were not your own, children could take over a woman's time, energy, and love.

Rachel Anna spun around, tugging on her mother's skirt. "Mammi, tell Joshua I am," she demanded.

"You are what?" Leah asked, smiling at the little girl.

"I am going to start school in another year. He says I'm not old enough."

"Not yet, you're not," Leah said. "But in another year, you will be."

"See, Joshua?" Rachel Anna turned to him with that determined little nod of hers.

Naomi could see Joshua mulling that information over in his mind. He looked at Naomi, his frown a miniature version of Nathan's.

"Naomi, if Rachel Anna is starting next year, then I should have started this year, because I am a year older than she is, ja?"

The question left her unprepared. True, she'd

hoped to interest Joshua in school, but she hadn't expected such a direct challenge. If she said anything in response that Nathan didn't like—

The teacher clapped her hands, and the room fell silent. Swept with relief, Naomi put her finger to her lips. Hopefully she'd have found a tactful answer by the time the program had ended.

The youngest children came on first, their eyes wide with excitement. Nervousness showed in feet that couldn't quite be still and in a reluctance to look straight at the audience, but they recited their Christmas welcome poem faultlessly. Naomi thought she detected relief on the teacher's face when they reached the last line.

The program went on with poems and recitations, every child in the school taking part. Sometimes they carried simple props, like the candle each child held for one reading. There was no mention of Santa or Christmas trees, of course. Each piece focused on the true meaning of Christmas or on the importance of giving and sharing in humble ways, just as Jesus had been humble.

Naomi glanced at Sadie's and Joshua's faces. Sadie was watching, smiling and nodding. But Joshua—Joshua was rapt, leaning forward, his shining eyes focused on the children. Naomi could practically feel the longing in him to be up there participating.

He is ready to be in school, Nathan. What can I do to convince you of that?

The program moved from simple to complicated presentations, from the youngest children to the oldest. Whatever their poem or reading, the messages were consistent: humility, appreciation, thankfulness. They spoke the joy of the season in the simplest way and even Naomi, who had witnessed so many Christmas programs, felt the sweet message as if it were brand-new.

Joshua wasn't the only one with longing in his heart. She longed, as well. She longed to give Joshua and Sadie her very best for as long as she had them in her care. If she could do that, she would be content.

The final recitation came to an end, and the applause was loud and long. Everywhere Naomi looked, faces were filled with happiness, and she felt her heart swell with gratitude that she was a part of this community.

Once the applause died down, the refreshments were brought out. No Amish event would be complete without feeding people. That was certain-sure.

"Can we go to the table for a cookie, Naomi?" Sadie tugged at her sleeve. "Please, please, please?"

"Ja, but don't cut in front of anyone. Wait, I'll come with you—" But it was too late. Sadie had already scampered off through the crowd with Joshua right behind her, weaving their way between and around pairs of adult legs toward the serving table.

As one of the grown-ups, Naomi had to behave with a little more circumspection. Leah was hugging her little stepson, congratulating him on a fine recitation. Gesturing to let Leah know where she was going in the din of chatter, Naomi followed the children.

The crowd was thickest, of course, near the table, and now she couldn't see Sadie and Joshua at all. Not that she was worried about them, of course, but she wanted to be sure that Sadie wasn't letting her enthusiasm carry her away. Naomi stepped around a group of women and then froze when she heard the sound of her name.

". . . father walked right into the harness shop and told Bishop Mose what an undutiful daughter she was in front of everyone. I heard it with my own ears."

Mary Esch, of course. Nothing pleased Mary more than to have something negative to say about someone. And to as big an audience as possible. Sometimes Naomi felt embarrassed at having her for even a distant cousin-in-law.

This time her audience was aware of Naomi's presence. Maybe their sudden silence alerted Mary. She spun and stared right at Naomi.

Maybe someone braver than she would have been able to snap back at Mary. Naomi could only stand there, wishing she could sink right into the floor.

There was a rustle of movement behind her,

and an arm swept around her waist. "It's too bad you can't put your ears to better use, Mary Esch." Lovina's voice was even, but her eyes sparkled dangerously. "Komm, Naomi, let us get some punch."

Naomi allowed herself to be led away, gratitude sweeping through her for her sister-in-law. Surely Lovina's support would still the clacking tongues. But—

"Lovina?" She struggled to get the words out. "Is it true?"

Her sister-in-law didn't answer. She didn't have to. The pity in her face was all the answer Naomi needed.

So Betty had been right. Daad had gone to the bishop about her.

Naomi plunged one of the supper plates into the hot sudsy water. In hot water—that was as good a description as any of where she found herself.

Daad had spoken to the bishop about her behavior. She'd said those words to herself several dozen times since they'd left the school-house this afternoon, but she could still hardly believe it. No wonder she'd sensed a reaction to her presence at the program. Probably half the people there already knew what Mary had been so gleefully passing on, and if they hadn't, they would by now.

Too bad Mary hadn't mentioned what Bishop

Mose's response had been. Nerves fluttered in Noami's stomach. Would the bishop come to see her? If he made a formal call, accompanied by one of the other ministers, that visit meant he considered her behavior a serious breach of conduct.

She picked up a towel and began drying the plates, looking absently out the window over the sink. It was dark out already, but she had a strong flashlight, and she didn't worry about her safety, walking across the field to her little house. She'd be far more nervous walking along a street in town after dark.

A squeal came from the living room, where Nathan had been reading to the children to settle them down before bedtime. It sounded as if the reading had turned into a game of some sort.

Nathan came through the doorway, carrying Sadie under one arm like a sack of feed, with Joshua hanging on to his leg.

"What has gotten into these kinder, Naomi?" he asked, laughter in his voice. "They want to put on a Christmas program instead of listening to a story."

"Excitement, that's for sure." She dried her hands, turning to smile at them. Sadie, upside down, was giggling helplessly. Joshua stood up very straight and held up an imaginary something over his head.

"I'm a little Christmas candle," he chanted, "shining my light for all to see."

Naomi's eyebrows lifted. "That's pretty close to what we saw today. Did you memorize the lines, Joshua?"

"I just remember." His eyes shone with the memory. "I want to do a program."

She thought quickly. "Maybe I can get hold of one of the poems," she said. "You could learn it and say it for your grossmammi when you visit her. That would cheer her up, ain't so?"

"Ja, ja," Sadie said. "Me, too." Nathan set her on her feet, and she ran to Naomi and snuggled against her. "It was the best day ever, Naomi."

"I'm glad you liked it." She smoothed back the hair that had been disarranged by their play.

"It sounds as if the school program was a big success," Nathan said. He leaned against the counter, as if ready to stay and chat.

"Ja, it was. Everyone was so pleased with how well the scholars did. Especially their teacher, I think."

He grinned. "She probably had her hands full. I remember how excited we used to get when it came time for the program. Jumping beans, the teacher called us, remember, Naomi?"

"I remember." Her heart seemed to give a funny little twist in response to his smile. "But I think it was mostly you boys who were the jumping beans. Not us girls."

"Not you, certainly." His voice was teasing.

"Daadi?" Joshua still stood very straight, his

head tilted to look up at his father. "Why am I not in first grade?"

There it was—the question Naomi had known would come from him. Oddly enough, Nathan looked startled, as if it hadn't occurred to him that Joshua would wonder.

"Well, I . . . I guess because you didn't turn six until after school started in the fall. Next year you will go." Nathan said that with a note of finality.

But judging by Joshua's expression, he didn't consider the subject finished. "Amos Zook is in first grade, and his birthday isn't until after mine. So if Amos could start when he was not quite six, why couldn't I?"

Nathan was beginning to look harassed. "It was farther than I wanted you to walk, and no one was free to take you. It would have been too much to ask Grossmammi to come that early. Now—"

"Naomi could take me. Couldn't you, Naomi?" His gaze fixed on hers.

"That would be up to your daadi," she said.

Joshua swung that pleading look back to Nathan. "You see? Naomi could take me, and I could start now, couldn't I? I could easily catch up. I already know all my letters, and I can print my name and—"

"Don't argue, Joshua." Nathan looked as if he was pinned in a corner, and he didn't like it.

"I'm not arguing. I'm just saying. Please, Daadi?"

"We'll see, all right? After Christmas, we'll see."

Joshua, taking encouragement where he could get it, smiled and clasped his hands together, as if he wanted to clap but didn't feel he could. "Denke, Daadi. I would love to go to school."

"Ja, well, right now I would love for you two to get ready for bed. Scoot on upstairs now. I'll be up as soon as I have a word with Naomi."

Naomi suspected she knew what that word was going to be, but even if Nathan was angry, she still felt she had done the right thing by taking the children to the program.

The look he turned on her was serious, but not angry, so far as she could tell. "That was what you hoped would happen if the kinder attended the Christmas program, ain't so?"

"It was what I thought might happen," she said. And then, when he frowned, she rushed on. "Komm, Nathan, you said you'd think about it, ja? I know it's hard to let the first one go off to school, but Joshua is ready."

"I don't want—" he began, and then stopped. "It *is* hard to let him go off on his own."

"Not exactly on his own," she said, her tone gentle. "He'd be just down the road a mile and a half, ja? With all the other kinder his age." She didn't want to have to say that it was what Ada would have done. He knew that well enough himself.

Finally he shrugged. "You may be right. If Ada were here . . ." He let that trail off. "After the Christmas holiday, maybe I'll talk to the teacher. See what she thinks. Will that satisfy you?"

She smiled, relieved. "It is Joshua you must satisfy, not me."

His lips twitched. "That Christmas program has a lot to answer for, I think."

The words struck home in a way Nathan couldn't possibly have intended, as Naomi was once again in that crowded classroom, hearing Mary Esch's words.

"Naomi?" Nathan touched her arm lightly. "Was ist letz? I'm not angry, if that's what you're thinking."

She shook her head, her throat tight.

"Komm." His voice was as gentle as if he spoke to one of the children. "Tell me what has happened."

She shook her head, not in refusal but in a futile attempt to shake off the memory. "Something was said today after the program. Someone had overheard my daad talking to Bishop Mose in the harness shop. About me."

"And that someone had to repeat it, ja?"

She nodded, misery weighing down on her. "Well, I shouldn't be surprised, I guess. Betty told me Daad was thinking about talking to the bishop about me. I just never thought he would actually do it."

"Your daaad . . ." Nathan paused. "Well, I would not speak ill of a brother. But I think he is so fond of his own way that he doesn't see what is best for anyone else."

"But to go to the bishop about one of his own children—" It was done so rarely it was seldom talked about. More likely, in fact, someone else might complain about a youth's behavior and cause the bishop to talk to the parents.

Nathan clasped her hand in a firm, warm grip. "I won't say to forget about it, because I know you can't. But Bishop Mose is a fair man. You can count on him to listen and understand."

Naomi nodded, trying to smile. "You are right, Nathan. I will try not to worry." But it occurred to her in that moment that she would rather have Nathan's support than anything else right now.

Chapter Fourteen

Nathan stepped off the back porch, looking up at the afternoon sky. Clouds were thickening, and they'd probably have snow by nightfall. Since he'd promised to take the children to the rehab center to see Emma this afternoon, he'd be thankful if it held off until then.

Still, Ben was a careful driver—that was one reason why so many Amish depended upon him to get them where they needed to go. Even if snow started to fall before they returned, he'd be ready to handle the roads.

Nathan heard the door behind him and turned, but it was Daad coming out, not the children. Daad paused to pull on his mittens before making his way down the few steps.

"Snow coming," he said.

Nathan nodded. Daad didn't depend on a weather forecaster to tell him when it was going to snow, any more than Nathan did. When your livelihood depended on understanding the weather, you learned to judge such things for yourself.

"We should be back before it starts, I think. Ben will be here any minute now." He glanced toward the house. "Is Naomi getting the kinder ready?"

"Ja." Daad smiled. "Sadie had to run back upstairs to get a picture she made. They will be ready on time. Naomi will see to it."

They'd all grown to depend on Naomi in such a short time. The least she deserved was to be able to depend upon them as well.

Nathan suspected he should have done more last night to show her his support when she'd told him the latest about her father, and that niggling sense of guilt annoyed him. He certain-sure didn't want to get entangled in a dispute with a member of the community, even if his private opinion was that Sam Esch was being both pigheaded and foolish.

And he certain-sure didn't want the bishop to think he had anything to do with Naomi's choices.

Don't you? The small voice at the back of his mind was active.

All right, he had to admit that he had maybe taken advantage of the situation out of his own needs, but that didn't make him responsible for it. Sam had done that all on his own, trying to dictate his daughter's future for her.

Somehow that argument wasn't doing the job of silencing the voice of his conscience. Luckily, at that moment, Ben's car turned in the driveway, distracting him. He glanced toward the house, ready to call to Naomi, but she was already bringing the children out.

Joshua and Sadie ran to him, Sadie waving a paper while Joshua carried another tin—this one of coffee cake, so he'd heard. Wrapping a black shawl over her blue dress and apron, Naomi followed them.

"I know you'll hold the tin nice and level." She smiled at Joshua with the reminder.

"Ja, for sure," he said. "Maybe Onkel Seth will like coffee cake. Do you think so, Daadi?"

Nathan tried not to stiffen. He shouldn't pass his doubts on to Joshua. "I'm sure he will."

The car drew up next to them, Ben giving a cheerful wave and a playful toot on the horn. Sadie bounced in response. "I love to go with Ben in the car."

Now didn't seem to be the moment for a reminder of why Amish did not own cars. Nathan opened the door of the backseat. "In you go. Sadie, in the booster seat."

Sadie pouted a little at the idea, but she climbed in, pulling the belt around her. Joshua put the tin carefully onto the floor and then hopped in.

Nathan was just opening the passenger-side door when he heard a hail. He turned to see Isaiah running across the pasture toward them.

"Cows are out," he called. "The fence must be grounded, and they're into Mickelson's cornfield."

George Mickelson, Nathan's neighbor on one side, worked in Lewisburg and played at being a farmer, but while all the Amish cornfields had been cut long since, his still stood, a temptation to the dairy herd. It would be a job to get the cows back in the field. Nathan hesitated, hand on the door.

"Daadi? Aren't we going?" Sadie's voice had a bit of a tremor.

"Go on to see Emma," Daad said. "Isaiah and I can take care of the cows."

But the last thing Daad needed was to be rushing all the way to Mickelson's field. "No, we'll have to cancel," Nathan said. "Maybe we can go later."

Daad frowned, probably guessing the reason for Nathan's answer and sensitive to the idea he couldn't do what he used to. "You don't want Ben to drive out here for nothing. Besides, Emma and the kinder will be disappointed. You go."

"No, I—"

"Why don't I take the kinder?" Naomi interrupted. "I would be happy to have a little visit with Emma."

It was the obvious answer, but . . .

"Jessie will probably be there," Nathan said quietly. "As well as Seth."

Her gaze flickered. "It is all right," she said. "I will deal with Jessie. And it would be interesting to see Seth again."

Interesting, ja. But Nathan could count on Naomi's level head where the children were concerned. "Denke," he said.

She nodded. "I'll just get my coat."

He appreciated it, he thought as he started across the field in Isaiah's wake. And it just made him feel even more guilty.

The rehab center was a pleasant place, with its bright colors, lively murals on the walls, and a general air that said, "Good things are happening here." Naomi had visited in the past, but never with quite this sense of apprehension. If only Jessie were not with her mamm this afternoon. Or, barring that, if she were so preoccupied by the presence of her brother as to forget her prejudice against Naomi—well, then there might be some hope of having a nice visit with Emma.

"Here we are." Naomi paused outside the door to Emma's room to help the children off with their coats and be sure they looked tidy. "Remember, be careful not to rush at Grossmammi or climb on her. Her hip is still very sore, and that might hurt, ain't so?"

They both nodded, but as an extra measure of precaution she took Sadie's hand as they entered the room.

"Ach, here they are," Emma exclaimed. She was sitting in a wheelchair by the bed, her hair fixed and her kapp in place despite the fact that she wore a robe and slippers.

"What are you doing here?" Jessie, standing behind her mother, glared at Naomi, not bothering to conceal her dislike.

So, obviously neither of Naomi's wishes had come true. She managed a smile, focusing on Emma as she brought the children to her, glad to see that they remembered not to rush.

Joshua handed over the tin. "Here is coffee cake for you." He seemed to give a sigh of relief once it was safely in her hands. "Can we give you a kiss without hurting you?"

"For sure you can." Emma leaned forward so that they could each kiss her cheek.

"Nathan is sorry he couldn't be here. The cows got out right when he was ready to leave, and he didn't want to keep the driver waiting. Or you."

Naomi bent, careful not to touch the chair, and pressed her cheek against Emma's.

"I am wonderful glad to see you." Emma clasped her hand briefly, sending a warning look at her daughter. "And here is someone else who was wanting to see you. You remember Seth, ja?"

"Ja, that's certain-sure. Wie bist du heit, Seth?"

"Fine, thanks. So this is Naomi." He moved as if to hold out his hand and then seemed to think better of it. "I would have known you anywhere."

She smiled. "I don't think I could say the same about you. You've made your mamm happy with this visit."

And why didn't you come more often? Emma could certain-sure have used your support when Ada died.

Still, it wasn't for her to judge. She studied Ada's big brother, seeing little there of the boy she remembered. The Seth of her memories had been laughing and teasing, with a headstrong streak that led him into mischief more often than not.

The man facing her looked like any Englischer, a businessman, maybe, with his stylishly cut hair and clean-shaven face. Where was the big brother Ada had looked up to and loved?

Fortunately for Naomi, Emma claimed Seth's attention before she had to say anything else.

"Here are Ada's kinder. Joshua and Sadie, greet your onkel Seth."

Seth smiled, his eyes softening as he looked at

the young ones. "I'm very happy to meet you at last. Sadie, you look just like your mamm. And Joshua, you're almost grown-up now."

"I'm six, Onkel Seth," Joshua said politely. Sadie hung back, not sure she wanted to get too close to this Englisch stranger.

"Naomi says you were my mammi's big bruder, like Joshua is mine," Sadie said, with the air of not quite believing it.

"Naomi is right." Seth didn't make any move to embrace the children, and Naomi was glad he had that much sense. He couldn't force a relationship with a niece and nephew who had never seen him.

"Naomi is always right," Joshua said suddenly.

Naomi blinked, surprised by his assertive tone. What undercurrents in the room was he responding to?

"She knows how to make things and all about the bees," Sadie said, following her brother's lead.

"Nobody could know all about the bees," Naomi said, embarrassed. "They are their own creatures." Maybe that was part of their fascination. There was a sense the bees would go on doing their own things in their own way, regardless of what went on outside the hive.

"Bees?" Seth looked puzzled for a moment, but then he nodded. "I remember. Your grandmother was a beekeeper, wasn't she? So you've inherited her talent, have you?"

"Grossmammi had a lifetime with the bees," she said, wondering why on earth they were talking about this when they'd come to see Emma. "I'm still learning. And speaking of learning, the kinder have learned something special for their grossmammi." She looked at Joshua and Sadie. "Are you ready?"

Joshua nodded solemnly, standing very straight in front of Emma. Sadie, with a slight giggle, hurried to stand next to him. Naomi handed each of them the candle she'd brought for them to hold. Then she moved to the side so that they could see her face while still looking at their grossmammi. She'd promised to mouth the words with them, just in case they forgot.

"All right?" she said. "Now."

"We are two little candles . . ." Joshua began, holding his candle high. Sadie joined in. She glanced frequently at Naomi to be sure of the words, but Joshua, his gaze fixed on Emma, recited the entire piece without a slip.

"Ach, that is wonderful gut," Emma exclaimed, clapping while the others joined in the applause. "It makes me feel like Christmas."

"We heard it at the Christmas program at the schoolhouse," Joshua said.

"Naomi took us," Sadie added. "It was fun. We got to have cookies afterward. Do you think they have cookies all the time in school?"

Emma chuckled, some of the lines of pain in her

face seeming to vanish. "Not all the time," she said. "But the Christmas program is a special time for the scholars."

"I want to go to school," Joshua announced. "I'm old enough. When I asked Daadi, he said, 'We'll see,' and, 'Maybe after Christmas.'"

Emma sent an inquiring look over their heads at Naomi.

"Nathan is thinking about it," she explained. "Joshua knows all his letters and numbers and he is already printing very well."

Emma nodded, but Naomi couldn't tell what she thought of the idea. Was she thinking that Naomi was pushing in too much, changing the way she'd done things?

Sadie began telling her grandmother about the presents she was making, and Joshua joined in. Relieved that the talk had moved off the subject of school, Naomi stepped back, letting the children entertain Emma.

She found herself standing next to Seth and sought for something to say to him. He lived in such a different world now. What was there in Pleasant Valley that might interest him?

"Do the children remember Ada?" he asked in an undertone, relieving her of the responsibility of finding something to talk about.

Naomi took a step or two farther away from the young ones, cautious always in what she said about their mother in their hearing. "Joshua does, since he was four at the time. Sadie . . . well, I think Sadie remembers more the idea of her mamm rather than anything specific."

"It was a waste." Seth's voice, soft though it was, was suddenly filled with anger. "She shouldn't have been doing anything so dangerous. She should have known better."

It almost sounded as if he was angry at Ada for dying. People did feel that way sometimes. It was part of grieving. But after two years, Naomi would have expected him to be past that point. And after all, how often did Seth even think of his sister in his busy, alien life?

"No one ever could stop Ada from doing something she really wanted to do," she said, keeping her voice mild.

He glared at her. "Aren't you going to tell me it was God's will?"

"I do not think you are ready to hear that yet, Seth. And I think we should talk of something else before the kinder hear us. Are you enjoying being back at home again?"

He glanced away, seeming to struggle for control for a moment, and then he shrugged. "Pleasant Valley hasn't changed any, as far as I can see. But I'm not staying at the house, if that's what you mean. I'm at the new motel out of town along the highway."

"I see." That surprised her. She'd naturally

assumed he'd be staying at his mother's house. Surely he didn't feel unwelcome there.

"I can't do without modern conveniences," he said, maybe understanding her thoughts. "As long as I'm in Pleasant Valley, I have to stay in touch with my business associates, so I need a high-speed Internet connection."

She could understand that, she supposed. The Englisch seemed to pride themselves on being constantly connected to the world, as if that was always a good thing.

"Are they making you comfortable there?" she asked politely.

His smile had an edge to it. "They aren't stuffing me with food, if that's what you mean."

"People who do physical work need plenty to eat." She answered the implied criticism. "I'm sure your mamm fed you well when you and your daad were working the farm. I seem to remember you were very partial to her apple dumplings."

This time his smile was genuine. "I haven't had any to equal hers since I left," he said. "You didn't happen to bring an apple dumpling in that tin, did you?"

Smiling in relief that they'd gotten past his edginess, she shook her head. "Only walnut streusel coffee cake," she said. "I don't think apple dumplings—"

"I don't know why you're spending all your time talking to her." Jessie's voice cut across what she was saying, and Naomi turned, mind racing, searching for something to head off the approaching storm.

"I think I—"

"You should leave," Jessie said, her voice as sharp as a knife. "You're not wanted here."

"Jessie, what's gotten into you?" Seth was looking at his little sister with such perplexity in his face that Naomi guessed this was the first time he'd been treated to one of Jessie's tantrums.

"You don't know." Jessie whirled on him. "How could you? You haven't been around to know. Naomi was always jealous of Ada, and now she's doing everything she can to get Nathan to marry her so she can take Ada's place."

"Jessie—" Emma began, but it was too late. Jessie ran to the door, rushed out, and set it swinging, leaving an appalled silence behind her.

It took a moment for Naomi to gather her wits together, unsure whether she was shaken or humiliated by the sudden attack. If the others saw her that way—

But there was no time to worry about the adults' reactions now. It was Joshua and Sadie who needed all her concern.

"Goodness," she said, trying to smile. "Aunt Jessie left in a rush, didn't she? I'm sure she'll come back in time to say good-bye to you, though."

Galvanized by her words, Emma nodded,

patting Joshua's shoulder and taking Sadie's hand. "That's our Jessie, for sure. Always in a hurry. But she did love your poem, you know. Did you see how she clapped at it?"

Joshua nodded, wary, while Sadie looked straight at her grandmother.

"Why is Aunt Jessie mad at Naomi?" Sadie's high voice seemed to puncture the smoke screen they were trying to erect.

"She isn't mad, Sadie." Emma snuggled her close. "Aunt Jessie just has a sharp way of speaking sometimes, but it doesn't mean anything."

"You know, I think I saw a vending machine down the hall. Why don't we go and see what some change might buy for Sadie and Joshua?" Seth jingled coins in his pocket.

"Vending?" Sadie's brow wrinkled.

"You know," Joshua said, with the lofty assurance of a six-year-old. "Like that thing with the bubble gum in it at the hardware store."

"Does it have gum?" Sadie, perfectly willing to be bribed, took Seth's hand. "Daadi doesn't let us have gum."

"Well, then, Onkel Seth won't, either," Naomi said, with a warning glance at Seth. "But there might be candy or crackers. Do you need any more change?" This last was aimed at Seth.

He shook his head. "I have enough, I think." He held out his hand to Joshua. "Coming, Joshua?"

Joshua looked at Naomi, and when she nodded,

he took the offered hand and the three of them went out into the hallway, leaving Naomi alone with Emma.

Naomi had to steel herself to turn, half afraid of what she might see in Emma's face. If Emma believed that what Jessie had said was true—

But one look relieved her. Emma's cheeks were flushed with embarrassment, and she held her hand out to Naomi pleadingly.

"Ach, Naomi, can you forgive her? I am so embarrassed and ashamed. I never thought to hear a child of mine speak such nonsense."

"Of course it's forgiven." She went quickly to clasp Emma's hand. "And it's not your fault, that's certain-sure."

Emma shook her head, and a tear escaped to trickle down her cheek. She looked shrunken suddenly, and older than her years.

"Ach, I am so weak I want to cry over every little thing. You know that Jessie doesn't take easily to change, and the poor child has had too much of that, with me away and now helpless in this chair." She smacked her hand against the arm of the wheelchair, as if it were to blame.

"Maybe . . ." Naomi stopped, censoring the words she wanted to say. Clearly Emma was not ready to admit Jessie needed more help than she could give, despite this most recent outburst. And with Emma in a weakened state herself, Naomi could hardly press the issue.

"Maybe what?" Emma asked.

Naomi shook her head. "I don't know. It seems I bring out the worst in Jessie, but I don't know why. Maybe it's because Ada and I were so close."

She spoke at random, trying to cover the direction her thoughts had actually taken, but she might have inadvertently come close to the truth. Emma was nodding.

"I think you might have it," she said. "Jessie always admired her big sister so much and wanted to be like her. She maybe resented the time Ada spent with you."

Naomi nodded, but whether that had been the starting point for Jessie's resentment or not didn't really seem to matter. Something had to be done. Perhaps Seth, coming back after so long a time, would be able to look at the situation more clearly than Emma could.

"But maybe Jessie was right in one thing." Catching Naomi's eye, Emma shook her head. "Ach, not about her idea of you chasing Nathan. That's foolishness. But maybe Jessie senses that it would be a gut thing for Nathan to marry you."

"Emma!" Naomi could barely catch her breath. "I'm sure the thought never occurred to him. Or to me," she added hastily.

"Maybe it should," Emma said. "Look at me." She gestured to the chair. "Whether Nathan has realized it or not, I'm not going to be able to take on those kinder full-time again. I'm not what they need. They need a mammi."

Naomi's throat was threatening to close. "Maybe one day Nathan will fall in love again."

Emma shook her head. "He buried his heart with Ada, I fear. And Joshua and Sadie need a mamm now, not off in the future sometime." Emma's grasp tightened on Naomi's hand. "You wouldn't be taking Ada's place, Naomi. But it could still be a gut life, having a husband and young ones to call your own."

Meaning she thought it impossible that Naomi would ever find someone to love her for herself, apparently. Naomi tried to smile, gently loosening her hand from Emma's grasp. "I think that is the weakness from your accident talking, Emma. You must stop worrying. The children will be all right. Now I think I'd better find them and send them back in to you."

Naomi stepped into the hall, glad to be away from Emma and her disturbing ideas. Surely that suggestion was the product of her accident and current weakness as she fretted her way through each day.

But there was no solitude in the hallway, as Sadie came rushing up to her, waving a half-eaten candy bar. "Look, look, Naomi. I put in the coins, and this candy bar came out."

"Amazing," she said. "Let's try not to get the chocolate on your dress, ja?" She glanced over

Sadie's head at Joshua. He had his own candy bar, eating it slowly as if to relish every bite.

"Did you remember to thank Onkel Seth?"

"They did," Seth said, joining her. His face softened when he looked at the children. Did he see himself and Ada in them?

"You two go back in and visit with Grossmammi," Naomi said. "Scoot, now. We'll have to leave before too long. We don't want to keep Ben waiting for our ride home."

"I could drive you," Seth offered.

"Denke, but we have already made arrangements." And she suspected that Nathan wouldn't be best pleased if she allowed Seth to drive the children.

Joshua and Sadie, clutching their candy, vanished into Emma's room, and for a moment before the door swung closed Naomi could hear Sadie's high voice exclaiming about her candy.

"I can't imagine a kid being that excited about vending machine candy." Seth was frowning. "I guess I'd forgotten how much you miss, growing up Amish."

"I do not think they would trade their faith and their family for a vending machine," Naomi said.

"Like me, you mean."

She shook her head. "I don't suppose your leaving had anything to do with vending machines, either." She reminded herself to be cautious. If she hoped to enlist his help for Jessie, she shouldn't antagonize him. "But you are back now, and that has made Emma very happy at a time when she needs cheering up."

"I hope I'm making this time easier for her." He frowned, and she wondered if he was thinking about Jessie. "What was all that business with Jessie, anyway?"

"It's not the first time she has spoken that way to me," Naomi said carefully. "It is troubling."

"I know my mother has been worried about her. But Mamm always says she's just immature."

"Is that what you think?" she asked directly.

Seth shrugged, as if trying to rid himself of a burden he didn't want to carry. "I think it's not my business. My mother is the best judge of what my sister needs." His tone made it clear that he wouldn't discuss his sister with her.

Naomi could hardly force him to talk about it. But was she the only one who saw that something was very wrong with Jessie?

Chapter Fifteen

Saturday's snow had only dropped an inch, which quickly melted. But snow was threatening again on Sunday morning, and Naomi had a feeling they wouldn't get off so lightly this time. Fortunately worship was being held just a couple of miles down the road at the Weaver farm.

Naomi rode with Libby and Isaiah, their buggy closely following the one carrying Nathan and the children. When they'd reached the Weaver place, it had seemed natural for Sadie to run to Naomi. When she'd walked into the Weaver family's basement to take her place holding Sadie's hand, she had felt as if the appearance were the reality —that they were any Amish mother and daughter.

But it wasn't true. Sadie leaned against her, eyes drooping closed, and Naomi moved her gently to a more comfortable position. She might look like the children's mother, but she wasn't.

Emma's disturbing comments zigzagged through Naomi's thoughts like lightning, illuminating the painful truth of her situation. She had gotten herself into just the place she'd vowed she wouldn't, raising someone else's children, loving them without having the right to be loved in return. In fact, everyone believed it impossible for her to be loved for herself.

Sadie sighed a little, drifting into sleep with her head on Naomi's lap. Naomi patted her, love clutching her heart. A slight movement from the row behind caught her eye, and she turned her head.

Leah, with little Rachel Anna dozing on her lap, smiled at her. She returned the smile, feeling a bond with the young mothers who filled the bench behind her. Leah, Anna, and Naomi's sister-in-law Lovina sat next to one another with their children, and it occurred to Naomi that it wasn't an accident that they were so placed. They were wordlessly showing support for her.

Tears stung her eyes, and she blinked until her vision cleared and she could see the minister's face again. What was she going to do about Daad? That worry had nagged at her for weeks, it seemed, but with the news of his complaint to the bishop it had taken on fresh urgency.

She did not want to be at odds with her father. She did not want to give up the work she was doing with Nathan's children. Surely it didn't have to come down to one or the other.

Please. The prayer was so incoherent it was nearly wordless. *Guide me.*

When the service wound to its close, Naomi realized that even though it had given her no answers, it had comforted her. More, she knew one thing she must do as soon as possible. She must speak to Bishop Mose.

There was a bustle of activity as men began the task of transforming the worship space into the eating space, while women scurried up and down the stairs with trays of food. Sadie woke, obviously refreshed by her nap, and ran off to find her brother. Across the large open area Naomi spotted Elijah helping to move a table. Beyond him, Daad stood against the wall with several of his friends, deep in conversation.

Momentarily adrift in a crowd of people, all of

whom seemed to have jobs to do, Naomi sidled toward the steps. She would go up to the kitchen and see what she could do to help. She'd just reached the top when someone moved into her path. Her fingers gripped the railing when she saw it was Bishop Mose.

Forcing a smile she didn't feel, she took the remaining two steps to reach him. She realized she was holding her breath, and she let it out, scolding herself. This was Bishop Mose. She'd known him all her life.

"Naomi, I was chust hoping to see you." When Bishop Mose smiled, the resulting crinkles in his face seemed to testify to his years of caring for his people. "I wanted—" He stopped, noticing that he was blocking the path to the basement. "Komm," he said. "Let us find a place a little less crowded." He nodded toward the back door. "Out on the porch, maybe, if you don't mind the cold."

"I could do with a breath of air." Naomi opened the door and followed him out onto the porch.

Bishop Mose steered her to the corner of the porch, and she realized that was deliberate. Here, no one would spot them and wonder what they were talking about.

"I hoped we could talk today." Her breath came out in a cloud on the cold air. "Someone . . . I heard at the Christmas program that my daad had come to you about my behavior." That much came out in a rush, and then she stopped, unable to say more.

"Ach, you should not have heard about it that way." Bishop Mose looked vexed, but not, so far as she could tell, with her. "I suppose someone who was in the harness shop that morning couldn't wait to pass on the story."

She blinked, determined not to give way to tears. "If the story is true, it doesn't matter how I heard, I suppose." For an instant she hoped against hope that Mary Esch had been making up the tale, but she couldn't quite believe that comforting thought.

"Did the person who passed on the story mention how I responded to your father?" Bishop Mose's blue eyes surveyed her shrewdly, and she suspected he knew full well who the tale-bearer had been.

"N-no." It startled her to realize that she had barely even considered Bishop Mose's response in all her worrying.

"I thought as much." He leaned against the porch post, seeming willing to stand here in the cold for as long as necessary. "I told your daad that it was not appropriate to air his complaints with his child in a public place. Further, that Scripture tells us that if we have a quarrel with a brother or sister in the faith, we must go to that person and try to make it right." There was a suspicion of a twinkle in his eyes. "I think you can guess how he responded to that idea."

She could, and she was emboldened by that twinkle. "I think Daad would say that Scripture also tells us a child should obey its parents."

"Ja, you have it." Bishop Mose shook his head slightly. "Sam Esch is a gut man, but that is not the same as being wise. You are his daughter, but no longer a child."

"Denke." Naomi breathed the word, her throat tight.

Bishop Mose frowned slightly. "You are doing a gut thing, I believe, taking care of those motherless kinder. Sam would probably agree if he were not so stubborn. There is no fault in the choice you have made, Naomi. But is there a fault in how you have dealt with your father? Have you tried to talk to him and explain what you are doing and why?"

Humbled, she shook her head. "I am at fault, too. Daad has not tried to talk with me, but I have not tried to talk with him, either. At least, not as much as I should. I must try again to explain."

Would it do any good? She didn't know, but her conscience convicted her of not trying hard enough to bridge the gap between them.

"Ja, that is what you must do. And if your daad still will not do his part to mend things between you, then he is the one to carry the burden of that failure."

The words sounded so final that they hurt

Naomi's heart. But she had asked for guidance, and it had come. Now she had to follow it.

When Isaiah drove the buggy between his place and Naomi's on the way to the stable, the first huge flakes were starting to fall. He halted the horse by the back porch. "Libby, you and Naomi go ahead and climb down. No point in you getting wet."

"It's snow," Libby exclaimed, sounding like one of the children to Naomi. "It is worth getting wet just to see it."

Isaiah met Naomi's eyes and grinned. "Ja, I know. I'd like to stop and play in it, but I think the mare would just as soon be in her warm stall."

Libby spun around once, holding out her arms as Isaiah drove on. Then she stopped and smiled at Naomi just as Isaiah had done. "Isaiah thinks he has to act like a grown-up just because we are married."

"Even grown-ups can enjoy the first big snowfall," Naomi said. "I heard some folks at worship saying that we are supposed to get several inches. Joshua and Sadie will be clamoring to get out their snow saucers, I think. Maybe they will let you borrow one for a ride."

"Don't tell anyone," Libby said, "but I have my own saucer up in the barn rafters."

"I won't tell if you'll let me have a ride," Naomi promised. Her young sister-in-law constantly amused her. She and Isaiah made a good match, both able to take things as they came and find joy in each day. That was a valuable gift.

"I promise," Libby said. "Don't forget you're coming over to share supper with us."

"I won't. I'll bring the apple pie." Naomi headed for her own house. She couldn't deny that she'd like to be out in the snow as well, but she'd rather change clothes first. Enjoying the snow required her thicker socks and her old jacket, as well as a muffler and mittens.

She went on in the house. Libby's playfulness had distracted her for a few minutes from that conversation with Bishop Mose, but the moment she was alone, it all came flooding back.

Well, at least she had to be grateful that the bishop understood and agreed with what she was doing. But the feeling that she had disappointed him by not doing more to mend the breach with her father wouldn't go away easily. Somehow she had to find a way to talk to Daad on her own, even though her heart cringed at the thought of receiving another dose of his anger.

Making peace was never easy, it seemed. Maybe it wasn't meant to be, or folks wouldn't value it so much. She would just have to pray that God would give her the right words to say to her father.

Gathering her sewing, she sat down in the rocker by the kitchen stove. The world was so quiet when it was snowing. That provided peace of a different kind, but none the less valuable. She would sit and rock and glance out at the drifting flakes while she worked on the doll for Sadie's Christmas gift.

Soon the snowflakes were driven, not drifting, and the white powder began to pile up on the ground. The weather predictions were right, it seemed. She had just about finished stuffing the doll when she heard noises outside. A muffled clop of hooves, the faint jingle of bells . . . She went to the window and peered out just in time to see Nathan's buggy horse come up the lane, pulling the old cutter she'd noticed in his barn.

Nathan and the children, well bundled up, waved to her and shouted greetings to Isaiah and Libby, who were already hurrying out their back door.

Naomi tucked the sewing out of sight and grabbed her jacket, as excited as a child herself. In moments she had joined the others at the sleigh. Snowflakes swirled around her, and she wrapped the muffler more securely around her neck.

"What is all this?" she asked. "Surely it can't be Joshua and Sadie in a sleigh!"

"It is, it is!" Sadie crowed, bouncing on the narrow seat. "Daadi got the sleigh out."

"It's a cutter," Joshua said, with his passion for being exactly right.

"Ja, so it is," Isaiah said. "And aren't you lucky that Daadi had it in the barn?"

"We almost sold it last year," Nathan said. He

grinned, the sparkle in his eyes about as bright as the children's. "It's a gut thing we didn't, ja?"

"Why would you sell it?" Libby stroked the curving runner, looking as if one of her Christmas wishes had come true.

Nathan shrugged. "As fast as they plow and cinder the road these days, there's not much use for it. And the lane has to be clear, as well, for the milk trucks. You can't drive a cutter over the cinders very well."

"So this is the perfect day," Naomi said, smiling at the excitement even as it bubbled in her, as well. "The plow drivers won't be in any hurry since it is Sunday."

"They certain-sure won't be out while it's still snowing." Nathan smiled down at her and extended his hand. "Komm, Naomi. You get the first ride."

Something about his smile, about the way he extended his hand, reminded her forcefully of those moments in the bee yard when they were covering the hives. She took a quick step back.

"Let Libby go first," she said. "I know she's dying for a ride but she won't ask."

"Ach, I can wait—" Libby began.

Isaiah cut her words off by lifting her bodily up into the cutter. The children scrunched over to make a space for her, and she laughed as she grabbed hold of the side. "All right, ja, I'm as excited as the kinder," she said.

Isaiah stepped back, Nathan slapped the lines, and the horse trotted off, the cutter running smoothly behind her. Off to the barn they went, turned, and slid back past them and out to the road, the children squealing, and Libby making just as much noise as they were.

"Ach, look at her." Isaiah watched his wife with a doting expression in his eyes. "She is just like one of the kinder. It was ser kind of you to let her go first."

"It's nothing. I knew how much she wanted a ride." To say nothing of the fact that she'd needed a moment to gather her wits.

Come now, she told herself firmly. *Maybe you'd best be careful about being alone with Nathan if you don't want him to guess that you feel . . . something. But as long as there are others around, you won't feel a thing.*

She hoped.

The cutter came flying up the lane, and Nathan drew to a stop in front of them. Libby jumped down, the tails of her muffler flying and her cheeks flushed. "That was so much fun. Your turn, Naomi." She gave her a little shove toward the cutter.

"Ja, up you go." Isaiah grabbed her arm and helped her up.

She settled on the seat, realizing how narrow it was—barely enough room for two adults, let alone two adults and two children.

"Here, Joshua, stand between my legs and you can help me drive, ja? Sadie, if you sit on Naomi's lap, she will have more room."

Joshua moved over importantly, his mitten-clad hands small on the lines. Nathan covered them protectively with his.

Naomi settled Sadie on her lap, and the child snuggled against her. "I'm glad you get to ride in the snow with us," Sadie said. "I love you, Naomi."

Touched, Naomi wrapped her arms around the child. "I love you, too, Sadie."

Nathan darted a smiling glance at her before concentrating on the lines, and Naomi's heart seemed to flutter.

"All right, Joshua. Flick the lines just a bit and tell her to step up."

"Step up, girl." Joshua attempted to mimic the way his father addressed the mare. Well-trained, she moved off instantly.

"Oh, my goodness." Naomi's stomach seemed to bounce. "It is nothing like riding in a buggy. It's more like flying."

They sailed along the lane, the runners making only a soft crunching sound on the snow. Snowflakes dusted her bonnet and gathered on the black sleeves of Nathan's jacket. She laughed with the sheer exhilaration of the ride.

"See what fun it is, Naomi?" Joshua didn't take his eyes off the lines, even when he spoke. He looked so serious and responsible standing there.

"It is great fun," she echoed.

"It's the best day ever," Sadie said, making Naomi smile.

"That's what you said about the day we went to the Christmas program at school," she pointed out.

Sadie considered. "This is the best day, 'cause Daadi and you are both here. That was the second best day."

"Gut thinking, Sadie," Nathan said. He reached across to pat his daughter, the movement bringing him even closer to Naomi.

Her breath caught in her throat again, and she forced herself to inhale and exhale evenly. Apparently they didn't have to be alone for her feelings to get out of control. She cared about Nathan. And there wasn't one thing she could do about it.

The storm ended up dropping more than four inches of snow overnight. Nathan came out of the barn the next day, blinking in the hazy sunlight reflecting from the whiteness, and paused to enjoy the view. Snow still rimmed the edges of the fences, and the branches of the hemlocks bowed gracefully under the weight. Before winter was over he'd be sick of the sight of snow, but at the moment it was still something to wonder at.

Joshua and Sadie had been overjoyed by their first sleigh ride yesterday. As had Naomi. It made

Nathan smile, remembering the fun they'd had.

Even now, Naomi and the children were out, bundled up and tramping through the snow toward the woods, pulling the plastic boat-shaped sled Nathan had bought for them last year. He smiled at the sight until he realized what it was Joshua carried over his shoulder—the heavy clippers he used to trim the trees.

Nathan headed toward them before he thought through what was happening. Well, whatever it was, he certainly didn't want his son using those heavy clippers. He'd be lucky if he didn't cut a finger off trying to manage them. What was Naomi thinking?

He'd worked up a head of steam by the time he reached them. "Where are you going with those clippers?"

Naomi looked at him, her smile freezing at his tone. "We're going to the woods to cut some greens for decorating, of course."

"No." Realizing how harsh that sounded, he quickly added, "If you need greens, I will cut some for you later. The kinder don't need to be doing such a job."

"But, Daadi, we want to." Sadie's voice trembled. "We're going to have fun."

"Ja, we are big enough to help," Joshua added.

"Why not ask Daadi to come with us?" Naomi said. "He can help us get the greens, and that will be even more fun than doing it by ourselves."

There was, he realized, a challenge in her eyes, a challenge that seemed to say that if he insisted on being foolish, at least he should join the children instead of forbidding them.

"Ja, ja, ja," Sadie chanted, running at him to grab his hand and swing on it. "Komm, Daadi, komm. We want you to komm to the woods with us."

"Please, Daadi." Joshua looked at him confidently.

Naomi had trapped him into this outing, it seemed. "Ja, all right. I guess I have time now," he said.

The smile on his children's faces made him think again of the fun of yesterday's sleigh ride. Naomi was right that they could have fun cutting the greens. Just not without him watching over them.

Hadn't he made it clear that he didn't want the children doing anything dangerous? Maybe he'd have to be more specific about what activities he considered dangerous.

"I'll take—" He reached toward the clippers his son carried and read disappointment in his face. "Why don't you put the clippers in the snow boat? Then you can pull them along instead of carrying them."

"That's a gut idea," Naomi said at once. "Will you pull for a while, Joshua?"

"Ja, sure." Joshua dropped the clippers in and

grabbed the rope. "I can get to the woods before you, Daadi." He started to run, his progress slow in the snow, the sled bouncing behind him.

"I'll catch you," Nathan said. He gave the boy plenty of lead and then jogged after him.

"Hurry, Naomi," he heard Sadie urge. "Hurry."

He made sure he and Joshua arrived at the woods in a dead heat, and they were congratulating each other when Sadie and Naomi arrived, laughing and breathless.

"This is about cutting the greens for our Christmas decoration, not about racing," Naomi said.

"Here are some greens." Joshua pulled on a low branch of hemlock.

"It's pretty," Naomi said, looking at the branch with a serious expression. "But hemlock needles fall off easily once the branch is cut. We probably don't want needles falling all over the house, do we?"

"But look at the pretty baby cones." Sadie touched one of the hemlock's small cones.

"We can find some cones on the white pine," Nathan intervened, no more eager to have hemlock needles all over the place than Naomi was. "Look, there's one right over here."

Sadie still pouted.

"You can pick some of the baby cones to decorate with," Naomi suggested. "We'll collect cones while Daadi and Joshua cut the greens."

"Ja, ja." Sadie clapped her mittens. "I'll put them in the sled."

"Daadi, here's the clippers." Joshua hoisted them out of the sled and handed them to him.

"Denke." He took them, lifting them well out of reach of the kinder.

"I love it when we put greens and candles in the windows," Joshua said, watching intently as Nathan cut a branch. "I remember when Mammi did it."

The reminder made his breath catch in his throat. "Do you?" he managed to say. "I'm glad." He glanced at Naomi, to see that the comment had affected her, as well.

"Naomi says we'll make strings of stars and angels to hang up," Sadie said, never wanting to be left out. She had few, if any memories of her mother, Nathan suspected, and the thought made his heart hurt.

"When you get some Christmas cards, we will hang those up as well," Naomi said. "That will remind us to think of the people who sent them."

Naomi's kindness shone through in all she said and did, it seemed. Nathan couldn't ask for anyone better to bring up his children, even if he didn't always approve of her ideas.

"How about this one?" Joshua asked, pulling on a branch. "This one is nice and thick. I think you should cut it."

Nodding, he reached out with the clippers, and

then he hesitated. He looked at his son, so eager to help.

"Let's do this one together," he said.

"You mean it, Daadi?" Joshua's face lit up.

"Ja, sure. Just like we drove the horse together yesterday." He drew the boy close to him, making sure the branch wouldn't spring back and hit him. "Put your hands here, like this. It's like cutting with scissors, ain't so?"

Joshua nodded, his face intent as he placed his hands exactly the way Nathan told him. With Nathan steadying the clippers, Joshua cut the branch, and when it fell, he broke into a huge grin. "I did it."

"You did," Nathan said, tossing the branch into the sled. Just a little thing, to make his son so happy.

Sadie chattered away, running back and forth, mostly finding pine and hemlock cones but sometimes burrowing in the snow or chasing a squirrel. Joshua worked steadily, seeming to model himself on Nathan's actions, and in short order they had filled the sled with greens and cones.

They started back toward the house, and it seemed to Nathan that his son walked a little taller as he pulled the sled. Naomi caught Nathan's eye and smiled as if approving his actions.

"Let's stop at the hives for a minute," she called as the children moved ahead of them.

Joshua and Sadie obediently swerved, waiting

for them next to the hives with their black winter blankets.

"You remember when I said that it's an old tradition to tell the bees about all the important things in your lives?"

They nodded solemnly.

"Well, I thought perhaps you would tell the bees your Christmas wishes."

That immediately caught the children's attention. "Me, first," Sadie said. "Me, first."

Naomi nodded. "Go ahead. Nice and clear, so the bees can hear you." She glanced at Nathan, and he realized she was answering his request. He'd wanted to know what to give the children for Christmas, and now he would.

"Can you hear me, bees?" Sadie whispered loudly. "I wish . . . I wish that I would get a doll cradle for Christmas." She spun, clapping her hands together. "Did I do it right?"

"Just right," Naomi said. "Now you, Joshua."

Joshua stood up very straight. "I wish for a wagon. If I had one, I could help Daadi and Grossdaadi haul things to the cows."

"That is ser gut," Naomi said, her voice a little husky.

She was affected by Joshua's wish, just as Nathan was. That his son wanted so much to help—the thought had his throat going tight. He had learned something valuable about Joshua today, and he had Naomi to thank for it.

He met her gaze. A smile trembled on her lips, her eyes were bright, and her cheeks were pink with the cold. He had never seen her look lovelier.

Longing swept through him, so strong it nearly had him covering the space between them. He wanted . . . he wanted . . .

Something startled and awareness came into her face, and her eyes darkened. For a moment it was as if they were touching each other.

"Daadi?" Sadie tugged at his sleeve, pulling him back to the here and now. To the truth of what he had almost done.

Guilt swept through him, as strong as the longing had been. Stronger. He couldn't feel anything for Naomi, not when his heart had been buried with his wife.

Chapter Sixteen

"More dessert, anyone?" Leah stood at the table with a knife poised above the pumpkin cheesecake she'd made for the Christmas lunch.

A series of groans greeted the suggestion of more food. Their rumspringa crowd from over ten years ago still had dessert plates in front of them, but no one seemed able to take Leah up on her offer.

"If I eat another bite I'll burst." Rachel, Leah's

best friend since childhood, spoke for everyone, Naomi thought. Certainly for her.

"It was scrumptious." Myra Beiler, Leah's sister-in-law, sighed at her inability to eat any more. "I hope you saved enough for Daniel and the kinder."

"Ach, don't worry about them. Elizabeth helped me, and we made three so there would be plenty. I wanted to try a new recipe, so I needed a little moral support."

"You are lucky to have such a sweet step-daughter." Lovina shook her head. "The boys are dear and I love them, but a daughter would be nice."

"It's not too late," Naomi teased. "The boys would love a little sister, and I'd certain-sure like a niece."

"We'll see," Lovina said, and something about the way she smiled made Naomi wonder if the idea of a daughter was more than just a wish. She eyed Lovina surreptitiously, but couldn't detect any change in her figure.

Still, Amish dress did a gut job of hiding a pregnancy.

"Is there something you're not telling us, Lovina?" Leah asked as she carried the basket of small gifts they'd brought to the table.

"Nothing I'm ready to talk about."

Lovina's answer had some knowing looks going around the table, and Naomi suspected she wasn't the only one counting up a probable birth month and thinking about baby quilts.

Leah clinked her spoon against her saucer. "Attention, please. It's time for our presents. Remember, no guessing who gave what until they are all opened."

The gift exchange was a little ritual they had enjoyed every year since the first time they'd met. In theory, you didn't know who had drawn your name, but in such a small group it wasn't hard to guess, especially once you saw the gift.

Naomi had pulled Rachel's name at the last meeting, and it had taken a bit of thinking to come up with something different. But Rachel, who was well-known for her greenhouses, would surely like the packets of heritage seeds Naomi had sent away for. They were all for varieties of vegetables or flowers that were seldom seen these days, and if anyone could grow them, Rachel could.

The gifts were opened amid laughter and squeals as they acted like the girls they'd once been. When they left, they'd all go back to being mature wives and mothers, but for a time this afternoon they were young again together.

Naomi's gift was a set of beautifully hand-quilted place mats, and it wasn't hard to figure out that Myra, a devoted quilter, had probably made them. Once all the gifts were opened, each person held up her gift and the giver identified herself. Sure enough, hers was from Myra.

Naomi turned from hugging Myra to be enveloped in a huge hug from Rachel. "Clever Naomi," she whispered. "You knew exactly what I'd love. I'll bring you the first ripe heritage tomato."

Mary Ann and Elizabeth Yoder, who were married to brothers, were laughing together over the fact that they'd gotten each other exactly the same thing—a quilted teapot cover. The two of them really seemed to have tastes in common.

In a moment Leah was coming around with the coffeepot again, and the group settled down for the talking and laughing that was always the best part of their Christmas lunch. There had been a time when Naomi and Leah were the single ones, listening to everyone else talk about their kinder.

Then Leah had married, acquiring Daniel's three young ones and having her little Rachel Anna, and Naomi had been left the only maidal.

At least now she had Sadie and Joshua to talk about, and her story of the children telling their Christmas wishes to the bees brought on laughter and maybe a tear or two. After all, Ada had been a key part of their group for years.

"I hope the young ones weren't too upset by Emma's fall," Myra said, her gentle face going solemn. "That would be frightening for a child."

"I think they feel better since they've visited

Emma at the rehab center. She looked like herself again and was so happy to see them that maybe it wiped away the scariness."

"That's gut to hear," Mary Ann said. "And I know you've been keeping them too busy to brood about it."

"Busy kinder are happy kinder." Leah voiced the common Amish belief.

And she was right, Naomi had found. Children who had no responsibilities and nothing to occupy them seemed to get lost. If Nathan had begun to see that he needed to allow Joshua some responsibility, she had done something good.

"You are so gut for those kinder," Myra said. "When you are really their mamm—" She stopped, turning pink. "I . . . I mean—"

Naomi struggled to understand. Why would Myra think such a thing? She glanced around the circle of faces and realized to her shock that Myra wasn't the only one.

"You all think Nathan and I will wed? But that's ridiculous."

"Naomi, I'm so sorry. I didn't mean to speak." Myra looked on the verge of tears. No one who knew gentle Myra could think she'd intended to spread gossip or to hurt Naomi.

"It's all right." She tried to keep her voice calm despite the fact that she was shaking inside.

"Ach, we might as well confess. We were talking about it before you came in." Rachel smiled ruefully. "But it's only natural, isn't it? We know you love those kinder. And we love you. We want you to be happy."

"Ja, I love them," Naomi said carefully. "I love taking care of them. But that doesn't mean either Nathan or I have thought of marriage." Nathan never would, she thought, her heart clutching.

"Don't be hurt by our chatter," Leah said, reaching out to pat her hand. "We think about how much you missed, taking care of your brothers and sisters all those years. As Rachel said, we want you to be happy."

Naomi had been foolish not to realize some might think her taking care of Nathan's children would lead to marriage. Not maliciously, the way Jessie thought it, but with kind hearts and good intentions. Maybe she'd known what people were thinking and just didn't want to admit it to herself.

"It does seem like the perfect solution," Lovina said, with a wistful look that one seldom saw on her capable face. "Then Daad Sam would stop trying to make you move in with us." She stopped, looking a little flustered. "Not that you wouldn't always be wilkom . . ."

"Lovina Esch!" Naomi stared at her sister-in-law, unable to repress a smile. "You don't want me to move in and take care of your kinder after all, ain't so?"

Lovina looked at her for a moment, eyes wide,

and then suddenly they were both laughing helplessly.

"I'm sorry." Lovina mopped at her eyes. "It's just . . . you know how your daad is, and sometimes Elijah is chust as bad. It never occurs to them that I might want to raise my own kinder. But you would always be wilkom . . ."

"Ach, Lovina, don't say it, or you'll start me laughing again." Naomi realized the others were watching them with expressions ranging from amused to perplexed. "I love you like a sister, but I don't want to live with you. And I know you feel the same way. So why didn't you tell Daad and Elijah that at the very beginning?"

Lovina's cheeks turned pink, but she didn't answer.

She didn't need to. Naomi knew. Lovina, like the rest of the family, relied on Naomi to deal with Daad for them, only this was one time when it seemed she'd failed.

Daad's farm was only a short detour on Naomi's route back to Nathan's house. Plucking up her courage, she turned the mare down the lane.

Bishop Mose had been right. She had to try again to make peace with Daad. She couldn't put it off any longer, hoping for some miracle. If she really was the adult woman she claimed to be, she would make the effort.

The mare, sensing familiar territory, quickened

her pace, and soon they turned into the narrow road that led to the house and barns. The fields still wore a blanket of white from the weekend's snow, but the lane was bare, beginning to freeze into winter's ruts.

The animals were in, which no doubt meant that Daad was at the barn or the milking shed. Naomi bypassed the house, driving to the barn and stopping at the hitching post.

A few quick steps took her to the open barn door, where a shaft of watery sunlight made patterns on the heavy plank floor. One of the stall doors was open. Bessie, the oldest of the workhorses, stood patiently while Daad knelt, applying fomentations to her off foreleg.

Naomi moved into the stall, stroking the horse's neck, and Bessie whickered in recognition. "Problems?"

Daad grunted, not turning from his task. "Cold weather's hard on her anymore. I noticed this foreleg swelling up a bit last night. Ach, well, she's getting old."

"Poor old girl." Naomi smoothed her hand over the velvety muzzle. "Daad will make it better."

The words sent a pang to her heart. Everyone knew how much patience and care Sam Esch had for his animals. She sometimes wished he'd had the same patience for his children.

"Ja, I'm not ready to give up on the old girl yet." Daad rose, running his hand up the fetlock. He shot Naomi a glance before bending again to check the mare's other legs. "You are here to talk to me, ja?"

At least his temper wasn't flaring at the sight of her. "I don't want to be at odds with you, Daadi. Can't we make up this quarrel between us?"

He didn't respond immediately, but Naomi thought she saw a bit of softening in the quick glance he sent her way. Then he bent again to check the poultice.

"I've heard some talk." His voice was a bit muffled by his position. "It seems some folks are thinking that Nathan might want to marry you."

Naomi's heart sank. It would have been too much to hope that Daad wouldn't get wind of what seemed to be a common assumption.

"I wouldn't have thought it myself," Daad said. "But if so, well, a marriage like that could be a gut thing." He straightened, facing her. "So I'm asking you, daughter. Is it true?"

Her stomach clenched, making her regret that piece of pumpkin cheesecake. She had to say what she felt sure was true.

"I know some people have been wondering, and I'm sorry. But I'm sure Nathan hasn't thought of such a thing." To her surprise, her voice stayed steady.

"No?" Daad's eyebrows drew down over his eyes. "Then he is exposing you to gossip and making you a laughingstock." His voice rose a little, and she recognized the signs. Daad was working himself into a fit of anger, and when he was angry, there was no chance he'd listen to reason. Still, she had to try.

"Folks will soon stop talking when they realize there's nothing to it. I am working for him, taking care of the kinder. That's all."

"That's not all." Daad's face reddened. "Do you think I want folks talking about one of my daughters that way? You must stop this nonsense and move in with Elijah and Lovina immediately."

There they were, back at the same sticking point. If only Lovina would speak up for herself—

"Daad, have you even considered that Elijah and Lovina might not want me moving in to take care of their kinder? Maybe Lovina doesn't want to spend her days working in the store." That was as close as she would go to betraying what was in Lovina's heart.

Daad brushed her words away with a sweep of his hand. "Nonsense," he said again, his gaze furious. "Never did I think you would be so willful, Naomi. If you will not do what I think best, I have nothing else to say to you." He turned his back.

Naomi reached out, nearly touching him. Her throat was tight with pain. "I'm sorry you are disappointed in me," she murmured.

She slipped out of the stall and went quickly outside. Her vision blurring with tears she didn't

278

want to shed, she unclipped the mare from the hitching post and climbed up to the seat.

She had done what she could. She had not returned anger with anger. As Bishop Mose had said, if Daad could not forgive, the burden was on him. But if that was the case, why did her heart feel so heavy?

She'd nearly reached the farmhouse when she realized that Betty had come outside and was standing by the lane, clutching a heavy black sweater around her shoulders. Steeling herself for more recriminations, Naomi drew to a stop.

"You have been talking to your daad," Betty said, not bothering with pleasantries. "How did it go?"

"Not well." Naomi kept her tone guarded. Whatever she said to Betty might well be repeated to her father.

Betty shook her head. "I feared as much." She put her hand on the buggy, as if to keep Naomi from driving off before she'd had her say. "I must tell you that I am sorry for how things ended between us the day you came to the house. I never meant . . ." She stopped, shook her head. "Ach, I'm sure you know that what I said was your father's idea. I didn't want to get involved in it at all, but you know what he's like when he gets an idea in his head."

She did, but she would think that a newlywed like Betty could figure out a way to manage

Daad. She reminded herself that she was out to mend fences today, not to erect them.

"It's all right, Betty. I'm not blaming you for this difficulty with Daad."

"Gut." Betty gave a sharp nod. "I am maybe the one person in the family who understands what you are feeling. After all, I lived on my own for a number of years."

Naomi nodded, cautious. She hadn't expected this overture of friendship from Betty, and she feared it would end in the same way the last one had, with a plea that she do what her father wanted.

"You were a widow, and people look at widows differently than maidals. Daad thinks he knows best for me."

"Your daad is a stubborn man," Betty declared. "Believe me, I thought long and hard about it before I agreed to marry him." She shrugged. "You're not going to find the perfect man, any more than you can find the perfect house or the perfect buggy horse. You just have to make the best decision you can."

That was the most honesty Naomi had ever heard from Betty, and it took her aback. "That's probably true, but I'm not sure why you're saying it to me."

Betty eyed her shrewdly. "Because you and I are more alike than you realize, Naomi. I will not go openly against your father's wishes, but I will do what I can to soften his heart toward you."

"Denke, Betty." She didn't think they were alike at all, but she would take help where she could get it.

Betty's tight mouth softened in a slight smile. "It is for my sake as well. Your daad is not comfortable to live with when he is in a rage."

Naomi nodded. That she could understand. She picked up the lines, thinking the conversation was at an end.

But Betty seemed to have one more thing to say, even as she stepped back from the buggy. "Remember what I said, Naomi. You'll never find the perfect husband, but if the chance arises, make sure you weigh the pros and cons before you answer."

In other words, Betty was among those who thought Naomi's job with Nathan could eventually lead to marriage. And she was bluntly advising her to weigh the advantages carefully.

She nodded and clicked to the mare, one thing clear in her mind. She would not choose as Betty had. She would not marry, even if the chance came, unless she could marry for love.

Nathan tucked the covers around Joshua, who had been unusually talkative at bedtime that night. "Time to stop the chatter and get to sleep."

He glanced at Sadie, who was most often the guilty party when it came to talking instead of sleeping, but her eyes were already drooping.

"But, Daadi, there is one more thing I wanted to talk to you about." Joshua clung to his sleeve. "Please."

"All right. One more thing." He sat on the edge of the bed. He probably shouldn't let Joshua prolong his bedtime this way, but these moments spent tucking the children in each night were precious to him. "What is it?"

"Sadie and me want to buy a present for Naomi for Christmas. Will you help us?"

"Don't you think Naomi would like to have something you made?"

But Joshua was already shaking his head. "She sees all the things we make. She teaches us how to do them. We want to give her something that would be a big surprise." Joshua's eyes shone. "Isn't that a gut idea, Daadi?"

"Well, ja, I think it probably is a fine idea." Joshua had obviously put a lot of thought into the subject. "I'll tell you what. Next time you and Sadie go with Naomi to get groceries in town, I'll go along. We'll find some excuse to get away from Naomi, and I'll help you pick out a present for her. Is that all right?"

Joshua, normally so undemonstrative, actually put his arms around him in a hug. "That's perfect, Daadi. Denke."

Nathan squeezed him, relishing the feel of his son's sturdy body. "Now you must go to sleep.

You can dream about finding just the right present to show Naomi you love her."

He tucked Joshua in again, kissed his forehead, and turned to Sadie. She was already asleep, snuggled into her pillow with one hand curled against her cheek. Smiling, he dropped a kiss on her head and went softly out of the room.

He found he was still smiling as he went down the stairs. Joshua was growing and changing, almost in front of his eyes. Sadie seemed to be changing as well, becoming less like a baby and more like a little girl. Naomi had a positive effect on all of them, it seemed.

He could hear Naomi rustling around in the kitchen as he reached the bottom step. The greens she and the children had arranged on the mantel and the windowsills made the living room look festive.

Now that Naomi lived so close, she stayed later, cleaning up the kitchen while he put the children to bed. It was comfortable, coming back downstairs to find her still there, busy about some task. It was almost like having a whole family again.

When he walked in, Naomi was gathering up some papers on the table. She looked up, smiling, when she heard him. "I was just getting ready to go. I'll put these away first."

"What is it?" He thought at first the papers were something of the children's, but on a closer look he saw that it was Naomi's writing. She seemed to have been drawing something. "I'm sorry. I didn't mean to pry into what you were doing. I thought it was some paper of Joshua's."

"It's not a secret." She turned the papers to show him, bending over the table and frowning at them. "I was trying to put together some sort of a label to go on the honey jars that I have for sale. Right now they just have a handwritten tag that says *honey*." She shook her head. "I guess I'm not much of a businesswoman."

"You're just starting out. You're not supposed to know everything about running a business at first." He sat down, pulling the papers toward him. "Maybe another opinion will help you decide."

Naomi sat down next to him. "I'd sure be glad of it." She fanned the papers out. "I'm not much of an artist, either. Maybe I ought to stick with what I have and be done with it."

She had been doodling, it looked like, trying out different versions of words and designs that might go on the front of a jar. Some said *Clover Honey*, others *Pure Clover Honey*, another one *Naomi's Honey*.

Nathan put his finger down on the last of those. "I think you should use your name. After all, the honey comes from your bees, and you are the one who processes it."

She looked up, her face a little troubled. "You don't think it would be seen as prideful?"

Being prideful was just about the worst accusation one could make about an Amish person, all of whom were trained to humility from birth. He could understand the idea troubling Naomi, especially now, with folks talking about the conflict with her father.

"I don't see why," he said, keeping his voice easy. "Plenty of Amish who create things for sale put their names to them. It's not a matter of pride, just of letting the buyer know what he's getting."

She nodded, but he could see a reservation in those deep blue eyes. "Still, your milk doesn't say *Nathan King* on it."

"True, but it does say *Pleasant Valley Cooperative*, and everyone who buys it knows what that means. Besides, our milk sells directly to people who know us. But plenty of Englisch, tourists even, will buy a jar of your honey. I'd think it would give them pleasure to put a name to the person who made it."

Funny, that he was taking so much time trying to convince Naomi of something that many people would take for granted. Even among the Amish, there were certainly those who were more prideful than others, though they'd be the last to admit it.

Maybe that was the key. A person like Naomi, with her genuine humility, worried about any hint of pride creeping into what she did, while those who already had a bit more self-confidence than they needed never considered it.

Naomi was nodding, her smooth forehead a bit

wrinkled in thought. "I heard Katie say once that Englischers who come in to buy a quilt from her or a piece of furniture from Caleb always want to have a bit of knowledge about the maker. She said they are looking for something handmade, because so much in their lives isn't."

"Since Katie Brand is a gut businesswoman, you would probably do well to listen to her. Those decorated jars she suggested have sold well, ain't so?"

Naomi's frown disappeared in amusement. "All right, you have convinced me. The jars should have my name. I just wish I knew how to make labels that would look a bit prettier." She glanced at the clock. "I should be letting you relax, not keeping you here talking about my labels, of all things."

"I enjoyed it." He found himself wanting her to stay a bit longer. He wanted to sit and talk over cups of cocoa, laughing over the events of the day.

The feeling was so strong that he nearly reached out to her. He managed to suppress it.

"I'm in no hurry to do anything, including relaxing," he said. "I was thinking a cup of that cocoa you made for the kinder would taste gut, if there's any left."

"I kept some in case you wanted a cup. Just let me warm it." Naomi swept up the papers in a single gesture and put them in her basket as she moved to the gas range.

He ought to tell her he could do it himself, that she could get on home. But that odd longing for even a pretense of a normal life held him in its grasp. He'd had it for a few minutes while they'd talked about her project. He didn't want it to end so quickly.

"Did you have a nice Christmas lunch today at Leah Glick's?"

"Ach, ja." She didn't immediately turn away from the stove, and when she did, she was smiling. "Leah is a wonderful-gut cook, and she made such a delicious meal."

"And you had lots of chatter about the old days, ja? Talking about who your come-calling friends were and who talked to which boy at the singing."

Nathan had a sudden vivid mental picture of that group of girls clustered under a cherry tree in blossom after worship one Sunday, all laughing and talking so much that it was a wonder anyone had listened. Ada had been at the center, of course, her face vibrant and alive.

"Ja, we did some reminiscing." Naomi poured the cocoa into a mug, holding the pan with a pot holder as the steam rose in her face. "Someone —Rachel, I think—was talking about the time some of you boys shot off fireworks and nearly set the woods on fire."

He grinned, remembering that night. "We were that scared when we saw the flames shoot up. It seemed like forever until we could get the fire out, but it probably wasn't more than a couple of minutes." He shook his head. "I get scared all over again when I think of Joshua taking such foolish risks as we took."

"Joshua's a sensible boy, and a responsible one for his age." Naomi set the mug in front of him. "But you know as well as I do what nonsense teenagers can get up to. Especially boys. Luckily you have a few more years before you have to deal with it."

He nodded, lifting his cup. "Aren't you going to have some, Naomi?"

She'd been reaching for her coat, but she stopped, drawing her hand back. "Well, maybe half a cup."

He grinned. "That's what Daad always says. Are you picking that saying up from him?"

"Maybe so." She lifted down another mug and poured. "When you're around people all the time, you tend to pick up their ways, I guess."

"Maybe Sadie will pick up some of your calm and patience, then." He paused, but surely he could voice this thought to Naomi. She was safe. "I worry, sometimes, when she goes from being happy to being upset in the blink of an eye. I mean, Jessie is Ada's sister, and I wouldn't want to see Sadie growing up like her."

The thought of Jessie's mood swings and uncontrollable temper transferred to his Sadie gave him chills.

"Sadie is like her mammi," Naomi said, her tone reassuring. "Ada always showed her feelings—that was what people loved about her. But Jessie—" She frowned, shaking her head and staring down into the cocoa as if she expected to find answers there. "What was normal and lovable in Ada is somehow twisted in Jessie."

Nathan wanted to repeat the familiar assurances, that Jessie was just immature, that her tantrums didn't mean anything. But he couldn't, not to Naomi, who knew her so well. Maybe it would be a relief to speak the truth about Jessie for once.

"Twisted," he repeated thoughtfully. "That is as gut a word as any. When she is disappointed she doesn't cry or look sad. She takes it out on other people."

Naomi nodded, cupping her hands around the mug as if grateful for its warmth. "It worries me, her being at the house alone while Emma is in rehab. Emma can handle her, but—"

She stopped, head lifting, eyes alert, as if she'd heard something he didn't. And then he heard it, too, coming from the children's room—an odd, barking, shrill cough that sounded as if one of them was choking to death.

Chapter Seventeen

Naomi reached the children's bedroom a second after Nathan, her heart pounding. Nathan was already switching on the battery-powered light, and she went straight to Sadie, scooping the child up in her arms.

Sadie blinked in the light. A spasm of coughing hit her, and her eyes grew round and terrified.

"She's choking," Nathan cried. "Do something."

Frightened by the terror in her daadi's voice, Sadie began to cry, that shrill cough seizing her again.

"Hush, hush." Naomi held Sadie against her, rubbing her back. Obviously she was going to have to calm both Nathan and the child. "She is not choking. She has the croup, nothing worse."

"Croup?" Some of the fear went out of Nathan's eyes. "Are you sure?"

"Ja, I'm sure. I've seen it and heard it enough times with Isaiah." She smoothed Sadie's hair back from her face. "When Isaiah was little like you, he used to get the croup, too. It gives you a funny cough, doesn't it? It sounds like an animal barking."

Sadie nodded, still looking scared, but her frenzied grasp on Naomi's arm eased a little.

Then she coughed again, and she started to cry.

"It's all right." Naomi stood, holding the distraught child.

"I'll call for the doctor." Nathan started toward the door, bumping into Joshua's bed.

"No, don't bother to call. Go to the kitchen and start some water to boil in a large kettle on the stove." She understood his worry, but it was more important now to treat the child than to make a probably futile call to the doctor this late.

Nathan hesitated, and it was clear that his instincts all told him to rush to call a doctor.

"Trust me, Nathan. Please. Believe that I know what I'm doing." She began wrapping a blanket around Sadie, talking soothingly to her.

Would Nathan listen, or was his panic for his daughter too great to accept her word? She heard his footsteps hurrying on the stairs, and then the clatter of a pan in the kitchen.

Good, he was doing as she said. But she didn't have time to feel relief, because Joshua was sitting up in bed, rubbing his eyes. He stared at her, looking confused and frightened.

"Was ist letz? Naomi, is something wrong? Why is Daadi upset? What's wrong with Sadie?"

"Everything is all right." She had to take a moment to comfort him. "Sadie has a bad cough, but Daadi and I will take gut care of her. You can lie down and go to sleep again."

He shook his head, shivering a little in the cool

air of the bedroom. "I can't go back to sleep. I'm scared."

She didn't want to have both of them up, but she could understand how scary it would be for Joshua, lying up here listening to sounds from downstairs and imagining the worst.

Sadie began to cough again, catching her breath on a sob. Naomi had to get the child downstairs. She made a quick decision about Joshua.

"Bring your blanket, and put your slippers on. You can stay up for a little bit until we get Sadie settled."

She carried Sadie down the steps, not waiting to see if he obeyed her. Nathan waited at the bottom, his hand taut on the railing.

"I started the water heating. But I still think I should call the doctor."

Naomi hurried on past him and into the kitchen, Nathan following. "If you call, he will only say to take her to the emergency room. Then you will have to call for Ben or one of the other drivers to come, and by the time all that happens and you get her to the hospital, the attack will be over."

"How can you be sure?" Fear threaded through the question, and she suspected her mention of the hospital scared him as much as anything.

Forcing a smile, Naomi tried to put as much reassurance as possible into her voice and expression. "I know how scary the cough sounds. It scared me to death the first time I heard it, and I reacted just the way you did. But my mamm knew exactly what to do, and she showed me."

That had been a gut thing, now that she thought of it. In another year, Mamm had been gone and she'd been the one to get up in the night when one of the little ones was sick.

"Joshua never had anything like this cough. Colds, ja, but nothing that sounded like Sadie's cough." Nathan still sounded worried, but not as panicked as he had a few minutes ago.

"Some kinder are just susceptible to croup. I don't know why that is. My sister Sara had it once or twice, but Isaiah was the worst. He seemed to get it several times a year when he was Sadie's age, and then he suddenly outgrew it and never had it again."

Nathan didn't respond, and she had to hope he had begun to accept her words.

She carried Sadie over to the stove. "Look, Sadie, we're going to get the kettle nice and steamy. And then we'll make a little tent and you and I will put our heads under it. That will make it easier for you to breathe without coughing."

Sadie clung to her, still frightened, but she nodded. She pressed her face against Naomi's shoulder, and Naomi's heart swelled with love.

There was a shuffle of slippers and Joshua came in, trailing his blanket. Nathan swung toward him. "Joshua, what are you doing up?"

"I told him he could come down for a bit, just until he sees that Sadie is all right," Naomi said quickly. "He won't be in the way."

Sadie began that sharp, barking cough again, and Nathan winced. "Hush, hush, little girl." She stroked Sadie's back, trying to send comfort through her touch. "It will be better soon."

She sat down next to the table, pulling another chair over close to them for the kettle. Naturally it was taking what seemed an eternity to boil.

"What can I do?" Nathan sounded calmer as the initial panic wore off. "What else do you need?"

"Either a small blanket or a large towel. We're going to spread it over our heads to keep the steam in."

Nathan nodded, starting out of the room, and then paused, looking at his son. He seemed to come to a decision.

"Joshua, you can run upstairs to the closet where we keep the sheets and towels. Take the flashlight so you can see what you're doing, and bring that great big blue towel, ja?"

"I can do it, Daadi." Joshua ran to take the flashlight from its hook by the door. He darted toward the stairs, and Naomi could hear his hurrying feet above them.

"Gut," she murmured, and saw from Nathan's expression that he understood what she meant. He was trusting Joshua instead of instantly doing it himself. That was good for both of them.

By the time Joshua returned, the kettle was boiling.

"Denke, Joshua." Naomi took the towel from him. It was bath-sheet size, and it would work perfectly. "You sit on the chair over there," she said, gesturing to the other side of the table. "Wrap up in your blanket, so you stay warm. We don't want you getting sick, as well."

Joshua nodded, climbing onto the chair. He watched curiously as Nathan transferred the boiling kettle to the chair.

"Now, we must be careful not to touch the hot pan." Naomi wrapped Sadie's blanket securely around her so that she couldn't inadvertently move and bump the kettle. "We are going to lean over the steam like this, and Daadi will put the towel over our heads."

Nathan nodded, reaching for the towel. In a moment the dark towel stretched over their heads, cutting off the room.

Naomi pressed her cheek close to Sadie's, feeling the steam full in their faces. "Just breathe in like you always do. That's right. Nice, even breaths in and out. The steam is going to loosen up your throat inside, so that you won't sound like a barking animal anymore."

Sadie coughed again, but the sound was looser, not as frightening.

"There, you see, it's getting better already."

"I don't like it in here," Sadie said fretfully. "I can't see."

"Of course you can't see," Naomi said, relieved to hear Sadie sounding more normal. "We are two little bees in our dark beehive. But even though we can't see anything, we know we are safe with our family around us. We can hear their wings moving, helping to keep us warm. Can you buzz a little, just to say denke?"

That caught Sadie's imagination, as Naomi had hoped, and she produced a gentle buzz. She coughed again, but this time her little body didn't tighten with fear.

"That's right," Naomi said gently. "Everything is going to be fine, you'll see. Coughing is nothing to be afraid of."

Sadie began to relax, and the inevitable tension that Naomi felt eased as well. She'd been confident there was no reason to rush off to the hospital in the middle of the night. Still, it was a relief to know she'd been right.

If this had happened when she wasn't here, what would Nathan have done? She imagined him running out into the dark, trying to hold Sadie and call for help at the same time. It certain-sure wasn't easy, being the only parent.

Naomi felt Sadie droop as she relaxed, and she shifted so that Sadie was leaning against her. The steam had perspiration streaking down both their faces, and while Sadie would look adorable with her cheeks pink and her damp hair curling against her face, Naomi suspected she looked like a drowned rat. Still, her appearance hardly mattered.

Finally, as the kettle began to cool, she eased the towel back from over their heads. The air in the kitchen felt chilly against her damp hair.

Nathan regarded her anxiously. "Should I heat the water again? Is it over?"

"She may need another treatment. Let's just keep the water hot on the stove. I want to get her into a dry nightgown and towel her hair." She glanced at Joshua, nearly asleep on the straight kitchen chair. "And I think we can get that one back in his bed."

"Ja." Nathan smiled at his children as he set the heavy kettle back on the stove and turned the gas on to a low flame. "I'll carry him up, shall I? I can bring down another towel and a fresh nightgown for Sadie."

Naomi nodded, leaning back in the chair with the sleeping child. She felt as if she had been running some kind of race—winded and exhausted but unable yet to relax. From what she remembered of Isaiah's attacks of croup, the first one often led to several more.

Sadie's breathing still seemed tight, her heart beating faster than normal. It could be a long night.

She heard the sounds of Joshua being tucked

into bed upstairs . . . the creak of the bedsprings, a sleepy murmur from the child, Nathan's comforting bass rumble answering him. In a moment he was back, carrying a couple of towels and a small white nightgown.

"Let's see if we can ease this damp one off without waking her." Naomi kept her voice low. If Sadie could sleep, that was the best thing.

"Just hold her," Nathan said, bending over them. "I'll do it."

His face was very close to hers as he bent over his daughter—so close that at one point she could feel the warmth of his skin, see the fine lines at the corners of his eyes. She tried to close her mind, to shut out any foolish speculation, but she couldn't seem to breathe.

And then someone was knocking at the back door, calling Nathan's name. Naomi smoothed the nightgown into place and wrapped the blanket more securely around the sleeping child as Nathan went to answer.

She heard Isaiah's voice, and then his ruddy face appeared around the corner of the door between the kitchen and the back hall.

"Ach, I don't need to ask what's going on," he said. "I know croup when I see it."

Nathan pushed him into the room and came in behind him. "Don't hold the door open."

"Sorry." He lowered his voice to a whisper. "Poor little one. But Naomi will take gut care of her."

"Ja." Nathan didn't say more, but a message seemed to pass between them as he looked at Naomi. He trusted her, and her heart swelled.

"We were worried when we didn't see you get home," Isaiah said, touching Naomi's shoulder lightly. "Do you want me to stay and walk with you?"

She shook her head. "I don't know how long I'll be. You should remember that croup can go on for a while. You may as well go on to bed. I'm not afraid to walk back to the house by myself."

To her relief, Isaiah didn't argue. There was no point in any more people losing sleep because of Sadie's croup, and the cows had to be milked in the morning regardless of whether the humans had gotten any sleep or not.

"I'll see you in the morning, then." He squeezed Naomi's shoulder and went out, closing the door quietly.

Nathan glanced at the clock. Maybe Isaiah's visit made him aware of how late it was getting. "You should probably go on home. Sadie seems better now."

Naomi could hear the reluctance in his voice, and she shook her head. She couldn't leave Nathan alone to deal with a sick child. "She's still making that little noise in her throat. I'm afraid we're not over this episode yet. I'll stay."

He gave her a look of relief. "Denke, Naomi.

299

Truth be told, I'd not like to be managing this by myself."

"Croup sounds much scarier than it is." She wanted to allay the concern that lurked in his eyes, but she knew Nathan could never stop worrying about his children.

"Scary? That doesn't begin to describe it. I thought . . ." He stopped, running his hands over his face.

Her heart lurched. Nathan seemed bound to compare every bump in his children's path to Ada's death. She felt his pain. She also felt helpless to do anything about it.

It was nearly two in the morning when Naomi finally tucked Sadie into her own bed with a feeling of assurance that the worst was over. They'd had to resort to the steam tent twice more, but each time the episode had lasted a shorter time. She went back down the stairs, weariness dragging at her. She'd forgotten how tiring and stressful it could be, staying up with a sick child.

Nathan was in the kitchen. He turned from the sink when he heard her, and she realized he was clearing away the kettle and the cups they'd used what seemed an eternity ago.

"You don't need to clean up. I'll do that in the morning."

Nathan's face was tight, and her heart seemed to skip a beat.

"Nathan?" She went to him, reaching out as she would to a hurting child. "Was ist letz? Sadie will be fine."

"I know." His voice rasped as if it pained him to speak. "I just . . ." He swallowed, and she could see the muscles work in his throat. "I should not be afraid. I should trust in God's will. But—" His voice seemed to fail him.

"But Sadie's illness made you relive Ada's death." She finished the thought for him, knowing too well that was his nightmare.

He clutched the sink, the muscles standing out on his forearms like cords, staring blindly at the darkness beyond the window.

"I chust went into town after supper to pick up an order of feed. The storm started when I was ready to leave for home, so I waited at the mill." A shudder went through him.

Naomi wanted to tell him to stop, not to relive that night again. But she couldn't. Nathan was already caught in the nightmare of remembering.

"It was such a quick storm. A few lightning strikes and a couple rumbles of thunder. That was all." He sounded almost bewildered.

"I know," she said softly. "I remember." She had been at home, rushing into the house with some sheets she'd pulled off the line when the storm came up. She'd been thinking of nothing beyond saving her laundry from getting soaked.

"I started toward home the minute the rain

301

slacked off. The ambulance passed me on the road, the siren wailing. I think I knew then."

"It wasn't your fault." She touched his arm, but he seemed so far away he might not have felt it. "Isaiah and your daad were in the south field, but by the time they saw that the barn had been hit and reached it, it was too late."

He shook his head, lowering it like an animal in pain. His shoulders hunched. "If I had been here—"

"You would have been out with your daad and Isaiah in the field, fixing the fence." She moved her hand on his shoulder, gripping it, longing to comfort him and not knowing how. "Could you have done more? Run faster than Isaiah? Been more clever than your daad? You know that you could not."

Poor Isaiah. Her little brother had been the one to rush into the burning barn, to find Ada lying under the beam that had fallen when she'd tried to lead the workhorses to safety. The horses had gotten out with minor injuries, but Ada was gone all in an instant.

"I know." Nathan turned on Naomi with a sudden spurt of anger. "I know they did all that could be done. That doesn't stop me from feeling how wrong it is. It should have been me in that barn, not Ada."

His anger was like a flame, scorching her, but she couldn't falter now that Nathan was finally speaking.

"That is what Isaiah said," she replied softly. "When I got here I found him out behind the toolshed, weeping. 'It should have been me,' he kept repeating. But it wasn't. Ada was the closest, so Ada was the one who went into the barn."

"It's not right."

The words came out in one last burst of anger, and then tears spilled over. Nathan turned to her as naturally as one of the children would, and she put her arms around him, murmuring the soothing nonsense words she'd have used to any hurting creature.

It had been too long in coming, this outpouring of his grief. Nathan had held it back, trying to be strong, and now the dam was broken. She could only hold him and pray that this release would bring healing in its wake.

After what seemed a long time but was probably only moments Nathan straightened, rubbing his face with one hand. "I'm sorry. I should not have given way."

"Ja, you should." Her hands were still on his upper arms, and she wanted to shake him. "Holding grief inside hurts you, Nathan. And it hurts those around you. Do you imagine Ada would want that for you?"

"Always so wise, Naomi. So strong." It might have been said mockingly, but it wasn't. "That was what Ada always said about you, and she was right."

He almost smiled, his face relaxing. And then his gaze caught hers. His expression became arrested, as if he saw something he had not seen before. He raised his hand, his fingertips brushing her cheek.

Everything changed. He wasn't a child she was comforting. He was a man, and the look in his eyes made her heart stop.

"Naomi." He said her name softly, his fingers against her cheek. She couldn't move, couldn't breathe.

And then he was stepping back, turning away. "I . . . I'm sorry. It's late. You should be at home, ja?"

"Ja." She knew what he was feeling, because she felt it, too. He was searching for balance in a world that had suddenly shifted.

And he was right. They could not do or say anything here in the night that they might want back in the light of day.

But as she put her coat and mittens on and picked up the torch that would light her way home, she couldn't repress the tiny sprig of hope that seemed to be blossoming in her heart.

The torch sent a yellow circle of light ahead of her as she walked across the frozen field. She nearly didn't need it, so bright was the moonlight.

She tilted her head back, looking up at a sky that seemed overfull of stars, clustering across the darkness in points of light. The night was so still that she could hear the faintest creaking of the snow cover beneath her feet and a tiny rustle that might belong to some small creature burrowing into its hole. It would never occur to her to be frightened here, even though not a soul seemed awake.

Those moments in the kitchen when Nathan had touched her face—had they meant as much to him as they did to her? Or had that been just a natural reaction to the emotions stirred up by Sadie's illness and the release of finally talking about Ada's death?

She couldn't be sure, and she must not assume anything. When she saw Nathan again, she must act as if all was just as it had been between them. She—

Naomi stopped, as frozen as the earth. There had been an alien sound interrupting her thoughts. The sound was something that shouldn't be there in the quiet middle of the night, but what?

She listened, her finger on the switch of the torch, but the noise, whatever it had been, wasn't repeated. Well, sounds carried in the night. Maybe it was something fairly far away, some natural sound that she wouldn't even notice in the daytime.

It was gone now and nothing to worry about. Nevertheless, she walked a bit more quickly the rest of the way to the warmth and safety of her house.

Chapter Eighteen

"Let's go into this shop." Joshua had his face pressed against the window of the gift shop in town. "It has lots of pretty things. We can find something for Naomi for sure in here."

"We'll give it a try." Nathan had actually been heading for the quilt shop, thinking that Katie Brand might be able to guide the young ones in finding a gift for Naomi, but this might do as well. He pulled open the door of the gift shop, setting its bell jingling.

They had dropped Naomi at the grocery store, and he'd said they'd be back in an hour. Naomi probably guessed their errand, but she hadn't let on, delighting the children.

Naomi had been just as usual in the two days since the night he'd broken down talking to her about the way Ada had died. Or more to the point, since the moment he'd looked into her face and felt such longing that he had become a stranger to himself.

"Look around and see if you find anything you might like to give Naomi," he told the children, "but be careful about touching things, ja?"

They both nodded solemnly, and Joshua took Sadie's hand. He led her off through the aisles, leaving Nathan struggling with his thoughts. He pretended interest in the closest display, which happened to be of candles.

Naomi had been her usual serene self since that night. He was the one turned upside down, and he didn't know how to right himself. He just knew he couldn't possibly have the kind of feelings for Naomi that he'd had for Ada. He couldn't.

What had happened between them had surely been an accident. He had been upset about Sadie, and then doubly upset because he'd blurted out all his grief over Ada's death in a way he couldn't believe in the light of day.

What had possessed him to talk like that to Naomi? She grieved for Ada, too, and he had burdened her with his pain. And then he'd made things worse by imagining he felt something, by touching her face . . . For an instant he was back in that moment, with Naomi's soft skin warm under his fingers.

"Daadi? Komm, see what I found." Sadie's voice was a welcome interruption.

He tried to shove thoughts of Naomi to the back of his mind, no easy task when they were busy trying to find gifts for her. He went around a display full of baskets to find Sadie staring at a glass ball enclosing a nativity scene.

"Do you like the snow globe?" Mrs. Macklin, owner of the shop, smiled at Sadie and took the snow globe from the shelf. She shook it and set it down right in front of Sadie, so that the child could see the snow falling on the nativity scene.

Sadie clasped her hands together. "Ach, Daadi, isn't it beautiful? And Naomi said we should have a putz to remind us of Jesus being born."

The putz was the nativity set found in most Pennsylvania Dutch homes at this time of year. They had one, of course. With a jolt to his heart, Nathan realized he hadn't gotten it out since Ada's death. The putz had been hers from the time she was a little girl, and he hadn't wanted to be reminded.

"Ja, it is very nice," he said. "But it seems to me it's something you'd like, not something for Naomi. Let's keep looking."

Sadie pouted for a minute, but then she hurried off in search of her brother. Nathan handed the globe to Mrs. Macklin. "Will you put it in our package so the kinder don't see?"

She smiled, tucking it into her sweater pocket. "Don't worry. We're very good at keeping Christmas secrets."

Nodding, he started after the children and then stopped, his attention caught by a display of preserves in jars similar to the ones Naomi used for her honey. Each jar had a label indicating the type of fruit inside a curving border that looked like a vine.

Mrs. Macklin, perhaps sensing another sale, moved closer. "Do you like those?"

"Not the preserves," he said. "But do you know where I could get labels similar to those?"

"I can do that for you," she assured him quickly. "I would just need to know what you want on the labels and what sort of design you'd like."

"You can actually design the labels?" He seemed to be back at the kitchen table with Naomi, talking about what she should do for her labels. He'd nearly forgotten that conversation, with everything that had happened afterward.

"I'm not an artist, but I have a computer program for creating labels, and it has all sorts of designs. I'm sure we could find one that would work." Lisa Macklin gestured toward the counter. "Do you want to come over to the computer, and I'll show you what I have? Don't worry about the children. I'm sure they won't get into anything they shouldn't." She smiled. "Not like some of the tourists we have in here during the summer."

Naomi would like the labels for sure, and he'd seen enough of her sketchy designs to be able to pick something out. He could almost imagine the pleasure on her face when she saw them. And maybe the gift would be a way of saying he supported her business, too.

"Ja, that would be gut." He followed Mrs. Macklin to the computer.

A few clicks and the computer displayed a bewildering array of labels. Each one had a border with words in the center.

"If you tell me what it's for, I can narrow down the selections a little."

He nodded, knowing that made sense. "It is for Naomi Esch's honey." He had an urge to explain why he was buying something for her, but why would Mrs. Macklin care? "Do you know it?"

"Yes, definitely. I bought a jar when I was in the bakery just a few days ago. And I think I have the perfect design." She clicked the keys again, frowning at the machine as if that would force it along.

"There," she said. "What do you think?"

The design that had come up on the screen had a curving border of vines and tiny blossoms. At the very top was a honey bee, seeming to hover in flight.

"It's just right." Nathan could picture the light in Naomi's eyes when she saw the image.

"Great. I can put any wording on the labels you'd like. It would just take a day to give me time to finish and print the labels, and then you can pick them up." She handed him a pad. "Just put the wording you want and how many. I'll have them ready for you to pick up by tomorrow."

"I'm not sure I'll be in town tomorrow." He would not want her to think he'd ordered something and then not come for it.

"No problem." She smiled. "I trust you. They'll be ready at the counter with your name on the package whenever you stop by."

"Denke." Nathan hesitated, pen poised over the paper. The Amish didn't go in for fancy labels, of course, but he thought he'd convinced Naomi that she should use her name.

Naomi's Honey, he printed carefully. Four dozen seemed a good number to start with, and he could always get more if need be. He could have put *Clover Honey*, but Naomi had talked about the different honeys she'd get, depending upon what nectar the bees had access to.

He was smiling as he went in search of the children again, imagining Naomi's happiness when she opened the gift. Maybe it wasn't something fancy, but he knew she would understand the thought.

He found Joshua and Sadie admiring a napkin holder painted with a distelfinks design.

"Do you think Naomi would like this napkin holder, Daadi?" Joshua's small face was very serious, as if choosing the right gift was the most important thing in his life right now.

"I don't know," Sadie said. "Maybe we should look some more."

He suspected Sadie would be happy to look around the shop all day. "I think it is a wonderful-gut gift. It is both useful and pretty."

"Like Naomi," Joshua said, the serious look dissolving into a smile. "She is useful and pretty too, ja?"

Before Nathan could respond, someone else

spoke. "Doing your Christmas shopping?" Seth Miller stood there, seeming perfectly comfortable to be shopping in Pleasant Valley instead of whatever big city stores he usually frequented.

"We found a present for Naomi, Onkel Seth." Joshua seemed to have gotten over whatever reservation he felt about this new uncle. "Do you think she will like it?"

Seth looked over the napkin holder gravely, as if the choice were as important to him as it was to Joshua. "I'm sure she will."

Joshua nodded, satisfied. "Komm, Sadie. We'll take it to the counter." They ran off, with Joshua clutching the napkin holder, leaving Nathan alone with Seth.

"I didn't know you were still in town." Nathan hoped that didn't sound unfriendly, but he couldn't deny that Seth's presence made him uncomfortable.

Seth shrugged. "I've made arrangements to stay until Christmas. It seems important to Mamm, so I figured it was the least I could do."

"Ja." As far as Nathan was concerned, it really was the least Seth had ever done.

"You don't like me much, do you?" Seth's voice had hardened, but it didn't sound as if Nathan's feelings bothered him.

Nathan blew out a breath, trying to organize his chaotic thoughts. "My liking doesn't matter, does it?" he said finally, torn between the truth and kindness. "Your mamm is glad you are here, and that's all that counts."

Seth nodded, as if he hadn't expected anything more. "Will you let the children accept Christmas presents from me?"

The simple question presented a difficult choice. Nathan could not easily forget the pain Seth had caused his parents and sisters when he went away. He didn't want his children added to the list of people Seth had hurt.

Then he heard Naomi's soft voice in his head. *What would Ada want?* Nathan couldn't doubt the answer to that question.

"As long as it is something appropriate," he said finally. "That would have pleased Ada."

Seth nodded, as if understanding that pleasing Nathan probably wasn't a possibility. "Denke, Nathan," he said, using the Pennsylvania Dutch word without hesitation. "I'll be careful in what I choose."

With that, Nathan supposed he had to be content. He went in search of the children, trying to dismiss the idea that he had been unkind.

If asked, he would have said that he had forgiven Seth for what he'd done to his family. But Nathan had to admit, if only to himself, that if he couldn't forget it when he saw the man, he probably hadn't done a very good job of forgiving, either.

• • •

Nathan and the children weren't back yet when Naomi emerged from the grocery store. She suspected that Christmas secrets were under way, and she'd have to be careful when they returned not to look too closely at any packages.

She loaded the groceries into the buggy and closed the door. A glance down the street told her that Nathan and the children weren't even in sight. Maybe she had time to run into the harness shop for a word with Bishop Mose while she waited. Since he shared a hitching rail with the grocery, she'd be able to see when Nathan reappeared.

Patting the mare, snug under the blanket Nathan always put on when the animal had to stand in cold weather, she went quickly toward the shop door. If Bishop Mose had customers with him, her conversation would have to wait, but if not, it was in her mind to tell him that she had tried to make peace with Daad, even though it hadn't turned out well.

The shop was warm and quiet, redolent of the scents of leather and oil. New harnesses and halters hung on pegs along the wall, but much of the work was in repairing and remaking used harnesses, along with saddles and bridles belonging to the Englisch customers.

Bishop Mose sat at one of his work benches, a strip of leather in front of him, but he stood when he saw her and came to the counter, smiling. The heavy apron he wore over his clothes was stained with neat's-foot oil.

"Naomi, I thought that was you I saw going into the grocery."

She approached, feeling the familiar sense of welcome that always seemed to flow from the bishop. "I'm waiting for Nathan and the kinder to return from doing some shopping, so I thought I would drop in to see you."

"And to tell me something, I think?" His shrewd blue gaze rested knowingly.

Her throat tightened. "Ja. I spoke to my daad, to say how sorry I am for the breach between us. I tried to explain why I prefer working for Nathan to moving in with my brother. But he seemed . . ."

She stopped, not sure she wanted to bring up Daad's assumption about her and Nathan.

"Ja?" Bishop Mose waited, seeming patient enough for however long this conversation might take.

She ought to tell him everything, so that he heard it from her and no one else. "He had heard some foolish talk about Nathan perhaps wanting to marry me." She suspected her cheeks had turned scarlet. It would be a relief to press her cold hands against them, but she didn't. "When I told him I was sure Nathan had no such idea, I thought that would reassure him, but it just made him angry. He wouldn't listen to me, and he said that if I wouldn't agree to do as he said, he had nothing else to say to me."

Tears stung her eyes, and she tried to blink them back. There had been moments when she'd been able to forget Daad's words, but talking about them brought the pain back.

"This has hurt you." The bishop's voice was quiet, maybe even weary with the weight of his people's problems.

"Ja. I do not want to be at odds with my father. But what else can I do?"

He shook his head slowly. "Nothing," he said simply. "Sometimes that is the hardest answer to receive. We always think that there is something we can do, ain't so? It's hard to accept that there are times when we can't do anything except wait for the good Lord to act."

"But Daad—" *Will he ever forgive?* She couldn't seem to say the words, but Bishop Mose probably knew without her saying them.

"Your Daad is hurting himself by his unbending attitude, but he doesn't know that yet. We will have to pray that he comes to see the truth for himself."

"You are right." She managed a smile. "It is hard to do nothing."

Bishop Mose smiled in return. "Listen for God's guidance, and don't close your heart. Perhaps you'll even find that Nathan is not so opposed to marriage as you suppose."

She shook her head. The bishop was wise, but on this subject he was wrong. Despite those

316

moments in the kitchen when Nathan had touched her, she knew him well enough to know the answer.

"Nathan never thinks of that, I'm sure." *Or did he?* There had been moments when she'd seen his awareness of her. But she couldn't build hope on something so fleeting. "In his heart, he is still married to his first love."

And what of her? She had told herself she only wanted to be Nathan's friend, but was there something deeper buried in her heart? If so, she must ignore it. She was afraid to hope, and the suggestions of others that she and Nathan might marry only emphasized that if Nathan did think of marriage, it would be for the children's sake.

"Ah." Bishop Mose paused for a moment, looking at her. "Do you remember my wife?"

"Ja, of course," she said, surprised at the turn of subject. "Everyone remembers how devoted you were to each other."

"Ja, we were." He smiled, as if the memories were happy ones. "There is something everyone does not remember, though. My Sarah was not my first love."

Naomi blinked. "I didn't realize . . . No one has ever mentioned . . ." She let the words trail off, not sure what to say to this unexpected confidence.

"They have forgotten." Bishop Mose's eyes were misty, as if he were looking back into the past. "I have nearly forgotten, myself, but it is true. Sarah always knew that she was not my first love. But to my great good fortune, she was my last love." He reached across the counter to pat Naomi's hand. "Life sometimes has great surprises in store for us."

Someone else had said something like that to her, and she couldn't think who it had been. But it made sense. Certainly her life had changed completely in only a month.

"Denke, Bishop Mose." She hesitated, thinking that there was something more she should say. "I do not think that Nathan and I will ever be together, but I am content to know that I am doing what I should."

He glanced over her head, and she realized he was looking out the window. "I see Nathan and the kinder coming, so you must go. You are in my prayers."

Nodding a good-bye, she went back out to meet Nathan and the children. Joshua and Sadie came running to her, and her heart filled with love for them.

Love, yes. But not hope, because hope dashed would be too painful to bear.

Nathan climbed down the ladder from the attic, balancing the box containing Ada's nativity scene under one arm. It was dusty from not being used, and that gave him a sense of shame. He should not have let the putz sit in the attic for so long.

Sliding the ladder back into place, he closed

the attic hatch and carried the box downstairs. He had been wrong to keep Ada's putz shut away from her children for so long, but now he would make that right.

The aroma of baking lured him to the kitchen. Naomi turned from the oven, smiling, and deposited a sheet of Peppernuts onto the cooling rack.

Sadie, standing on a chair at the counter, clapped her hands. "Can I taste one, Naomi? Please?"

"They must cool first, or you will have a scalded tongue." She glanced at him. "Besides, I think your daad has something to show you."

"Ja, I do." He set the box on the end of the table. "But where is Joshua?"

"He's outside, helping Isaiah and your daad finish up some shoveling."

A fresh layer of snow had fallen overnight, delighting the kinder. Naomi gave Nathan an assessing glance, as if to wonder whether that would arouse his protective instincts.

"They will see that he doesn't get hurt, I know. But Daad should not be shoveling." Frowning, he headed toward the door.

"But, Daadi, what's in the box?" Sadie hopped down from her chair to pursue him.

"I know," Naomi said, answering him, not the child. "But I also know it's impossible to keep your daad from doing what he thinks he should. That's why Isaiah and Joshua are there, sharing the shoveling with him."

Nathan nodded, admitting the truth of what Naomi said. No one could convince Daad he couldn't do everything he used to.

"Maybe I can get him to komm in and see this, as well." He nodded toward the box and then smiled at Sadie, her hands clutched in eagerness. "Just be patient, my little girl. As soon as Joshua and Grossdaadi are here, I'll show you what that box has in it."

Naomi headed for the stove. "Some hot cocoa wouldn't go amiss, I'm thinking. Maybe by then the Peppernuts will be ready to eat. Can you get some mugs out, Sadie?"

She nodded, dashing toward the cabinet while Nathan went out the back door.

He realized he was smiling. Naomi was having such a good effect on Sadie. A month ago she'd have been wailing about opening the box right this minute, and now she was cheerfully helping Naomi while she waited.

How had Naomi come by such skill? By having inherited the responsibility for her younger brothers and sisters when she was so young herself? Perhaps it was simply a God-given gift. If so, God had blessed Nathan's family with that gift, too.

Getting everyone to stop shoveling involved some negotiating, but finally Nathan had all of them inside, shedding coats and mufflers and exclaiming at how wonderful gut the cookies smelled.

"Pfeffernuse," Daad exclaimed, bending over the cookies to inhale, giving them the Pennsylvania Dutch name. "I haven't had these since your mamm used to make them. Smell the spice in them."

"You can eat, not just smell," Naomi said, sliding some warm cookies onto a plate. "Komm, sit down. There is coffee, and the hot chocolate will be ready in a moment."

"Now will you tell us what's in the box, Daadi?" Sadie slid onto her chair while Joshua pulled off his boots.

"Ja." Nathan lifted the lid off and was visited by a sudden memory of Ada packing the figures away after that last Christmas they had together. She had put the newspaper, now yellowing, around each of the figures. She . . .

He swallowed, pushing away the thoughts. This was about the kinder, not about him. He lifted out the topmost figure—a shepherd holding a lamb in his arms.

"It's the putz." Joshua crowded close to him. "I remember. We put it up at Christmastime."

"I remember, too," Sadie echoed, but Nathan felt quite sure she didn't. His throat tightened.

"The putz helps us remember the story of Christmas," Naomi said, as if she knew he needed help. "We can look at the shepherds, the animals, the wise men, and the angels all there to worship the baby Jesus."

"There is a stable, ain't so?" Joshua furrowed his forehead. "I think Mammi had us put fresh straw in it."

Nathan couldn't speak for the pictures that were crowding his mind, so again, Naomi did it for him.

"I'm sure your mammi did. This was her putz when she was a little girl, and I remember her putting straw around it every year. We used to play with it when I came to see her, telling each other the story of that first Christmas."

Nathan stepped back from the table, inviting Naomi to take over with a quick gesture of his head. She slipped into the chair nearest the box.

"Let's see what else we can find." She handed a wrapped figure to each of the children to open, and they aahed with the appearance of a golden-winged angel and a gray donkey.

Isaiah leaned over the box, his face as excited as those of the children. "We had one of these when we were little, remember, Naomi? You brought it out and we set it up while you told us the Christmas story."

"Let's do that," Sadie said instantly. "Tell us the story, Naomi."

"I think we should get the straw first," Joshua said, not willing to give up the one detail he had remembered. "And decide where to set it up. It can't stay on the kitchen table."

"Why not?" Sadie demanded. "I want it here."

"Joshua is right," Naomi intervened. "Once we

have all the pieces out, we will find a spot for the putz in the living room, where we can look at it and remember the story and tell it every day. But Sadie is right, too. We can tell the story while we get the pieces out. We will tell it many times in the next few weeks, because it is a very important story, ain't so?"

The kinder nodded, both mollified. They continued to uncover the pieces. Naomi began telling the story, her narrative interrupted by interjections from Isaiah and comments from the kinder as each figure emerged from its wrappings.

Nathan took a few steps back from the hubbub around the table and realized Daad was standing beside him, watching.

"I am ser glad you got Ada's putz out again," Daad said, his voice quiet. "It is gut for the kinder to have it. They will remember their mamm as well as remember the story of Christmas."

"Ja." Nathan's throat still seemed too tight to say more. He didn't regret the decision to get out the putz, but he hadn't expected it to provoke such strong feelings.

"Christmas is a time for missing the ones we love who have gone on ahead of us." Daad seemed to know exactly what he was thinking. "I long for your mamm more at this time of year. Sorrows seem deeper, but joy seems brighter, as well. And Naomi has brought much joy to this house, I think."

Daad's words startled Nathan. They confused him a little, as well.

But they were true, weren't they? He could see for himself how happy the kinder were under Naomi's guidance. And he knew how happy he was to have Naomi here, as well.

He felt a moment of panic. What was he thinking? Naomi could not take Ada's place. No one could. And yet he couldn't seem to get the idea out of his head.

Chapter Nineteen

To Naomi, the days seemed to fly past. That always happened in the weeks leading up to Christmas, but this year she was busier than she'd been since Isaiah and her sisters were small and she'd had all the running of the house to do as well.

The doll she was making for Sadie was nearly finished. It had taken longer than she expected, since she could only work on it in the evenings after she'd returned to the grossdaadi house. Sadie was too inquisitive, and there was no place at Nathan's where she might easily hide it. Tonight she was putting the final stitches in the cape, sitting in her rocker near the stove in her small, cozy kitchen.

Naomi let the sewing rest on her lap for a moment as her gaze moved around the room. Even though she spent most of her time at the farmhouse, she still appreciated the fact that here she had her own things around her—the rag rug on the floor that Grossmammi had made, the chair where her mamm had rocked the kinder, the tea towels her sister had made for her hung neatly on their hooks.

Despite the grief Naomi felt over the breach with her father, she was content. That was what she'd told Bishop Mose, and she believed it was true. Still, she couldn't help the tiny hope in her heart as every day seemed to bring Nathan closer to her. Perhaps, one day . . .

A flicker of light from the driveway between the houses startled her, even as she heard the crunch of tires on the gravel. Who would be coming to see her after dark? More likely it would be someone for Isaiah and Libby.

But the car drew into the pull-off by her back porch, and she heard women's voices along with the slam of car doors. It must be Paula—who else could it be?

She hurried to the door and swung it open. Paula, for sure, stepping carefully over a patch of snow, but it wasn't Hannah, her niece, with her. It was Leah Glick.

"Paula, Leah, wilkom." She couldn't help an edge of anxiety in her voice. "Is anything wrong?"

"What could be wrong?" Paula pressed a cold cheek against hers. "Ach, that old heater of mine doesn't work so well anymore. I near froze Leah to death getting here."

"It wasn't any colder than riding in a buggy in this weather," Leah said, already hanging up her bonnet and coat in the hall.

"Komm, schnell. The kitchen is nice and warm." Naomi hurried them in, her thoughts revolving around the unexpectedness of this visit.

Paula set a laden basket on the table. "I wanted to bring you some Christmas goodies to share with the kinder. I'm sure you have cookies of your own, but what is the sense of being a baker if I cannot share with my friends?"

Naomi smiled and nodded, moving automatically to put the kettle on, but concern threaded along her nerves. Leah was not saying enough, and Paula was saying too much. Something other than Christmas cookies had brought them here tonight.

She looked from Paula, still chattering about the bakery, to Leah, who smiled but avoided her eyes.

"What is it?" She interrupted Paula's tale of the number of jars of honey she'd sold. "I can see that something is wrong. Please, just tell me what it is." Her mind leaped ahead to possible answers. "Something is wrong with Daad? Or one of Elijah's family?"

"No, no, nothing like that." Leah put an arm around her waist and guided her to a chair. "I told Paula you would guess there was a problem the minute we came in."

"Ja, well, no point in starting out with trouble," Paula said, her voice a little testy. "We'll sit down here, and when the kettle boils we'll have a nice cup of tea, and we'll talk about it."

Naomi sat, clutching Leah's hand. "Tell me."

The two women exchanged glances, as if neither one was willing to start. Then Leah nodded, accepting responsibility.

"There are rumors flying around the valley. You have not heard anything?"

"If you mean about Daad talking to Bishop Mose about me—"

"Ach, no, that is old news," Paula said. Her round, kindly face was set in worried lines that contrasted sharply with her usual good humor. "This is about you and Nathan."

Leah's fingers tightened on Naomi's. "Ugly talk has started, and no one seems to know with whom. But they are saying something is improper in your relationship with Nathan."

"Improper—" Naomi could hardly take it in. "But that's ridiculous." Impossible, that her friends and neighbors could be saying such a thing about her. "Surely no one believes such a foolish rumor could be true."

Leah and Paula exchanged a look.

327

"This is more than an idle rumor, I'm afraid." Leah's blue eyes were dark with worry.

"The talk is about a particular night. They are saying that someone saw that you didn't come home from Nathan's until nearly morning." Paula rushed the words out, as if she were giving nasty medicine and eager to get it over with as quickly as possible.

"We have both heard it from different sources," Leah said. "We each had the same reaction—that it was foolish and wicked to say such a thing."

"We both tried to stamp it out right away." Paula looked as if she wanted to trample someone or something underfoot. "But it was like a wildfire. As soon as I'd scold one person for saying it, the story would pop up someplace else, even worse."

"But I didn't. I wouldn't." Naomi's hand twisted in Leah's. "You know that about me."

"Of course we do. We know you well enough, and plenty of others do, as well. But still, there is the talk. Was there something . . . anything . . . that might have led to folks misunderstanding?" Leah leaned toward her, face intent.

"It must have been the night Sadie was sick." Naomi pressed her fingers to her forehead, trying to make sense of it all when her stomach was churning so badly she wanted to throw up. "She came down with the croup just when I was getting ready to leave for the day. Nathan didn't know what to do. I had to stay and take care of her."

"There, I knew there was an answer," Paula said, relief in her voice. "No one could expect you to leave a sick child."

"We were sure there would be some explanation," Leah said, echoing the thought. "But you can understand how it looks. What time was it when you came back to the house?"

"It must have been close to three in the morning. I know it was about two when I got her to sleep after the final attack." And then she'd stayed still longer, listening to Nathan, holding him while he wept. But she couldn't say that, not to anyone. "I suppose it looks bad, but there was nothing improper. I had to stay until I felt sure Sadie was well."

"Nathan will back you up, for sure, but people with nasty minds will say that he would anyway. What about Isaiah and Libby? Did they come over?" Leah asked, her mind obviously lining up a defense for Naomi.

"Isaiah came to the farmhouse to check when he didn't see lights here." She gestured around the kitchen. "He knows that Sadie had the croup."

"If he stayed to bring you home . . ." Paula began, but Naomi was already shaking her head.

"I knew it would be a long siege, and I didn't want both he and Nathan losing a night's sleep when they had to be up for the milking so early. I sent him home."

"That's too bad. If he'd stayed, he could have

scotched the rumors in a hurry." Paula shook her head. "So there's no one to say when you came home."

The kettle whistled, and Paula rose with a light touch on Naomi's shoulder. The clink of cups was a soothing and somehow incongruous background to the turmoil in Naomi's thoughts and the pain in her heart.

"But that is exactly what someone is saying," Leah said, frowning at Paula. "You're forgetting how exact the story was. Someone seems to know what time it was when you came back to the house. Someone knows about that night. How? Who could possibly know about it and feel enough ill will toward Naomi to spread a rumor?"

Memory came back, sharp and clear. "There was something," she said slowly. "When I was walking back here in the darkness, I heard something unexpected."

"What?" Leah shot the word at her.

She shook her head helplessly. "I'm not sure. I'd been looking up at the stars, thinking how beautiful the sky was, maybe not paying a lot of attention. I just knew that there was some sound that I didn't expect."

"A car going by on the road?" Leah asked. "Maybe someone saw you."

"I'm sure it wasn't that, because I'd have noticed the lights of a car." She shrugged. "The nearest I can come is that it might have been the creak of a buggy or wagon, but I just don't know. And anyway, sound carries a long way at night. It could have been something at a distance."

It was Leah's turn to shake her head. "Maybe, but I'm not ready to dismiss it as a coincidence."

Paula cleared her throat, as if preparing to say something unpleasant. "I hate to say it, Naomi, but do you think it's possible your daad would spy on you? Or that he would say such a thing if he thought it would make you do as he wants?" She set a cup of tea in front of Naomi and pushed the sugar bowl nearer.

"I can't believe that of him." She got the words out quickly, but a shadow of doubt lingered. She would not have expected Daad to do a lot of things he'd done lately.

"Well, who else?" Paula asked, her tone practical. "I don't see anyone else with a grudge against Naomi."

"I can think of one." Leah's gaze sought hers. "Jessie Miller has been downright nasty about Naomi taking over with her sister's kinder."

"But how would she know about that night? How could anyone know?" The more they talked, the more impossible it seemed to Naomi. "I can't seriously believe anybody would be out in the cold watching on the chance of catching me doing something wrong."

"Maybe Isaiah said something in all innocence, and it got repeated in the wrong quarters," Leah said. "After all, he wouldn't think it necessary to keep your being at the farmhouse a secret. You were just doing what you've always done in taking care of a child."

"Ja, or even Nathan or his daad might have said something," Paula added. "Things get out, one way or another, it seems. Well, at least now that we know what really happened, we can fight the rumor with the truth."

"Some people would rather believe the rumor." Little though Naomi wanted to say it, she knew it was true. Rumors were easy to start but not so easy to stop. Her cheeks burned at the thought of what people were saying and thinking about her.

"One thing is certain-sure. You must talk to Nathan about it." Leah was using her school-teacher voice, the one that assumed obedience.

"How can I?" Naomi wanted to weep in pain and frustration. "How can I possibly say something like that to Nathan?"

"If you don't tell him, he'll find out from someone else. It's better that he hears it from you." Paula hesitated. "Do you want us to be with you when you talk to him?"

"No." She fought to smile. "You are right. This is for me to do."

No matter how much Naomi dreaded it, Leah was right. It was better for Nathan to hear it from her, so he was forewarned. But how he was going to take it, she couldn't begin to imagine.

• • •

As they finished the midday meal, Nathan took a second look at Naomi. Her eyes seemed heavy and shadowed, and there had been a tension about her since she'd arrived this morning, although she'd been as patient as she always was with the children.

He hoped she wasn't getting sick, with Christmas just a few days away. It might be selfish, but he didn't want anything to disrupt the joy of this holy season.

There was no doubt about it, he decided. His thought was definitely selfish. Of course he wanted Naomi to be well for her own sake, not just for theirs.

The children were scrambling down from their chairs when Naomi turned to his daad. "I'm sure the kinder would like to take an apple to the pony. Would you go with them?"

"I will," Nathan said. "Let . . ." He stopped, realizing he was getting a distinct, if wordless, message from Naomi.

Daad had already headed for the hall and his coat, shooing the kinder ahead of him. "Komm, let's go and see what Coalie is doing, ja?"

"I'll get the apples," Joshua said, darting for the basket they kept in the cool back hall.

"Me, too," Sadie said.

The door closed on their chatter, and Nathan turned to Naomi. "You have something upsetting you to talk to me about, ain't so?"

Naomi nodded. The pain in her eyes shocked him, and he realized she must have been hiding it all day. A bad feeling sank into him. Naomi might be going to tell him that she'd decided she must do what her father wanted. He knew how much the breach with her daad had grieved her.

It had always been a possibility she'd give in to her father to keep peace in the family. He should have been prepared. Instead, all he could do was wonder what life would be like here without her. How had she become so indispensable to his happiness in such a short time?

Not his, he corrected himself quickly. The children's happiness.

"Naomi, what is wrong? Has your father been making you unhappy?" *Please don't say you're moving out.*

But that question simply generated a surprised expression. "No, no. It's nothing about Daad." She sucked in a breath and took hold of the nearest chair back with both hands. "Last night Paula came to see me. With Leah Glick."

"Ja?" It must have been more than just a friendly visit if it had left Naomi this upset.

She nodded, obviously having difficulty getting the words out. "They said—they told me—" She closed her eyes for an instant. "They said that people are talking about us. About you and me and that night I stayed late when

334

Sadie was ill. Saying that something went on."

"Something went on?" His mind was blank. "What went on was that Sadie had croup and you took care of her."

"No." Color mounted in her cheeks. "They are saying that something improper went on between you and me that night."

He could only stare at her. "Leah and Paula think that about us?"

"No, of course not. But they both heard the same rumors yesterday."

Anger flicked its tail in him like an upset animal. "So they rushed out here to tell you and make you feel bad? They'd do better to mind their own business."

"Ach, Nathan, Paula and Leah had only my well-being at heart. How could they not tell me that folks were saying such things? I had to be prepared to deal with it."

He could only be surprised that Naomi had allowed a few rumors to upset her so much. "I don't see what you—we—can do. If people are determined to talk, they'll talk. Don't worry. Those who know us won't believe it, and the others will soon go on to some other gossip."

"Don't you see how serious it is?" A flash of something that might have been anger lit her eyes. "People are accusing us of sin."

"Wait." He held up a hand. "No one is accusing us, ain't so? People are passing around a rumor, that's all. They should be ashamed of themselves. We have done nothing wrong."

She shook her head as if impatient with his dullness. "Nathan, don't you understand? Someone started this story, and they knew about the night I stayed so late. How did they know? Who told them? And how can we defend ourselves? It is true that I was here until nearly daybreak."

"Taking care of a sick child," he reminded her, still unable to take this seriously. People were always talking. That was part of living in a small community where everyone knew everyone else's business. "Just because a few blabbermauls chose to make the worst of that fact doesn't mean that people we know will believe it. As for how they knew about it . . ."

He hesitated, the unpalatable truth sinking in. How would anyone know? It was not as if they had any near neighbors. The only house in sight was Isaiah's place and the grossdaadi house.

"You walked across the field to go home, ja?" he asked abruptly.

She nodded.

"I suppose someone passing could have seen your flashlight from the road." He knew even as he said it how unlikely it was that anyone had passed by at that hour. And even if they had, the logical assumption would have been that it was Isaiah.

Naomi rubbed her arms as if she were cold. "I would have noticed if someone had been passing on the road. This feeling that someone wishes me ill . . . it's not very nice."

"No." He could point out that he was a target as well, but that would hardly make Naomi feel any better, and at this moment, that was the most important thing. "Maybe we should talk to Bishop Mose about it." Before someone else does. That was the thought in his mind.

She glanced at him. "Talk to the bishop?" The color came up in her cheeks again and then drained away almost as quickly, leaving her white and strained. "Nathan, do you think that Jessie could be the one spreading rumors about us?"

"Jessie?" His first instinct was to scoff, but he controlled himself. "Jessie is troubled, I know. And she has some funny ideas about you taking care of the kinder. But how could she possibly know anything about the night Sadie was sick?"

"I don't know," Naomi admitted. "Could Isaiah or your daad have mentioned it someplace that she got to hear about it? Or did you talk about it to Emma when you went to see her?"

"I did tell her about Sadie having the croup, but nothing about how long it lasted or how late you stayed." He shook his head. "Jessie has a reckless tongue, I grant you, but I don't see how she could have known enough to spread such a rumor."

He moved closer to Naomi, wanting to put a

comforting hand on her shoulder but not quite daring to. This ridiculous rumor had made it impossible to behave naturally, and his anger welled up again.

"Naomi, I still think—"

The back door opened, and there was Isaiah, wiping his boots on the mat.

Nathan's frustration mounted. "Isaiah, can you leave us alone for a bit? We're talking."

"I can't." Isaiah looked scared and determined, and he was nearly as white in the face as Naomi was. "I bring a message from Bishop Mose. He wants to see you this afternoon at four at our house. He's bringing one of the ministers with him."

The words fell into a shocked silence. Nathan had been wrong. Naomi was right to be concerned. They were being called before the bishop and the minister to account for themselves.

The ticking of the clock was Naomi's only company as she waited for it to be time to go across the lane to Isaiah's house. She had paced around the little house for a while, but now she simply sat in the rocking chair, her hands loose in her lap.

She had wept. She had prayed. But she had no answers. All she could hope now was that whatever happened, it was God's will.

Pushing gently with her feet, she was soothed

by the creaking of the old rocking chair and the rhythm of the movement. She could almost imagine she was a child again, sitting on Mammi's lap in this same chair.

But Mammi wouldn't be there when she faced the bishop. Daad and Betty were coming, as well as Elijah. Nathan's sister had taken Joshua and Sadie to her house.

Naomi felt a wave of gratitude for Sarah's calm good sense. She'd talked to the children cheerfully about having a holiday sleepover at her house with their cousins, planning on the popcorn balls they'd make even as she eased them into their coats.

It was a good thing someone could act normal with them. Naomi had felt too frozen, even though she'd tried, and Nathan hadn't bothered to disguise his expression that resembled a thundercloud. Surely the kinder had known something was wrong, but they'd gone off with Aunt Sarah cheerfully enough in the end.

Naomi heard the clop of hooves in the lane. A quick glance told her it was Daad's buggy, followed closely by Elijah's. Since she had no desire to face Daad's inquisition first, she'd decided that she would not go over until the bishop arrived. That would be time enough to confront all of them.

How had matters come to this pass? She still didn't quite know. If she had it all to do over again, she couldn't say that she'd do things any differently.

Please, God . . .

Her prayer seemed to end there. She couldn't think what else to say, any more than she could imagine how she was going to defend herself.

Another buggy, Bishop Mose's this time. Ready or not, she must go.

By the time she'd put her coat and bonnet on and crossed the lane, the others were already seated in Isaiah and Libby's small living room. Daad, Betty, Elijah, and Lovina sat in a row, while Isaiah and Libby hovered in the background. Nathan and his father sat opposite them, faces stoic, while Bishop Mose and John Fisher, one of the ministers, had two chairs brought in from the kitchen and placed at the end of the room.

Libby came quickly to greet Naomi, her voice as hushed as if it was a funeral. She took Naomi's coat and bonnet, squeezed her hand, and then vanished toward the hall to hang them up.

One chair was left, next to Betty. Naomi slipped into it, eyes downcast. Daad leaned forward, looking past Betty at her, his mouth opening to say something, but Bishop Mose got in first.

"We are all here, so I will begin." The bishop's voice could have a note of command when he wished, and it did now. "I am sorry this call is necessary. However, when I heard the rumors that some people have been spreading in our community, it seemed important to deal with the situation right away, before the talk becomes any worse. Truly the unbridled tongue can be an instrument of destruction."

The room was completely silent; not even the ticking of a clock sounded. Naomi imagined that she felt Bishop Mose's gaze resting on her, and for an instant she couldn't breathe.

"No formal charge of improper behavior has been brought against Nathan and Naomi. I would rather dismiss this story as unfounded rumor, but a specific night has been mentioned repeatedly. Naomi, is it correct that on last Wednesday night you did not leave Nathan's house until nearly dawn?"

"Ja, that is true." She heard a quick, indrawn breath from someone, but that was all. She prayed to keep her voice steady. "Sadie became ill with croup just when I was ready to leave at about seven thirty. She has never had it before, and it was a bad attack. I could not leave Nathan alone to deal with it, so I stayed until I felt sure she could sleep through the rest of the night. It was nearly three by the time I walked back here to my house."

That was her defense, and she could do no more. She felt a little surprised that the words had come out so easily. She expected more questions from Bishop Mose, but he turned instead to Nathan.

"Nathan, is Naomi's account of what happened correct?"

"Ja." The word sounded as if it had been chipped from a block of ice. "Sadie started to cough. It was a terrible sound, like she was choking. I didn't know what to do, but Naomi did." Nathan kept his eyes focused on the bishop. "If she hadn't been there, I don't know what I would have done."

The bishop nodded, and it seemed to Naomi that a little of the tension went out of the room. "I understand that Isaiah has something to contribute."

Isaiah, realizing that all eyes were on him, flushed. "Ja. I . . . We noticed that no lights were on in Naomi's place, and she is always back by around eight at the latest. So I walked over to the farmhouse to see if everything was all right." He seemed to run out of steam.

Naomi's heart twisted. It was unfair that her little brother should be brought into this and forced to speak before the bishop.

"And what did you find?" Bishop Mose asked, his tone encouraging.

"Like Naomi and Nathan said." Isaiah's Adam's apple bobbed. "They were in the kitchen, and Naomi had been treating Sadie with a steam tent. Like she used to treat me," he added with a quick smile.

"You did not stay?" John Fisher asked, speaking for the first time.

Isaiah shrugged. "There was nothing for me to

do, and I would have to be up early to do the milking. Besides, I knew Naomi would take gut care of the little girl."

Bishop Mose nodded. His gaze moved from Isaiah to her. "Naomi, has there been any improper behavior between you and Nathan?"

"No." She kept her eyes fixed on his face, feeling that he would know she was telling the truth.

He nodded, and then turned to Nathan. "Nathan, has there been anything improper in your relationship with Naomi?"

"No." Nathan's mouth clamped shut.

Bishop Mose nodded again. He looked around the room from one face to another. "Does anyone know how this rumor might have started?"

Silence again. Jessie's face appeared in Naomi's mind, but she pushed it resolutely out again. She would not cast suspicion on another without proof.

"Very well." Bishop Mose shot a glance at John Fisher, and some wordless communication seemed to pass between them. "I am satisfied that no wrong has been committed here, save by the people who have repeated an unfounded rumor. There is no blame attached to Naomi for her actions in nursing a child in her care, nor to Nathan for allowing it. Does anyone have something to add?"

Daad slapped his hands on his knees, the sound

sharp in the stillness. "I am not satisfied. My daughter is still the subject of rumors and slanderous talk."

"If I can find the one who has started the rumors, that person will be brought before the congregation," Bishop Mose said.

"And if not?" Daad's face was red, and he ignored the placating hand Betty laid on his arm. "The talk doesn't matter so much to Nathan. It is always the woman who carries the blame."

"It matters to me." Nathan was angry. She didn't think she'd ever seen him angry, not like this, anyway. His fists were clenched, and he shot to his feet as if he couldn't sit still for another minute. "It matters. I don't want folks talking about Naomi any more than you do. Or talking about me, and my kinder maybe hearing about it."

"Then do something." Daad shot the words at him.

"All right. I will do something." Nathan's voice was loud in the room. "I will marry Naomi, and that will stop the rumors once and for all."

Every eye in the room turned toward Naomi. She prayed for the floor to open up and swallow her, for an earthquake to hit, anything rather than having Nathan proposing to her out of anger and embarrassment.

They were waiting. All of them waiting for her answer.

Two things were suddenly very clear to her. She

loved Nathan King with all her heart. And she could not possibly marry him, not like this.

She rose, surprised to find that her legs could hold her up. She faced Nathan.

"No," she said clearly. "I will not marry you." She turned and walked out, aware of the stunned silence behind her.

Chapter Twenty

Naomi went back to the grossdaadi house. Where else could she go? She didn't know, just as she didn't know what she was going to do next.

The family wouldn't leave her alone for long. She ought to be making plans so that she'd have something to say to them.

Naomi pressed her hands to her face, feeling tears sting her eyes. How could she have said no to Nathan right out in front of everyone?

A flicker of anger went through her. As well ask how he could have proposed marriage to her in that way. She just prayed he would not attempt to talk to her.

The back door opened, and Naomi's breath caught in her throat. But it was Lovina, thank the good Lord. She could just about bear to talk to Lovina.

She started to rise, but Lovina reached her

quickly and pushed her back down in the rocking chair.

"Sit," she said. She pulled one of the straight chairs from the table over next to her. "And I will sit, too, unless you want to kick me out." Her smile was a bit anxious.

Naomi shook her head. "I knew someone would come. I am glad it is you."

Lovina's smile became wider. "Ach, you threw the cat among the pigeons for sure when you turned Nathan down and walked out."

"I didn't mean to hurt him." She pressed her fingertips to her lips for an instant, but words already spoken could not be called back.

"He'll get over it." Lovina's tone didn't promise much sympathy for Nathan. "As soon as you were gone, your daad started in again on how he'd said all along that you should have come to us, and if everyone only did what he said, we'd all be happier."

"I'm sorry." She'd involved them in her troubles, it seemed.

"Don't be," Lovina said. "I did what I should have done before. I came right out and said I wouldn't be happier, because I didn't want to work in the store, I wanted to stay at home and take care of my own children. And Elijah tried to shush me, but I said he was just as bad, and he knew how I felt so why didn't he have courage enough to tell his daad."

"Lovina, you didn't." Naomi, caught between laughter and tears, could only stare at her sister-in-law.

"I did. And that shut the both of them up, I can tell you. And then Nathan—"

"He's not going to try and talk to me, is he?" Panic ripped through her. "I can't see him now."

"I can't promise he won't want to see you sometime soon, but it won't be tonight. Betty up and told him to his face that it was no wonder you'd turned him down, the ham-handed way he went about asking you to marry him. And when Daad tried to lay blame on Nathan, she turned on him and told him that he was at fault just as much or more."

Naomi's head threatened to split open. "I can't imagine—What on earth did the bishop think of all those goings-on?"

Lovina shrugged. "He just smiled. He told me to make them leave you alone for a bit. After he left, I got rid of Nathan and convinced Elijah to mind his own business. But Daad is outside waiting, and I think he won't go home without seeing you, at least for a minute."

Naomi might have known her father would have to have the last word. She nodded, the movement a bit shaky. "Ja, all right."

Lovina stood, and then she bent to hug her. "You were right about the coming boppli," she

347

whispered. "And we stand behind you, whatever you decide to do."

She had gone to the door before Naomi could find the words to thank her.

There was a murmur of voices, and then Daad and Betty came into the kitchen. Naomi rose, not wanting to face Daad sitting down if he was going to scold her.

But her father didn't look as if he were in a scolding mood. In fact, he seemed a bit ashamed, or maybe embarrassed. Betty had to nudge him to get him started.

"Naomi, I . . . I hope you are all right." He glanced at Betty, and then looked at his shoes. "I should not have spoken . . . carried on the way I did."

No one could not say it didn't matter, because it did. It had precipitated that foolish offer of marriage from Nathan, and that was no small matter.

"Denke, Daadi," she said finally. "I appreciate it." Even if Betty was making him apologize, she was grateful. She was sure now that she had underestimated Betty.

Daad met her gaze then. He took a step toward her, and his face worked as if emotions threatened to overcome him. "I am sorry," he said again, his voice husky. "I should not have let a wall grow between us. You are a gut daughter, Naomi."

A sob broke loose from her control, and she

went quickly into his arms, feeling them close around her, inhaling the familiar scent of him. "Denke, Daadi," she whispered. "I love you."

He hugged her as if she were a small child again, and then he let her go. "Gut, gut. And if you want to komm home, you are wilkom."

She didn't, but she appreciated the offer more than she could say. "I must think about what I am going to do."

Daad opened his mouth as if he planned to tell her. Then he closed it again. He nodded.

"You will tell us when you decide," he said. "We are your family. We will stand with you, whatever the decision is."

He edged toward the door, and Naomi suspected he would be glad to leave the emotional displays behind. She hugged Betty, whispering her thanks in Betty's ear. Betty nodded, and in a moment they were gone.

Naomi was alone. Now she could think about what she meant to do. The only trouble was that she didn't have any idea.

The house had been so empty when Nathan awoke that it set up lonely echoes in his heart. He'd been eager to leave it behind to come out to the barn for the morning milking. He leaned against the warm side of a cow and aimed a squirt of milk at the barn cat, who lapped it from her whiskers and then set about busily washing her face.

He couldn't distract himself from his troubles so easily. The children were safe with his sister, for the moment. But what about when they came home? And what about Naomi?

He'd made a mess of that situation, and it was his own fault. If he hadn't let Sam Esch make him angry, if he'd simply let the bishop handle Sam, everything would be back to normal by now.

Well, maybe not normal. Folks would still be talking, but when Bishop Mose's attitude became known, the talk would die off.

The clop of hooves announced Daad's arrival. At least the effort of talking to Daad might take his mind off his troubles.

"You are here early," he said.

Daad slid the barn door closed behind him, cutting out the cold. "Ja." He rubbed his hands together to warm them as he approached the next cow in the row. "Thought maybe you'd want to talk before Isaiah got here."

So it looked as if there was no avoiding the subject. At least, as Daad settled on the milking stool, Nathan couldn't see his face.

"The kinder are all right?" he asked, delaying the moment when they'd have to talk about what had happened yesterday.

"Ja, they are fine. Sarah kept them all so busy they were ready to fall into bed when the time came." The rhythmic sound of the milk hitting the pail punctuated his words. "But soon they will ask questions. What will you tell them?"

"I don't know." The cow flicked her tail, maybe picking up on his edginess. "I made a mess of things, didn't I?"

Daad grunted. "You were ferhoodled for sure, asking Naomi to marry you in that way."

"I know, I know. I let Sam make me mad, and now I've hurt Naomi. If I'd just kept quiet, well, it might have been awkward for a while, but she'd be back here where she belongs."

"I doubt she thinks she belongs here now," Daad said, not letting him off easy.

"I was stupid. I know."

"The women lost no time in letting you know what they thought of you, that's certain-sure." There might have been a smile in Daad's voice over the way Lovina and Betty had reacted.

"At least they blamed Sam, as well," Nathan said.

"That is not a defense for what you did."

"I know," he agreed hurriedly. Daad might be soft-spoken, but he never made light of it when one of his children did something wrong and tried to get out of the blame. "Naomi has been nothing but kind and generous to the kinder and to me. And in return I insulted her with that stupid proposal."

Daad didn't speak for a moment. Nathan heard the scrape of his milking stool, and then Daad

351

appeared, standing there looking at him with a question in his face.

"The way you did it was stupid, that's certain-sure. But is it such a far-fetched idea, marrying Naomi?"

Nathan opened his mouth and then shut it again. He would not admit that when he'd thought about being married to Naomi, it had seemed . . . what? Comforting? Right?

"I don't think—"

The evasion he was fumbling for didn't have to be spoken, since the barn door slid open and Isaiah came in. Daad could hardly think Nathan would talk about Naomi in front of her brother.

Isaiah unwrapped the muffler that covered his mouth. "I will take over for you, Nathan. You are needed back at the house."

"Naomi?" He stood up so quickly he knocked the milking stool over.

Isaiah shook his head, frowning a little. "No. I have not seen her this morning. It is Jessie Miller, here already and wanting to know where the kinder are."

Jessie. Nathan exchanged glances with Daad. What on earth was Jessie doing here this time in the morning? He shrugged. Whatever the answer, he would have to deal with it.

"Denke, Isaiah. I will go."

When he stepped outside, the cold air smacked his face, and his feet crunched on the patches of icy snow. He heard steps behind him and turned to see Daad coming, too.

He waited until Daad caught up with him and looked a question at him, smiling a little. "Do you think I cannot handle Jessie on my own?"

Daad did not have a returning smile. "Maybe so, maybe not. But with Jessie—I think it best that you not be alone with her."

Nathan could only stare at his father. "Why? What do you think might happen?"

Daad shrugged, his face setting in determined lines. "Jessie is unpredictable. I think maybe Naomi has been right in thinking Jessie needs help."

Nathan turned this unexpected comment over in his mind. How many times had he made the excuses Ada had always made, ones Emma continued to make? Jessie was immature. Jessie was emotional. She just needed to grow up a bit. The familiar phrases sounded hollow.

He glanced at Daad as they reached the steps. "Are you thinking that it was Jessie who started the rumors about me and Naomi? But she couldn't have known."

Daad didn't answer. He just walked up to the door and paused, letting Nathan go inside first.

The instant Nathan stepped into the kitchen, Jessie spun toward him.

"Nathan!" She reached out as if to hug him. Daad moved from behind him, and she froze. "Ezra." She nodded toward him.

"Jessie, what are you doing here?" Nathan said. "You should not be out this early. It must not have been light yet when you left home." He moved toward the stove, busying himself with pouring a mug of coffee for Daad.

"Why shouldn't I be here?" She elbowed him aside. "I will do the coffee. You don't need to bother." She swung around with the mug so quickly that some of the coffee sloshed out. She didn't seem to notice, handing it to Daad.

Daad nodded his thanks. Setting the mug on the table, he began taking his jacket off, moving deliberately as if announcing that he was here to stay.

Nathan tried to gather his thoughts. "I'm sure your mamm would be unhappy if she knew you had driven out here so early. Are you going to see her today?"

Jessie shook her head, kapp strings fluttering with the movement. "I can't go to see her. I'll be too busy here." She turned, hurrying over to the stove and picking up the coffeepot again. "I should make more coffee. Men need something hot when they're working outside on such a cold day."

Nathan seized the pot from her and set it down. "That is ser kind of you, but I don't want coffee. What do you mean, you'll be busy here?"

"Watching the kinder, of course." She grabbed a dishcloth and began rubbing it over the counter

354

as if she'd wear right through the surface. "Cooking and cleaning and taking care of you and the kinder. That's what Ada would have wanted. Where are Joshua and Sadie? I want to see them." She dropped the cloth as quickly as she'd picked it up.

Nathan felt as if his wits had slowed to molasses. What was she going on about? "The kinder are with my sister, Sarah. They're fine. You'll have to see them some other time."

"But I want them to be here. This is where they belong." She spun again, her quick movements making him dizzy, and he longed for Naomi's calm, serene presence. "I'll go and bring them home."

"No." He caught her wrists to keep her from bolting out the door and then let her go just as quickly when she leaned toward him. "I want my children to be just where they are, do you understand, Jessie? Now calm down and tell me what you are talking about."

She looked at him as if he were being dense. Maybe he was. Naomi had tried to warn him, and he hadn't listened.

"Naomi isn't going to be around here anymore. She won't be trying to take Ada's place. But you can count on me. I will take gut care of you and the children."

Nathan's stomach twisted. "No, Jessie. You will not be caring for the kinder. Do you understand what I am saying?"

She stared at him, anger flashing in her eyes. "Naomi has turned you against me. I should have known she would."

The last thing he wanted was to have Jessie direct her anger against Naomi. "This has nothing to do with Naomi. I make the decisions for my kinder."

"It's all right." The anger changed in an instant to a smile. "I understand. You think I'm not responsible enough, but I am. You'll see."

In an instant she was out the door, pulling her coat on as she went, her bonnet dangling from one hand. Before Nathan could decide if he should try to stop her, she was gone.

Daad put a hand on his shoulder. "Best to let her go. It would cause more trouble if you tried to stop her, ain't so?"

"Maybe, but one thing is sure." Responsibility weighed heavily on him. "You were right to be cautious. Something must be done about Jessie."

The sound of someone knocking sent Naomi cautiously to the back door, thinking of all the people she did not want to see today. But the visitor was Lovina, and she gestured with the suitcase she'd agreed to lend Naomi when they'd talked briefly after Daad and Betty had left the previous day.

"Lovina, komm. I'm glad it's you." She could

only hope her face wasn't showing the stain of the tears she'd shed during the night.

"I brought the suitcase," Lovina said unnecessarily, setting it down. "But are you certain-sure you want to go away, Naomi?"

She wasn't sure of anything, which seemed in itself a good reason for getting away for a bit. "I'm sure. It will be gut to spend a few days with Anna and her family." And Anna's house was a safe bus ride away from Pleasant Valley and all the gossip.

"Anna will be wonderful glad to see you, I know." Lovina took her bonnet off, showing she intended to stay.

Well, Naomi could hardly send her sister-in-law out into the cold again without something to eat and a hot drink. She reached for the kettle.

"Tea or hot chocolate?" she asked, knowing Lovina didn't have a taste for coffee when she was pregnant.

"Tea sounds gut." Lovina hung up her jacket and bonnet and took a seat at the kitchen table, where she sat looking at Naomi with a troubled frown.

"Please don't look so worried." Naomi set cups on the table and a wedge of coffee cake Libby had brought over last night. "I'm all right. It will be best to get away for a while, that's all."

"But to go right before Christmas . . ." Lovina shook her head. "I hate to think of you traveling then. Please, stay with us until after Christmas, at least. Then you can go."

"I can't." She pressed her lips together, and then she realized she had to say more. "It's not that I wouldn't enjoy Christmas with you and the family. But until all the talk has died down, I just want to be somewhere else."

"Ach, well, I'm sorry to see you go, but I do understand."

Lovina's loving concern nearly made Naomi's eyes sting. The kettle boiled, and by the time she'd poured the tea, she had regained control. She sat down opposite Lovina, who had already cut a slice of the coffee cake.

Lovina smiled. "I'm eating too much already, I know. I'm either starving or sick, it seems."

"These first few months will pass quickly," Naomi said. "Then you'll have your energy back. Have you talked to Midwife Sarah yet?"

The community's midwife was young and progressive. She always wanted to see expectant women as early as possible.

"I'm to go in after Christmas." Lovina was momentarily diverted by talk of the new boppli, but Naomi suspected that wouldn't last.

Sure enough, the concerned look appeared in her eyes again. "I understand your wanting to get away, at least until people understand that the bishop has confidence there is nothing wrong between you and Nathan. But afterward —will you go back to Nathan's children?"

Naomi pressed her palms against her cheeks. This was the question that had kept her up most of the night. What about the children? But how could she bear to go back, to be in Nathan's house every day, with the memory of that proposal that had been like a slap in the face?

I'll marry her then. Not exactly the words a woman wanted to hear. But Lovina was waiting for an answer.

"I don't see how I can. If Nathan hadn't spoken . . ." She let that trail off, Nathan's words pounding in her head again.

"Ach, Nathan is as foolish sometimes as most men can be when it comes to women. How could he think you would marry him after such a proposal?"

"He wasn't thinking at all. He doesn't want to marry me." Naomi said the words evenly, at the cost of considerable pain in her heart.

"I don't think Nathan knows what he wants." Lovina was more blunt than usual. "He convinced himself he could never love anyone else after Ada died, and now he feels guilty to think of anything else."

Naomi stared at her sister-in-law for a moment. "How did you get to be such a wise woman, Lovina Esch?"

"Ach, it's not wisdom, it's common sense." A

smile flickered across her face. "Betty saw it, too. That's why she scolded him so thoroughly. You know, I'm starting to like Betty."

Some of Naomi's tension slipped away, and she managed a smile. "I am, as well. If it hadn't been for her, I'm not sure how I'd have made peace with Daadi."

"Now that you have, you must not run away." Lovina reached across the table to clasp her hand. "No matter how people may talk or what Nathan may feel, you are still the same person you were. You have nothing to reproach yourself for."

"It's not so easy as you make it sound. And I'm not sure I am the same person I was before I came to work for Nathan."

Lovina's grip on her hand tightened. "I see. You love him, don't you?"

She may as well admit it out loud. Lovina would know if she lied. "Ja, I guess I do." She blinked back the treacherous tears. "If I didn't love Nathan, it wouldn't matter so much. I don't want to run away. I just don't see what else I can do."

Nathan couldn't help shifting restlessly as he waited at Bishop Mose's harness shop for Seth Miller to pick them up. Events had followed quickly once he'd decided that he had to speak to the bishop about Jessie.

Maybe too quickly. Should he have gone to Emma instead? But it seemed unfair to push the burden onto Emma in her current state. What could she do, tied to her wheelchair at the rehab facility?

Bishop Mose moved steadily through the shop, hanging up his apron, turning the sign on the door to CLOSED. Then he got his jacket and pulled it on.

"Seth will be on time, I think. He is used to punctuality, being a businessman out among the Englisch."

"Are you sure it was right to involve him?" Nathan couldn't help voicing his doubts.

"Seth is Jessie's older brother. Going Englisch didn't change the fact that they are his family." The bishop's tone was serene, his patience reminding Nathan of Naomi. "With Emma unable to help, Seth must take the responsibility."

"He hasn't taken the responsibility in the past."

"No. But now he has another chance to do what is right." Bishop Mose reached for the door handle. "Here he is."

A silver car pulled up in front of the harness shop. By the time the two of them reached it, Seth had come around to open the doors on the passenger side.

Bishop Mose climbed into the front without hesitation, so Nathan slid into the backseat. Once Seth resumed his place behind the wheel, he swiveled to look at them, frowning a little.

"Are you really sure this is necessary? I know

Jessie's behavior has been erratic and that my mother is worried about her. But maybe confronting her isn't the way to go about getting her help."

The bishop didn't seem any more affected by Seth's doubts than he had been by Nathan's. "I have spoken to Emma. She admitted to me that she has never seen Jessie's speech and behavior so wild. And I have talked with Lydia Beachy, Emma's next-door neighbor."

Seth gave him a sharp look. "Would she have been Lydia Weaver?"

"Ja, the same," Bishop Mose said tranquilly. "I thought you would remember her."

Nathan knew Lydia well, too. He had a lot of respect for her sound common sense. If she had told the bishop something troubling, it must be serious.

"What did Lydia say?" he asked, half wishing he didn't have to hear the answer.

"She has been troubled about Jessie since Emma first went away. She did not wish to be a tale-bearer, but she began to be worried when Jessie's horse and buggy were gone all night several times. She confronted Jessie, and Jessie insisted she had stayed with a friend." He paused. "I have checked with the friend. Jessie was not there."

Chapter Twenty-one

Seth pulled the car away from the curb, his hands tight on the wheel. Nathan felt as if there were a lead ball in the pit of his stomach. This was serious, very serious. The fact that the bishop would take such extraordinary steps testified to how concerned he was.

"I guess we don't have a choice." Seth clipped off the words. "But what are we going to do if she simply denies it?"

"It is in God's hands," Bishop Mose said.

That silenced Nathan. He wondered for a moment if Seth would make some comment, but he didn't. Apparently he accepted that, as he'd said, they had no choice.

Emma's house was about a mile from the edge of town along a sparsely traveled back road. Lydia's place was next door, but the lots were big enough that the houses weren't very close together. Lydia's orchard stretched between the houses up the gentle slope. Probably she would be able to see the lights from Emma's house. That might be what had first alerted her to the fact that Jessie wasn't where she should be.

"I have asked Lydia to meet us at the house."

Bishop Mose spoke as they turned in the lane that led to the house and beyond it to the small barn. "One of the sisters should be here, and I did not wish to bring anyone else into the business who didn't already know something of it."

Nathan nodded. "That is gut. We don't want to encourage any more rumors." He hesitated. "You are thinking that Jessie is the one who started the stories about Naomi and me, ain't so?"

The bishop got out of the car and stood for a moment, waiting until they had joined him. "One of the nights when Lydia says Jessie was not home was the night Sadie was taken ill."

Seth shot him a glance, obviously not knowing what they were talking about. But Bishop Mose did not offer an explanation. As country people always did, he went to the back door. Nathan and Seth followed, and Nathan wasn't sure which of them was the more reluctant.

It was Lydia who came to answer his knock. She nodded to Nathan, darted a quick glance at Seth, and turned to the bishop. "I have been trying to get her to sit down and have some tea, but she can't seem to stop pacing around the house." She gestured toward the living room. "I will take your coats."

"Denke, Lydia. It is gut of you to help in this way." Bishop Mose made it sound as if this was like any of the normal occasions on which an Amish neighbor helped as a matter of course.

"Why don't you brew some of your chamomile tea? That is always soothing."

Lydia nodded, taking their coats toward the row of hooks in the back hall.

Bishop Mose gathered the two of them with a glance and led the way into the living room.

Jessie was walking with quick strides across the room, and she spun around when she saw them. Ignoring the other two, she zeroed in on Nathan.

"Have you come to apologize for the way you acted this morning?" she demanded. "You were rude to me."

"I did not mean to be rude to you, Jessie." Nathan kept his voice as even and patient as if he were speaking to a jittery animal. "You took me by surprise, that's all."

"Well, it's time you came to your senses. All of you." Her gaze swept the other two, and Nathan's breath caught. People didn't speak to the bishop that way. Not rational people, anyway.

"Komm, Jessie." Bishop Mose was calm but firm. He took her arm to lead her to the sofa. "You must sit down here so we can talk to you. We are worried about you."

"Nobody needs to be worried about me." She jerked her arm free. "I'm fine, and I don't want to sit down."

Seth moved quickly to take her other arm. "You don't want to talk to the bishop that way, Jessie. Think how upset Mamm would be to hear you."

Surprisingly, she allowed Seth to lead her to a seat on the couch. "Mamm's not here," she stated. "I can do what I want."

Seth sat down next to her, exchanging glances with the bishop. "What things, Jessie? Like going out at night, maybe?"

She looked down at her feet. "Maybe." She shrugged. "I can take care of myself. I don't know why anyone should worry."

"It's dangerous to drive a buggy at night," Bishop Mose said quietly. "Especially all the way out to Nathan's place on that busy road."

"I did not take the main road," she said quickly. "I went on all the back roads. It took longer, but it was safer, and no one saw me." She stopped, her face puckering a little. "Why are you asking me? How did you know I went to Nathan's?"

"Because how else would you know about Naomi staying so late the night Sadie was sick? You wouldn't tell anyone that unless you knew for sure," Bishop Mose said.

"Of course I wouldn't. I'm not a blabbermaul. But I knew Naomi would do anything to try and catch Nathan. I had to protect him from her. I knew if I watched, I'd catch her, and I did!" She ended on a triumphant note.

Nathan's stomach seemed to be turning inside out. Little Jessie, Ada's baby sister, sitting here confessing to spying on him. Ada's heart would be broken if she knew how sick Jessie was.

"You spied on Nathan and Naomi." Bishop Mose's voice had taken on a stern note. "And then you bore false witness against them, telling people they were sinning when you had no proof at all."

"I did have proof! I did!" Jessie's voice rose and her gaze darted from one to the other of them, as if she had just realized that no one agreed with her actions. "I saw Naomi leaving the house in the middle of the night with my own eyes."

"Naomi stayed because Sadie was sick . . ." he began, but Jessie didn't let him get any further.

"It's a lie." Her words shrilled out of control. "You're lying, trying to protect Naomi. You want her to take Ada's place." She lurched to her feet, throwing off Seth's restraining hand. "She's tricked you!"

Without warning she launched herself at Nathan, swinging wildly, striking his face again and again as Seth struggled to restrain her. Nathan stood motionless, bearing the blows, until finally Seth and Lydia and Bishop Mose among them wrestled Jessie onto the couch.

She deflated all in an instant, bursting into sobs and curling into a ball on the couch. Seth looked at him, face white.

"Are you okay?"

Nathan nodded. "What are we going to do?"

"The hospital emergency room first, I think," Bishop Mose said, moving so that Lydia could bend over Jessie, murmuring something soothing. "They will be able to refer her to whatever care she needs."

Seth nodded, rubbing his face with his hands. "I'll drive her there. Someone had better come with me in case—" He left that unfinished, because all of them could visualize what it could be like trying to get Jessie to the hospital if she erupted again.

"I will go," Nathan said.

"No." Bishop Mose's tone was firm. "Your presence would just remind her of her grievance against you. I will go. Maybe Lydia . . ."

"Ja, I will komm as well," Lydia said. "My mamm is with the kinder."

It felt like shirking his responsibility, but Nathan could understand the wisdom of Bishop Mose's words. Why had he not realized how serious this obsession of Jessie's was? She had come close to ruining Naomi's life out of her jealousy.

"Someone must talk to Emma about what has happened," he said. "I'll get Ben to drive me over there to explain things."

Seth nodded. "Tell her I'll come and let her know what's happening as soon as I can." He paused, looking at Nathan. "You have no reason to believe me, I guess. But I won't be dumping this responsibility onto you. I'll stay here until things are stable with my mother and my sister."

Nathan saw the resolution in Seth's face, and it

seemed to him that he could feel Ada's approval. "Ja," he said. "That is gut."

Naomi was packed and ready to leave. Soon Daad would pick her up and drive her to the bus stop in Pleasant Valley. By evening—Christmas Eve, she reminded herself—she would be with Anna and her family.

She suspected that Daad would have taken the unusual step of calling Anna to tell her what had been happening in Pleasant Valley. Anna was the tactful one of the family—she'd make sure that no one mentioned a thing about Nathan or rumors or Pleasant Valley at all.

Naomi drew the collar of her black coat more closely around her neck. The chill wind blew across the field, sending a fine spray of snow through the air. She sent a cautious glance toward Nathan's farmhouse, but no one was visible, and she thanked the good Lord for that mercy. She couldn't see Nathan yet.

She had just one thing to do before she left. She must say her good-byes to the bees.

Superstition, some rational part of her mind jeered, but in her heart she knew her feeling ran deeper than a silly belief. The bees were a part of her life. Once, when Naomi asked Grossmammi why she talked to the bees, she had said that she found peace with life's changes by speaking them aloud to the bees.

Perhaps telling the bees would help Naomi to accept, even if peace seemed in short supply right now.

Satisfied that she had reached the hives without attracting anyone's notice, Naomi pulled off her mitten and put her hand against the center hive. If she listened closely, she imagined she could hear the whirring of countless tiny wings as the bees clustered closely around the queen, keeping her warm so that all of them could survive another year.

Grossmammi seemed very close at the moment, the thought soothing and comforting, like the feel of her gentle hand stroking the back of a crying child. The way Naomi had stroked and comforted Sadie when she was sick.

No going back, she told herself. She had come here to tell the bees she was leaving, not to think of all the reasons why she longed to stay.

"I'm going away for a bit," she said to the hives, hearing the weight of the words. "I do not wish to, but I must get away for a little bit of time, at least. It is too hard to stay here."

"Because of my stupidity."

She swung around, stumbling back a step. Nathan stood there, his face grim beneath the brim of his black hat. "Naomi, I—"

"Don't, please." She put up her hand, as if she could physically hold back his words. "I didn't see you, or I wouldn't have come."

"I was in the barn when I saw you. I thought you'd go back to the house if you saw me, but I have to talk with you."

"I don't want to talk about it now." She took another step away. She could hardly run off across the field, but she wanted to.

Nathan seemed to swallow whatever he'd started to say. "I understand. But I could not let you go away without telling you about Jessie."

"Jessie?" She blinked, trying to follow him. "What about Jessie?"

"She came here early yesterday morning." Nathan spoke with deliberation, as if choosing his words. "She was talking wildly, demanding that I let her take care of the children."

Alarms seemed to go off in her heart. "The kinder weren't here to see it, were they?"

"No. Thank the gut Lord they were still with my sister. Daad was with me. We could both see that you had been right all along about Jessie. Something had to be done." He blew out a breath, and she could see it misting on the cold air. "So I went to Bishop Mose."

Pain carved lines around Nathan's eyes, and Naomi's heart went out to him. "I am sorry. But you did the right thing."

"Ja, so the bishop said." Nathan rubbed the back of his neck in the way he did when tension ran high. "It turns out Bishop Mose was already worried about Jessie. He had found out from a neighbor that ever since Emma went away, Jessie had been going out at night."

Naomi's thoughts leaped ahead to the obvious conclusion. "You think she was spying on us."

"I know she was," he corrected. "She admitted it when we confronted her."

"You and the bishop?" She cringed at the thought of what it must have been like.

"And Seth. I wasn't so sure about him, but Bishop Mose said that Seth had to be told. So the three of us went to the house late yesterday. It was . . ." He stopped, passing his palm over his eyes as if to wipe out the images.

"I'm sorry." Her heart hurt for him as well as for Jessie. "It must have been so hard to do such a thing."

"Ja, but it was needed. Seeing Jessie get so hysterical, even striking me—well, there was no doubt about what had to be done. They took her to the emergency room, and she's been admitted to the hospital." He sighed, rubbing his hand along the back of his neck again.

"That is terrible news. Poor Emma."

"Seth says they will keep her there for a few days. Then she will go somewhere else for treatment." Nathan focused on Naomi's face. "So, if you're going away because of the talk, you don't need to. Everyone in the township will soon know the truth of it."

She let out a sigh. Here they were, right back to

the subject she didn't want to talk about. But maybe it was better to be telling Nathan instead of the bees.

"That is not the only reason for my decision."

"I know. Like I said, I was stupid and angry, and that is not a gut combination. I hurt you by asking you to marry me in such a way."

Her throat was too tight to speak, but it wasn't necessary, was it? He already knew what he had done.

"I don't blame you for saying no to me, Naomi. But won't you at least think about marriage?"

"Marrying you?" she asked faintly.

"Marrying me." He took a step closer, his face suddenly eager. "Naomi, the kinder miss you already. You and I . . . we work well together. Why shouldn't we be married? We could have a gut life. A comfortable marriage."

Comfortable. The word stuck in her heart like a barb. This proposal might be even more hurtful than the first one. Somehow, she had to find the courage to tell Nathan the truth.

"I can't," she said carefully, knowing that wouldn't be enough for him. "I can't because there is no room in your heart for me, Nathan. You know that and so do I."

"I care about you. I do."

"Ja." She closed her eyes for a second and then focused on his face. "Once, that kind of caring would have been enough for me. But I have learned something in the past month. I have learned to value myself too much to settle for a marriage without love."

She couldn't say anything more, because if she tried, she would break down. She turned and walked away, and she knew without looking that he wouldn't follow her.

Nathan watched Naomi, a solitary figure, dark against the snow as she trudged toward the grossdaadi house. What had he done wrong now?

He'd apologized for his thoughtless behavior. He'd asked her to be his wife and tried to be honest about his feelings.

Hadn't he come up with an answer that would solve all their problems?

Turning away from the hives, he marched toward the outbuildings as if he could outrun the sense that he had failed at something very important.

He had reached the barn before he let himself glance toward the grossdaadi house. A buggy was coming up the lane—Sam Esch's buggy, he could see from here. Come to pick Naomi up and take her to the bus, no doubt. She was going on a visit to her sister and no one, maybe not even Naomi, knew when she would return to Pleasant Valley.

Naomi must decide what was best for her. Nathan reminded himself of that fact several times while he completed the chores that had brought him out of the house in time to see Naomi talking to the bees. There was nothing else he could do.

By the time he returned to the house, he'd almost managed to convince himself that was the truth. But no sooner had he hung up his jacket than Joshua and Sadie ran to him—Sadie already crying and Joshua with tears sparkling in his eyes.

"Daadi, Naomi is gone," Sadie wailed and clutched his leg. "She's gone away."

Nathan patted her back. "Hush, little girl. It will be all right." But would it? He looked toward Daad and Sarah.

Sarah shrugged, looking both guilty and defiant. "They had to know, Nathan. There's no point in looking at me that way."

"It's not true, is it, Daadi?" Joshua stared at him, willing him to deny it. "We have to give Naomi her Christmas presents. You'll make it right and Naomi will komm home."

His son's innocent belief in him struck Nathan in the heart. He reached out to grip Joshua's shoulder. "Sometimes there are things we must accept. Naomi is going away. It is her choice."

He intercepted a skeptical glance from his sister that annoyed him. Did every woman in Pleasant Valley think he was the one to blame?

"She doesn't want to go away." Sadie lifted a tear-stained face to him. "She wants to be here with us. She loves us."

"Sadie . . ." He was left without words. Naomi did love the kinder.

More, she loved him. Hadn't that been what she was saying to him? She'd said she couldn't marry him when he didn't love her.

Didn't he love her? His mind seemed to be spinning in circles, showing him image after image of the past month with Naomi: laughing in the snow, glancing up with a smile from working with the children, emerging damp and rosy-cheeked from under the steam tent with Sadie, holding him while he wept for Ada.

The spinning stopped, settling on one sure thing. Naomi wasn't just necessary for his children's happiness. She was necessary for his own happiness. All the joy of the past month had come because of the changes that Naomi made in his heart.

"I am certain-sure that Naomi loves you," he said carefully. "Just as you love her. Just as I love her."

"Then she'll stay with us," Joshua said, his tone positive.

"I don't know. That is up to Naomi." Nathan tightened the grip on his son's shoulder. "But we will not let her go without telling her how much we love her. And we will not let her go without giving her our gifts."

The dawning hope of his son's face seemed to echo the hope blossoming in his own heart.

"Sadie, you run and get our gifts for Naomi. Joshua, you and I will harness the buggy. We must hurry if we are to reach Naomi before she gets on the bus."

"Komm, komm, Sadie," Sarah exclaimed. "I will help you get the gifts and put your coat on."

Joshua was already shrugging into his jacket. "I will help Daadi with the harness," he said to his grossdaadi.

"Ja, I know you will." Daad smiled at Joshua and then extended the smile to Nathan. "The gut Lord go with you."

He might need some heavenly intervention, Nathan thought as he and Joshua ran to the barn. If they didn't reach town in time . . . If they did but he couldn't find the right words . . . If Naomi was determined to leave . . .

Please, his heart murmured. *Please. Give me a chance to make this right.*

Joshua arrived at the stall before him, reaching up to clip a lead line to the halter of the buggy horse. "I'll lead her out," he said. "I can back her between the shafts. Grossdaadi showed me how."

Nathan nodded, lifting down the harness. His son was growing up before his eyes, and he had to allow that to happen. Naomi had shown him that truth.

In moments, working together, they had harnessed the mare and were driving up to the house. Sarah hurried out, clutching a shawl around her, with Sadie and a shopping bag full of gifts. She boosted Sadie up to the buggy and handed him the bag.

"Do it right," she said.

"I will try." He clucked to the mare, and they were off.

"Hurry, Daadi, hurry," Sadie exclaimed.

"Ja, hurry." Joshua leaned forward in his seat. "We can't miss her."

No, they couldn't miss her. Maybe it was superstitious, thinking he had to stop Naomi before she left. After all, he could go after her. If need be, he'd court her for the next six months if that was what it took to persuade her.

But somehow the children's urgency was his, as well. He couldn't let another moment go by without telling Naomi how he felt about her.

It was probably the fastest he'd ever covered the distance between the farm and town. When they turned onto Main Street, he saw a group of Amish standing at the bus stop. Naomi's family, come to tell her good-bye. The bus must be late, as usual.

Not good-bye, he prayed. *Please, not good-bye.*

"Naomi, look." Lovina, one arm around Naomi's waist, turned her toward the street.

A buggy was coming toward them, moving faster than most folks would ever drive a buggy in town. It swerved to the curb and halted at the bus stop, as if to block the bus when it arrived. Naomi's heart cramped. It was Nathan and the children.

A murmur passed through the small group that had come to see her off. Nathan slid down from the buggy seat, but the children beat him to the sidewalk. They came running toward her, and she thought her heart would surely break.

"Naomi!" The family around her parted to let Sadie rush to her, with Joshua close behind. "Don't go." Sadie clutched her coat. "Don't go away. We love you."

"Ach, I love you, too." Naomi loosed the clinging hands, holding them in hers. "Such cold little hands. Where are your mittens?"

"Mittens don't matter," Joshua declared. "We had to stop you. You can't go away. We love you."

"Denke, Joshua." She could sense Nathan's tall figure behind the children, but she would not look at him. "It means so much to know that you and Sadie love me." And it made it so hard to do what she must. "But—"

"We love you," Nathan said, his voice deep. "Not just the kinder." He held out a shopping bag. "We don't want you to leave. But if you must go, at least open our gifts before you do so."

Naomi took the bag, determined not to meet his eyes. *We love you,* he had said. But he didn't mean . . . he didn't mean he loved her the way he had loved Ada.

Lovina came to her rescue, taking a package out of the shopping bag and holding the bag for her. "Go on," she said. "Open it."

"That is from me and Joshua," Sadie said. "We picked it out all by our own selves."

Trying to smile, Naomi pulled the wrapping free. "Ach, a beautiful napkin holder from you. Denke. I love it." She bent, hugging the two children together, trying to hide the tears that stung her eyes.

"Now mine, Naomi." Nathan held out a small package.

She still couldn't look into his face, but she couldn't help seeing his strong, gentle hand as he gave her the gift, and her breath caught.

"Denke," she murmured. She pulled, and the wrapping came away, exposing a package of labels—beautiful labels for her honey jars.

"I had them made for the honey that you will be harvesting next year," he said. "It is my prayer that you will be there with us then and for every year. We love you, Naomi."

He looked around, taking in all the watching, interested faces. Grasping her hands, he drew her away from the others, into the small recess in front of the nearest shop.

As if a message had been received, her family started talking, their words forced with the effort to be tactful.

Nathan turned his back to them, shielding her

with his body so that no one else could see her face. "I love you, Naomi." His voice had roughened. "This is not about the kinder. It is about us. I love you."

She looked up, startled and half-afraid to see his face, her breath catching in her throat.

"I love *you,* Naomi Esch." Nathan's eyes were so intent that it seemed she could see into his very soul. "It wonders me that it took me so long to know the truth. I love you. I want you to be my wife. I'll spend as much time as you want proving that to you." He jerked his head toward the family, standing behind them on the sidewalk and trying to pretend they weren't listening. "I think everyone here knew it before I did. Please, don't say no to me again."

Even without looking, she knew that every person watching them was wearing a smile. This proposal would go down in the history of the Pleasant Valley Amish, that was certain-sure.

She seemed to hear Bishop Mose's wise counsel in her ears, but she didn't really need it. She knew her own heart.

"I love you, Nathan. I will marry you."

The exhalation of breath around her almost made her laugh. And then Nathan put his arms around her and pressed his cold cheek against hers. Suddenly Sadie was crunched between them, and Joshua was trying to hug them both at the same time. Caught between laughter and tears,

Naomi tried to put her arms around all three of them while Isaiah pounded Nathan's back and Daad actually laughed out loud.

The rightness of it settled in her heart. She might not be Nathan's first love, but she would be his last.

Epilogue

Naomi looked around the crowded table at Daad's house at the faces of those she loved. Second Christmas, the day after Christmas, was the time to celebrate and feast with family. Today her family had grown to include Nathan, the children, and his family.

Yesterday had been a quiet day, spent with just Nathan and the children in the house that would soon be hers, as well. They had gone for supper with Nathan's daad, his sister, and her family. Today everyone was celebrating together—celebrating Christmas as well as the joining of their two families.

Sadie, always irrepressible, went around the table to lean against Daad's chair. When he stopped what he was saying to look at her, she gave him an engaging smile.

"Are you going to be my grossdaadi, too?" she asked.

Naomi realized it was one of the few times when Daad was taken by surprise. He glanced toward Nathan's daad and then smiled at her. "Naomi will be your new mammi, ja? So that makes me your new grossdaadi. You can't have too many grossdaadis, ain't so?"

Sadie nodded. Tugging on his sleeve so that Daad leaned over, she kissed him on the cheek.

Everyone was smiling, quiet for a moment. Joshua looked around the table. "Our family got a lot bigger, didn't it, Daadi?"

"Ja, it did, Joshua. That is a gut thing."

Nathan reached under the cover of the table to clasp Naomi's hand. His grip was warm and sure and familiar, and her heart seemed to expand until it pressed against her skin. She had never known it was possible to feel so much happiness.

Naomi glanced at Betty and smiled, thinking of all that had happened in the month and a half since her birthday supper. Pain and pleasure, all mixed together—that was what life was like. You mourned the passing of the old and embraced the new.

The future would surely hold many more endings and beginnings, but together she and Nathan would cope with them. For now, looking at the joyful faces in the lamplight, she could only cherish the love and family that Christmas had brought.

Amish Christmas Customs

Christmas is probably the most important celebration in the Amish year. In fact, it's so important that it is actually observed by some Amish three times: Christmas Day, Second Christmas, and Old Christmas.

Christmas Day falls on December 25 for the Amish as it does for other Christians, a day when the miracle of Christ's birth is recognized with joy and awe. For such an important event, one day isn't enough, so while time spent with the immediate family is the norm for Christmas Day, the day after Christmas, also called Second Christmas, is a day to celebrate with the extended family. Visiting and sharing a meal can be an extraordinary event when your extended family is as large as that of most Amish. There might be more than fifty people there!

In many Amish groups, Old Christmas is still observed. Falling twelve days after December 25, January 6 is the celebration of Epiphany, the arrival of the wise men to visit Jesus, and in the Middle Ages this was the culmination of the Christmas feast. When the Gregorian calendar replaced the older Julian calendar, the Pope set

December 25 as the official Christmas Day, but many Protestants kept to the old calendar, celebrating on January 6. The tradition has hung on among some Amish who celebrate on both days, with Old Christmas usually being a more solemn and religious day.

Whether they recognize Old Christmas or not, an Amish holiday is one that most people in contemporary society would consider very plain. Amish children don't make lists for Santa Claus or pore through catalogs searching for the latest in electronic gear. Old Order Amish homes don't have Christmas trees or elaborate light displays. The Amish Christmas celebration, like all of Amish life, is focused on faith, home, and family.

Holiday customs vary from one Amish community to another. More conservative communities have low-key observances of the holidays. In Pennsylvania, the Amish are affected by the strong Pennsylvania German tradition, and they are more likely to have the customary Pennsylvania Dutch decorations.

Christmas decorations in a typical Pennsylvania Amish home may include lighting candles and placing them in the windows to symbolize the birth of Jesus. Many homes now use battery-powered candles that pose less threat of fire. Candles are sometimes also used with greens on the mantelpiece and tables. If you visit a home with young children, you'll probably find doorways and windows draped with strings of paper stars, angels, and sometimes popcorn. If the family receives Christmas cards, they'll probably be displayed so that they can be enjoyed time and again throughout the season.

Christmas cards are sent in some church districts and not others. With so many Amish working in jobs that bring them into daily contact with the Englisch, it has become more common for Amish families to send cards to Englisch friends, and the cards are almost always hand-made.

The putz, or manger scene, is an important part of the Christmas decoration throughout the Pennsylvania German communities. The putz developed very early in the church's history as a way of teaching children the story of Christ's birth. If you visit Bethlehem or Lititz in Pennsylvania during the holiday season, you can see some beautiful, elaborate depictions, some-times including other Biblical scenes in addition to the familiar manger. The typical Amish putz is much simpler, using clay or wooden figures and possibly a stable. Some families embellish the scene with natural materials like straw and greenery. Using the putz, the Christmas story is told over and over throughout the days leading up to Christmas.

The Moravian Star is a twenty-six-point star, first used in Germany in the 1800s. The Moravian community that settled in Lititz has preserved the tradition of hanging the multi-pointed star, and many Amish homes also include the Moravian Star in their decorations as representing the Star of Bethlehem.

School celebrations are an important part of the Christmas season in most Amish areas. The children begin preparing their parts a month ahead, but their teachers have probably been busy since last year's program in collecting materials to use! The program, presented before as many family and friends as can cram into the one-room schoolhouse, typically includes readings of prose and poetry, the acting out of skits, and the singing of Christmas carols. Every child participates, and parents hold their breath until their little scholar gets through his or her piece. Teachers sometimes exchange skits and poems with each other, building up a collection so that each year they can provide something new to the audience, which has probably seen countless Christmas programs over the years. The theme of every poem and skit is that of gratitude for the gift of Christ and of the proper response of humility and love. This may be the only time when an Amish child "performs" in any way, but the audience is always uncritical and enthusiastic.

Gift-giving is part of the Amish Christmas celebration, but it bears little resemblance to the avalanche of gifts common to a typical American household. The presents are often handmade and generally something that is useful. Younger children typically receive one toy from their parents, while other gifts might be handmade clothing, cloth dolls, or wooden toys. An older girl might welcome something for her future home, while tools are popular gifts for older boys. The Amish school often has a gift exchange among the children, and usually the children take great pleasure in making a gift for the teacher.

The Amish home will probably be filled with the aroma of cookie-baking and candy-making for weeks before the holiday. While you can usually find home-baked cookies on any day, the holidays call for something special, and Amish cooks preserve family recipes for the cookies and treats, passing them on from mother to daughter. Most Pennsylvania Dutch are known for the quality and variety of their Christmas cookies, and you'll find some traditional ones from my family in the recipe section. Enjoy!

In addition to celebrating with immediate and extended families, most Amish adults have various groups that plan Christmas lunches and suppers. In fact, there are so many of these that they might still be going on in February! Groups of cousins, people who work together, girls who went through rumspringa at the same time—all of these and more may share a special Christmas treat together.

But the focus of the Amish Christmas celebration, as of all Amish life, is the family. Gathered around a groaning table spread with roast chicken, all the trimmings, and an endless array of breads, cakes, cookies, and homemade candy, the family celebrates Christmas together with humility and gratitude to God for His amazing gift.

Folded Paper Stars

The art of paper strip folding is used to create the Moravian Star that is such a beautiful part of Pennsylvania Dutch Christmas decorating. The Moravian Star, with its 26 points, is a rather complicated project to master, but a simpler 5-pointed star is an easy introduction to strip paper folding.

To begin, cut a strip of paper that is ½ inch wide and 11 inches long.

1

At one end of the strip, form a standard overhand knot, being careful not to crinkle the paper. Slide it as close to the end as possible. Press the knot down to make it flat.

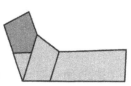

2

Fold the short end of the paper toward the center, cutting off any excess. Let the long end extend down and to the right.

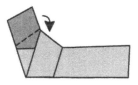

3

Using the long end of the paper, fold the strip so that edge A aligns with edge B.

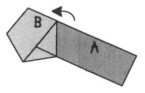

4 Flip the paper over so that the long end points down and to the right again. Now fold it across so that edge C aligns with edge D.

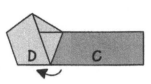

5 Flip the paper over so that the long end points down and to the right and repeat step 3.

6 Flip the paper over so that the long end points down and to the right and repeat step 4.

7 Continue flipping and folding, alternating the alignment, until you run out of paper. Tuck the end under a flap of the paper. You should now have a pentagon.

8 Hold the pentagon by the edge and use your fingernail to press in one of the five sides. Rotating the pentagon, press in each side. You'll end up with a perfect 5-pointed star! These can be made with colored paper and strung on thread to form garlands for Christmas decorating.

Your Finished 5-pointed Star

Recipes

Snickerdoodles

This is a traditional Pennsylvania German cookie, and perhaps the best known with its light brown, crinkled top. A great favorite with children!

½ cup soft butter or margarine
¾ cup sugar
1 egg
1¾ cups flour
1 teaspoon baking powder
½ teaspoon baking soda
½ teaspoon ground nutmeg
¼ teaspoon salt
2 tablespoons sugar for rolling
2 teaspoons cinnamon for rolling

Preheat oven to 400°F.

Cream the butter or margarine and sugar together. Add the egg and beat until fluffy. In a separate bowl, stir together flour, baking powder, baking soda, nutmeg, and salt. Blend dry ingredients into creamed mixture to make dough. Add more flour if needed to make the dough stiff enough to form balls.

Mix the remaining sugar and cinnamon together in a small bowl. Shape the dough into balls the size of unshelled walnuts. Roll cookie balls in the cinnamon sugar. Place on greased cookie sheet and flatten with a fork. Bake for 10–12 minutes or until very lightly browned. Remove to cooling rack, cool, and enjoy! This recipe makes about three dozen cookies, depending on their size.

Candy Jar Cookies

My mother called these date-and-nut balls Candy Jar Cookies because she liked to put them in quart canning jars, decorated with bows, and give them to neighbors at Christmastime.

1 cup margarine or butter
1 cup brown sugar
3 cups flour
1⅓ cups chopped dates
2 tablespoons orange juice
1 cup chopped walnuts
powdered sugar for rolling

Preheat oven to 300°F.

Cream the butter or margarine and sugar together. Add the rest of the ingredients, except the powdered sugar, and mix well. Shape into balls about the size of unshelled walnuts. Bake on an ungreased baking sheet for 18–20 minutes. Remove to a rack and cool slightly, then roll in powdered sugar. This recipe makes about four dozen small cookies.

Rolled Sugar Cookies

This is a traditional cookie dough for making cut-out cookies. Using shortening instead of butter gives the cookies a crisp texture and not-so-sweet taste, which combines well with the powdered sugar icing.

FOR COOKIES:
½ cup shortening
¾ cup sugar
1 egg
2 cups flour
½ teaspoon baking powder
½ teaspoon baking soda
½ teaspoon vanilla
2–3 tablespoons milk

Preheat oven to 350°F.

Cream the shortening and sugar together. Add the egg; beat. Add the other ingredients and mix well. Gather together a generous handful of the dough, and roll it out on a well-floured board until it is about ⅛-inch thick. Use cookie cutters to cut the dough into different shapes and arrange the cookies on an ungreased baking sheet. Repeat with the rest of the dough. Bake the cookies for 5–6 minutes. Remove to racks to cool.

FOR ICING:
3 tablespoons butter or margarine
1 teaspoon vanilla
2 cups powdered sugar
2 tablespoons milk

Beat the butter or margarine and vanilla together. Incorporate the powdered sugar in small increments, adding dribbles of milk as you go until the mixture reaches spreading consistency. Beat well. Add drops of food coloring to the entire batch, or to small batches, as desired.

Frost the cookies with the icing and allow the icing to dry for several hours before attempting to stack the cookies or place them in a container. This recipe makes about five dozen cookies, depending upon the size of the cookie cutters.

Dear Reader,

I hope you've enjoyed another visit with the people of Pleasant Valley. Although the place doesn't actually exist, it seems very real to me, as it is based on the Amish settlements here in my area of north-central Pennsylvania.

It gave me so much pleasure to write about an Amish Christmas in Pennsylvania. Because of the strong Pennsylvania Dutch heritage here, Amish customs are a bit different than they are in some other parts of the country, with a little more emphasis on decorations, although always those that draw attention to the meaning of the season.

Naomi is one of my favorite characters—a quiet, self-effacing woman who nevertheless has a deep well of spiritual strength. I'm sure we've all known women like Naomi, and I've developed a special appreciation for those who have such gentleness coupled with such fierce determination to do what is right.

I would love to hear your thoughts on my book. If you'd care to write to me, I'd be happy to reply with a signed bookmark or bookplate and my brochure of Pennsylvania Dutch recipes. You can find me on the Web at www.martaperry.com, e-mail me at marta@martaperry.com, or write to me in care of Berkley Publicity Department, Penguin Group (USA) Inc., 375 Hudson Street, New York, NY 10014.

Blessings,
Marta Perry

Center Point Large Print

600 Brooks Road / PO Box 1
Thorndike ME 04986-0001 USA

(207) 568-3717

US & Canada:
1 800 929-9108
www.centerpointlargeprint.com